FUGITIVE JUSTICE

Davis walked like a man who knew where he was going and had every right to be going there.

When he reached the corner of the building, he turned around it, relaxing slightly as he put himself out of sight of the trading post and the other businesses and cabins. The woods grew close to the back of the jail, and Davis headed straight for them, eager to lose himself in their thick, clinging shadows. It would have simplified matters if he'd had a horse, but the only way to get one here in Elkton would be to steal one. He wasn't going to do that.

No matter what else might be said about him, Davis Hallam was no thief.

But he was a man who had been terribly wronged, and he swore that by the time this night was over, he would have his vengeance on Andrew Paxton.

Books by James Reasoner

Wind River
Thunder Wagon
Wolf Shadow
Medicine Creek
Dark Trail
Judgment Day
The Wilderness Road

Published by HarperPaperbacks

The WILDERNESS ROAD

James Reasoner

HarperPaperbacks
A Division of HarperCollins*Publishers*

This is a work of fiction. The characters, incidents, and
dialogues are products of the author's imagination and are not
to be construed as real. Any resemblance to actual events or
persons, living or dead, is entirely coincidental.

HarperPaperbacks   *A Division of* HarperCollins*Publishers*
                    10 East 53rd Street, New York, N.Y. 10022

Cover illustration by Rick McCollum

First printing: April 1996

Printed in the United States of America

HarperPaperbacks and colophon are trademarks of
HarperCollins*Publishers*

❖ 10 9 8 7 6 5 4 3 2 1

For Randal Greenwood

1

The sky was the color of a flintlock's barrel, a hard gray that held no mercy. Davis Hallam hunched his shoulders forward and leaned into the cold wind as he rode toward his farm. Today the Shenandoah, usually a peaceful, pretty stream as it wound through this broad valley, was as flat and hard as the sky. Davis's horse plodded along the road that followed the banks of the river.

He had been down to the Bristow place. William Bristow had fallen out of his hayloft the week before and broken his leg, and the man had a wife and six little ones to look after. Even now, in the dead of winter, there was plenty of work to be done around a farm. Until Bristow's leg healed, Davis and some of the other neighbors were looking after the place for him. They all knew Bristow would have done as much for any of them. Here on the frontier, a man couldn't make it without good neighbors.

But that didn't mean it was easy. Davis was tired from doing his own work. When he got back to his farm, he had a plow to repair, and the chore would probably take him all afternoon.

The lane went around another bend and the farm came into sight. Davis felt something inside him like the glow from a fireplace far into the night when the wood had burned down to embers and still gives off heat and light but not much of either one. There had been a time when the fire in him burned brighter, but not for quite a while.

Not since Andrew had come.

The cabin was made of logs and chinked with mud so that it was tight against the wind. A stone chimney rose at one end. A large barn, also of logs, was behind the cabin. Pole fences formed pens for the cows, the hogs, and the mules. The chickens wandered loose. Davis had built a stone fence along the land, choosing each rock carefully and stacking them precisely. Some of them had weighed so much that he had trouble lifting them alone, but he enjoyed the struggle, the way the sweat popped out in beads on his forehead, the familiar ache in his arms and shoulders, the tremble of combined weariness and satisfaction when he stepped back and looked at how much he had gotten done each day. The fence had taken a long time, but he knew every rock in it.

On the other side of the fence was a large pasture where the cows and mules grazed in the summer, with the cabin and barn at the far end of the pasture and the plowed fields beyond the buildings. As Davis rode closer he saw the three children playing in the pasture. Mary, the oldest at ten, with her mother's bright fair hair and good looks, was telling her sister and brother what to do, as usual. Laurel was eight, darker, more slender, faster than Mary but for the most part unwilling to go against what the older girl said. The baby of the family was Theodore, though as a five-year-old he no longer tolerated being called a baby. He had his father's thick brown hair and already showed signs of having inherited Davis's rangy build.

Davis frowned. The children shouldn't have been outside. It was January, after all, in the Year of Our Lord 1790. Children didn't play outside during the winter.

They saw him coming and ran to meet him, each of them leaping onto the stone fence and dashing along it with the careless, sure-footed grace of the young and immortal. Theodore shouted, "Pa!" while Laurel greeted him with cries of "Papa!" Mary called a more dignified, "Hello, Father."

Davis reined his horse to a stop and said, "What are the three of you doing out here? That wind's got ice in it."

"Mother sent us out to play," Mary said. "She said the fresh air would be good for us, and for us to watch for you and sing out when we saw you coming."

Davis nodded, somewhere in his head understanding more than he really wanted to. At least the children were wearing their coats, and the thick garments kept them warm. Their cheeks were red from the wind, but they weren't shivering.

He looked past them. A big chestnut gelding, a much finer horse than the ewe-necked roan he was riding, was tied to the post in front of the cabin. He recognized the horse. It belonged to his half-brother Andrew Paxton.

Davis wasn't surprised that Andrew was here. Andrew had a way of showing up any time Davis had to leave the farm for very long.

Davis nudged the roan through the gap he had left in the fence. "You children go on inside. I'll be there as soon as I've tended to the horse." He paused, then added, "Sing out again before you get there, so your mother will know you're coming."

"Sure, Pa," Theodore said as he jumped down from the fence. Laurel followed him. Only Mary hesitated.

"How's Mr. Bristow's leg?" she asked.

"Getting better," Davis said. "I shouldn't have to help out much more."

"Good," Mary said, and then she jumped down from the fence and ran after her sister and brother. Theodore was already hollering toward the cabin.

Davis rode through the pasture and circled around the cabin and went to the barn. He dismounted, opened one of the double doors, and led the horse inside. The other animals were there, warming the place with the heat that came from their bodies, and it felt good to be out of the wind. An odor of earth and straw and manure, not that unpleasant once a man got used to it, filled the barn. Davis unsaddled the roan and put the horse in its stall. He patted its smooth red shoulder, checked to see that there was grain in the trough and water in the bucket.

He had to walk back around the cabin to reach the door. He paused at the corner and looked to the east, toward the Blue Ridge that could only dimly be seen today. Like the sky and the surface of the river, the mountains seemed not blue but gray. Sky, mountain, and river blended one into the other so that ends and beginnings no longer meant anything, at least not from a distance. It was only up close that such distinctions were important.

Davis pulled the latch string and opened the door. He heard laughter as he stepped inside. Andrew must have said something funny, because Laurel and Theodore were laughing. Even Faith was smiling, an expression Davis saw but seldom on his wife these days. Only Mary didn't seem amused. She sat on a three-legged stool in the corner, her features solemn. She looked so much like her mother that Davis felt a twinge of something deep in his chest, a knowledge of how Faith must have been when she was a child.

The only difference was that, when she was a child, Faith Larrimore had worn fine dresses and spent her days in the big house on the Tidewater plantation her father owned. Mary had to settle for homespun and this log cabin her father had built with an ax and his two hands. Not that the girl complained.

"Hello, Davis," Andrew said with a grin. "How's old Bristow?"

"Mending," Davis said.

"I've been meaning to get down to his place and lend him a hand. I'll do that next week."

Davis grunted and nodded. He doubted that Andrew would even go near Bristow's farm.

The air inside the cabin was filled with the smell of stew cooking in the big iron pot suspended over the low flames in the fireplace, blended with the sweet tang of Andrew's tobacco. His pipe was out now, tucked into the pocket of his leather vest, but obviously he had been smoking it earlier. Andrew was sitting on one of the benches beside the rough-hewn table, so Davis sat down opposite him.

There was little resemblance between them. Davis took after his father Michael, with features carved out as roughly as the table at which he now sat. Andrew had the finer looks of the mother they shared. Michael Hallam had come from Ireland to this land when it was still only a gathering of British colonies with a toehold on the vast, unknown continent. When he died, his widow Lydia had married Henry Paxton and in due course had borne him a son. Andrew had her darker hair and her slender build, too. Not many people would take Davis and Andrew for relatives, especially not a blood bond as close as it really was.

Davis took his own pipe from his pocket and placed it on the table, but he did not reach for his tobacco pouch. Instead he toyed with the stem of the briar and didn't look as he said, "What are you doing here, Andrew?"

Faith was stirring the stew. The ladle rattled against the iron pot as she said, "That's not a very friendly way to talk to your brother, Davis."

"Oh, I think it was a perfectly innocent question," Andrew said with a smile. "Wasn't it, Davis?"

"Just wondering," Davis said. "Takes a lot of work to get a farm ready for planting, 'specially a new place. Ever since Andrew came to the Shenandoah Valley last fall, he's spent as much time over here as he has on his own land."

Faith said quickly, "Not that we mind, Andrew. We certainly don't. We enjoy your company, don't we, children?"

"Uncle Andrew tells the best stories," Laurel said, and Theodore echoed her.

Davis finally took out his tobacco pouch, opened it, and began to pack the rough-cut Virginia blend into the bowl. "You're welcome here any time, Andrew," he said. "You know that. But I'd be glad to help out on your farm if you're having trouble getting ready for spring."

"No trouble at all," Andrew said easily.

"Well, just remember what I said."

Davis tried not to frown. He felt Faith's eyes on him, watching him.

He got up, took a glowing sliver of wood from the fire, and lit his pipe. By the time he had smoked it, Faith had a bowl of stew and a wooden spoon on the table in front of him. She served Andrew next, then the children and finally herself. Davis ate sullenly, barely able to conceal the resentment he felt. When he was finished, he stood up and said, "I'm going out to the barn to repair that plow."

"Need any help?" Andrew asked.

Davis shook his head and went to the door. He picked up his hat and put it on before he went out.

A fine mist had begun to drift from the gray sky, coming down so intermittently that it was almost as if God was dropping a handful of rain at a time. Davis walked around the cabin and went to the barn again. It was dim inside the barn, the only light coming from the gaps Davis had left between some of the logs to allow more air to circulate. After a moment, his eyes adjusted and the light was enough for him to see what he was doing. Some strips of rawhide were hanging from pegs driven between the logs of the wall. Davis took one of them, slipped his knife from the sheath on his belt, and began cutting the rawhide into shorter lengths. He would tie them around the joints of the plow that had begun to weaken. Once spring arrived and the weather warmed up, the rawhide bindings would shrink and tighten until they were almost as strong as iron.

He had been working at his task for about half an hour when he heard a horse leaving, the hoofbeats soft and muffled in the light rain. That would be Andrew going home. Ten minutes later, the barn door opened with barely a whisper of sound. Faith came in.

"You treated Andrew horribly," she said. "He's going to think you don't want him here."

Davis looked up from his work. She stood between him and the door she had left open. He saw swirls of moisture drifting around her. She had to be getting wet, but she was too angry to care.

When her hair was damp it drew up into tight curls that floated around her shoulders. Davis had always thought she was especially lovely like that. Now, however, there was a frown on her fine-boned face, and though he couldn't make out the expression in her blue eyes, he knew it was not a happy one.

He said, "Andrew doesn't care whether I want him here or not . . . so long as you do."

Faith's shoulders lifted a little as her back stiffened. "What do you mean by that?"

"Just what I said. It's you he comes to see, not me."

"Don't be ridiculous. He's *your* brother."

"Half-brother," Davis said. "And we were never close. I hadn't seen him in five years when he showed up here last fall and said he'd taken up a claim on that land east of here."

"He adores the children—"

"Then why did I find them playing outside, in the cold damp wind, when I got back from Bristow's place?"

"Andrew and I were talking," Faith said. "The children were bored. It was their idea to go outside."

Somehow Davis doubted that, but saying so would not have done any good. He looked down at the plow again and went back to what he had been doing.

After a moment, Faith asked, "You don't believe me, do you?"

"Doesn't matter if I do or not."

"Why don't you just go ahead and accuse me, if that's what you want to do?"

"Never said I wanted to accuse you of anything."

Faith took a step toward him, lifted her hands as if she wanted to either reach out to him or strike him, then dropped them at her sides again where they hung, pale smudges in the shadows like her face.

"We all might be better off if you spoke more, Davis," she said. "A person might as well be gazing off at the Blue Ridge as to look at your face. There's no way of telling what's on the other side."

His fingers tightened on the plow handle. "The mountains tell a story . . . if you know where to look."

"If you know what you're looking for," Faith said. She sighed, shook her head. Then she turned and walked out of the barn, pulling the door closed behind her. Davis had to let his eyes adjust to the dimness again.

Then he went back to work on the plow.

Faith was quiet at supper, and the children were subdued as well, even the normally boisterous Theodore. Davis didn't really taste the venison and potatoes, even though Faith had cooked them with wild onions. The mist had turned into rain, and in the silence Davis thought he could hear each drop striking the roof of the cabin. The wind had picked up as well. It found its way into the cabin somehow, making the flames in the fireplace tremble like the fingers of an old, old man. As soon as the meal was over, Faith worked with Mary and Laurel on their letters and ciphering while Theodore used his piece of board and a lump of charcoal to draw pictures. Davis sat at the table; as he smoked, he watched them and listened to the wind and rain. He could hear the strain in Faith's voice. Davis knew that Mary could hear it as well, but Laurel didn't seem to notice.

It wasn't that common for a woman to be able to read and write, let alone do sums, but Faith's father, old Hammond Larrimore, had hired a tutor for his daughter and provided the best education he could. Faith was an only child, and, with the profits from his huge tobacco plantation, Hammond and his wife Cornelia had given her everything that their money could buy.

And then, to hear Hammond tell it, Faith had thrown it all away by marrying a poor Irish lad who wanted nothing more than to till the earth and earn a living from his efforts. Worse still, once Davis and Faith were married, he had dragged her off to what Hammond and Cornelia considered a God-forsaken wilderness, leaving the Tidewater behind to live on a farm in the Shenandoah Valley.

But for more than a decade, Faith had been happy . . . or at least she had seemed to be. Until Andrew came, with his expensive clothes and his tales of having lived in Boston and Philadelphia and Charleston and Savannah and Richmond. Andrew, handsome Andrew with his stories and his jokes, who was everything his brother was not and never could be.

Davis's teeth clamped down tightly on his pipe and he told himself to stop thinking such thoughts. They were sly, though, stealing into his head like a fox or a raccoon into a chicken house, then striking without warning.

When the evening's lessons were done, Faith said, "Up to the loft with the three of you now." Theodore groaned about being sent to bed, as he always did, but within a few minutes the children had climbed up the ladder to the loft where they slept.

Faith came over to the table and sat down across from Davis. He didn't want to look at her, but when she said his name he turned to her. She said, "Things can't go on like this."

He felt as if he might have taken a chill. He wiped the back of his hand across his nose and said, "What would you have me do? Step aside so that Andrew can have you?"

"How can you say such a thing? And keep your voice down. The children are still awake."

"They'd be happy with Andrew for a father."

"You shouldn't talk like that."

"You said I didn't talk enough. Now you don't like what I say."

She sighed. Her eyes were moist as she reached across the table. She touched his hand. Davis didn't pull away from her fingers.

"Things change, Davis, and once they have, they can never again be the way they were. But they can be just as good. You don't have to throw everything away, all the years . . . "

"I'm not the one doing that," he said.

Her fingers twined in his. "Please, Davis. Don't think the things you've been thinking."

Maybe he had been wrong. He wanted to believe that. Faith stood up, still holding his hand, and he rose with her like a drowning man pulled from the waters of the Shenandoah. She came around the table and into his arms. Her lips were sweet and warm as she kissed him. The fingertips of her other hand, cool and sweet, touched his cheek. He leaned toward her. The desire that sprang up in him, the need for her, astonished him with its strength.

He *had* been wrong, he told himself, wrong about Faith and about Andrew and about everything. She was here in his arms and they were moving toward the bed on the far side of the room and the logs in the fireplace crackled, and this moment was all that was real, all that mattered.

2

Things were better for a while after that. Davis stayed close to home for a couple of weeks, and Andrew came around only occasionally; when he did show up, he stayed a short time and then left. Davis might have thought that all his suspicions were unfounded if he had not noticed the way Faith tried to watch Andrew ride off each time without being obvious about it. He saw the way her eyes moved to one side and followed the dwindling figure on horseback. He tried to tell himself that it was only his imagination, but he knew it wasn't. The longing was still there in Faith's eyes.

If that was all it was, he could live with it. Whenever Andrew wasn't around, Faith was pleasant to him, smiling and laughing, good with the children. Anyone watching her would have thought she was happy. Anyone except Davis, and he knew better. But life slipped back into its familiar patterns after that momentary lurch, and like the rolling of a wagon over a smooth road, it lulled Davis into a sense that things were going to be all right after all.

January turned to February, and with the new month came snow that moved in over High Knob and the Shenandoah Mountains to the west. The first storm merely dusted the fields with a spotty layer of white, but the second, following close on its heels, brought half a foot of heavy wet flakes. This was the time of year for folks to stay inside and sit by the fire, and that was what Davis did. Mary, Laurel, and Theodore rapidly grew bored, and Faith's eyes took on a restless sheen, too. Davis didn't seem to mind being cooped up in the cabin. . . but that was a pose. Inside, he seethed with the need for spring to arrive. He wanted to smell damp, freshly turned earth and feel it cling to his fingers as he pressed seeds into the ground, working itself into the lines of his flesh so that it left behind dark trails when he brushed his hands off.

That time was still weeks away, however, and all he could do until then was to make the best of the situation.

He might have made it to the spring, and everything might have been all right, if Jonas Kirby hadn't ridden up one afternoon, his horse leaving deep hoofprints in the snow. Davis didn't know Kirby was anywhere around until the man let out a yell.

"Hello, the cabin! Are you to home, Hallam?"

Davis was sitting at the table, smoking. He lifted his head and then stood up. Faith was molding johnnycake dough onto the shovel that would be placed in the fireplace so the dough could bake. The children were on the other side of the room playing some sort of game; Davis hadn't been paying enough attention to know exactly what it was. He walked to the door. The windows were shuttered for the winter and too much trouble to open just to see who was there. Besides, he thought he recognized the voice.

"Hello, Kirby," Davis said as he stepped out and closed the door behind him. He had not put on his coat and the temperature was still below freezing, but the thick homespun shirt he wore would keep him warm enough for a few minutes. The wind had laid down earlier in the day and no longer cut through anyone foolish enough to venture out into it.

"'Spose you're wonderin' what brings me here?"

Davis shrugged. He and Jonas Kirby were not friends, not by any stretch of the imagination. Davis couldn't have said what caused the friction between them, because nothing had ever happened to make them enemies. It was more a matter of nature, like the color of a man's eyes or the shape of his ears. Kirby was the same way. But the two men tolerated each other because they were neighbors and neighbors had to get along.

"There's trouble down at Bristow's place," Kirby said. "He's hurt his leg again."

Davis shook his head. "That's a damned shame. What happened?"

"I'm not sure myself," Kirby said. "Mordecai Duncan stopped by my place and told me about it. Thought I'd ride down there and see what Bristow needs. Want to ride with me?"

Davis hesitated, surprised by the invitation. More than likely, Kirby didn't want to go alone because a horse could slip and break a leg on the icy lane. It was better to travel in pairs during weather like this. Davis cast a glance at the sky; there were patches of blue between the grayish-white clouds, but the sunlight was weak and watery and held no warmth. Kirby was right. It was no day for a man to be out alone.

"I'll get my coat and saddle my horse," Davis said. "Get down and come inside where it's warm. My wife has some tea."

"Much obliged."

Davis turned and opened the door. "Here's Jonas Kirby," he told Faith. "We're going down to Bristow's place. Bristow's hurt himself again. I told Jonas he could have some tea."

"Of course." Faith reached for a cup, then smiled at Kirby as the man clomped through the doorway past Davis. "Hello, Mr. Kirby."

Without closing the door, Davis picked up his hat and coat, then carried them outside to put them on. Mary closed the door behind him. He went to the barn, saddled the roan, and led the horse around to the front of the cabin.

By that time, Kirby was stepping outside again. He was a lantern-jawed man whose gray hair and chin whiskers made him look older than he really was. He climbed onto his own horse again as Davis swung up onto the roan.

For the most part, they were silent as they rode south along the lane toward William Bristow's farm. The hooves of the horses made soft thudding sounds against the frozen, snow-covered ground. The mountains of the Blue Ridge were mantled with white in the distance, and Davis thought they were pretty. The same was true of the Shenandoahs to the west. The river wasn't frozen, but it was more sluggish than usual. In a couple of months, Davis thought, once the spring thaw hit, the river would flow fast and muddy from all the snow that melted and ran off. Every creek, every tiny rivulet, would be full and the whispery, chuckling sound of water flowing over mud and rock could be heard night and day. Green buds would begin to appear on the trees, delicate swellings that would soon burst into life. Shoots of fresh grass would appear in the meadows. It was one of Davis's favorite times of year.

They reached Bristow's farm and Davis called out to let the inhabitants of the cabin know someone was coming. There hadn't been any Indian trouble around this part of Virginia for quite a few years, but no one with any sense rode up to a man's cabin without announcing himself. Bristow's wife came out of the door with a rifle cradled in her arms. She was a tall, angular woman, her face hardened by work and child-bearing. Her features eased slightly as she recognized the visitors.

Davis reined in and nodded politely to her. "Howdy, ma'am. Hear Bristow's laid up again."

"He decided he had to get out and chop some ice," Mrs. Bristow said, her voice disapproving. "Slipped and twisted his bad leg, he did. Now he can't get around at all."

Kirby swung down from his saddle. "If you need some ice, Hallam and me will chop it for you."

"And anything else you need done," Davis added as he dismounted.

"That's mighty kind of you. We don't like other folks havin' to do for us."

Davis said, "That's what neighbors are for, to help out when we need it."

Pride and gratitude warred for a moment on the woman's lined face, then she nodded. "We'd be much obliged for anything you'd care to do."

Davis and Kirby spent the next couple of hours doing chores around the Bristow farm, aided by the three children who were big enough to help out. When they were through, they went inside and talked to Bristow, who was sheepish over his new injury and apologetic about taking the two men away from their own work. Davis assured him it hadn't been any bother. Mrs. Bristow fed them tea and johnnycake before they started back.

Davis experienced an odd feeling of camaraderie as he rode toward his own farm with Jonas Kirby. They didn't say much, but Davis thought Kirby felt the same thing. They reached the Hallam farm first, and Kirby started on down the lane toward his home with a friendly wave.

The cabin was still over a hundred yards away. Davis started toward it, then reined in sharply. Like birds searching for seeds, his three children were scurrying around the snow-covered pasture, leaving trails behind them in the white blanket. He could hear their laughter.

Nothing wrong with children going out to play in the snow, Davis told himself. It didn't have to mean a damned thing except that Mary, Laurel, and Theodore had grown so bored that they couldn't stay inside the cabin any longer. The fact that they were outside didn't really matter, as long as they were bundled up well.

The horse tied up at the cabin—that was what mattered.

It was Andrew Paxton's horse.

Davis's pulse was like a mallet striking his skull in a deadly rhythm. The cold air filled his throat, choking him. Andrew must have been watching the place. As soon as he had ridden away with Jonas Kirby, Andrew had come running. That was the way it must have been.

His stomach clenched, sending waves of sickness through him. What had been clean, crisp air only seconds earlier was now sour, filled with a stench that disgusted him. Bile rose in his throat. He had been betrayed, and it was the worst feeling of his life.

He couldn't let them get away with it.

His movements jerky, Davis slid down from the saddle and grasped the horse's reins. He started leading it across the pasture toward the cabin. The children saw him and started running toward him, but he waved them back and motioned for them to be quiet. Snow crunched underneath his boots as he walked. He had started breathing again without really being aware of it, and small clouds of steam hung in the frigid air in front of his face. He moved through them, feeling the condensation from his own breath wrap around his head. It smelled bad to him, too, as if there was something rotten inside him.

He had no idea what he was going to do once he got to the cabin, but he knew he had to do something.

He was aware of the knife in its sheath pressing against his hip. Faith might not be so interested in Andrew if his features were carved into something that resembled a statue hacked out of wood, much like Davis's. It was just a thought, but Davis's pulse quickened even more as it went through his head.

Maybe he was wrong and he would find them sitting at the table and drinking tea, nothing more. If that was the case, he would look foolish bursting in on them, his face dark with fury and a knife clutched in his hand. His fingers wanted to wrap themselves around the hilt of the blade, but he held them back. He took a deep breath and tried to compose himself. Once again he told himself that maybe he was wrong about them . . .

But as he let go of the horse's reins and strode quickly over the last few yards and reached for the latch on the door, he knew he had been right all along.

They must have heard his footsteps, must have known he was coming. There had been time enough for Faith to sit up in the bunk and for Andrew to leap out and reach for his breeches. But then Davis threw open the door and saw them there, Faith clutching the quilt around her, Andrew groping for his clothes. Faith's blond curls were disarrayed and her mouth had a bruised look.

"Wait a minute, Davis!" Andrew said desperately. "You don't understand!"

He might have lived if he had kept his damned mouth shut, Davis thought. But at the sound of Andrew's voice, all of Davis's rage welled up his throat and out of his body in a horrible roar as he lunged at Andrew.

Davis's fist crashed into his half-brother's jaw, knocking Andrew back away from the chair. Andrew caught his balance before he could fall to the floor. Davis went after him, arms swinging wildly as he threw punch after punch. Most of the blows didn't connect. Andrew was faster than he was. Stepping close to Davis, Andrew hit him twice in the belly. Davis grabbed his shoulders, swung him around, and gave him a hard shove. The push sent Andrew staggering next to the chair where his clothes lay.

Davis reached underneath his coat and pulled his knife from its sheath.

Faith came up out of the bed with a flicker of pale flesh, a scream ripping from her throat. "No, Davis!" she cried. At the same instant, Andrew plucked a small pistol from underneath his clothes. He twisted at the waist, turning toward Davis and bringing up the weapon. His thumb found the hammer and drew it back as the gun rose. His finger was already tightening on the trigger. Davis saw it all in shattered little instants of time. He saw Faith throw herself between him and Andrew, felt her hand against his chest pushing him back with a strength he would not have guessed she possessed.

And then she was turning toward Andrew, her mouth opening to say something, but the words never came because the pistol cracked spitefully and Faith's head jerked back and blood bubbled from her throat where the lead ball had torn the soft flesh. She stumbled backward toward Davis and he dropped the knife to try to catch her. Her nude form filled his arms and sagged lifelessly against him. His eyes widened in horror as his rough palms pressed against her breasts and he felt the warm crimson flow of her blood washing over them.

Andrew dropped the smoking pistol and sprang forward. He clubbed his hands together and swung them as hard as he could at Davis, who was still holding his wife's body and had no chance to ward off the attack. Andrew's fists smashed into the side of Davis's head and drove him against the wall. Faith slipped out of his grip to fall onto the puncheon floor, landing in a pool of her own blood. Before Davis could recover, Andrew hit him again, then kicked him in the groin. Agony flooded through Davis and he folded up, pitching forward to land beside his wife. Andrew kicked him again in the head, just for good measure.

Through the red haze that settled down over Davis's eyes, he saw Andrew frenziedly pulling on his clothes. Then, faintly, as if from a great distance, he heard his half-brother shouting, "Oh, God, Davis, what have you done?"

There were cries from outside the cabin. *The children!* Davis thought with the tiny portion of his brain that was still working. The children couldn't see this.

But then Andrew threw the door open and said, "Stay back! Oh, Lord, don't look!", but of course they did and Mary and Laurel began to scream and Theodore cried, "Mama!", and Andrew pushed them out of the doorway saying, "He went mad, your father went mad! He killed her and he tried to kill me!"

Davis tried to push himself up off the floor, tried to call out to his children and tell them that Andrew was lying, but the red haze filled his head now like blood-stained cotton and pain radiated out from his midsection to engulf his body. Faith was lying right there beside him, her face pale and lifeless, her eyes glazed in death, the pale pink tip of her tongue protruding just a little between her open lips.

His fingers moved a little, inched toward her face. But just as he reached her and his fingertips brushed against her waxy cheek, darkness claimed him and carried him away and the last thing he was aware of were the screams and cries of his children.

3

Something hard was underneath Davis's head. That was the first thing he was aware of as consciousness began to seep back into his head like melting snow. Whatever he was lying on prodded painfully against his skull. He groaned and tried to sit up but found that his muscles lacked the strength.

"You're awake, are you? Good."

The unfamiliar voice held a savage pleasure. Davis was not able to sit up, but he could roll toward the voice. Doing so, he discovered, took some of the pressure off the back of his head. He was able to pry his eyes open, but the effort required so much struggle that beads of sweat popped out on his face and slid slickly across his skin.

A grim-featured man with iron-gray hair pulled back tightly from his forehead was leaning over Davis and peering intently at him. Hatred was in the man's eyes. Davis had never seen him before.

Davis's tongue was like a piece of firewood in his mouth. His throat burned and was dry. He wondered if he had vomited. That was what it felt like. He said, "Wh-where . . . who . . . ?"

"I'm Constable Peter Abernathy, if that's what you're asking. And you're in my jail at Elkton."

Elkton. It was a settlement down the valley from his farm, Davis recalled. He and Faith and the children went there occasionally to pick up what few supplies had to be bought. The farm was, by and large, self-sufficient, and that was the way Davis liked it. For the life of him, he could not figure out why he would be waking up in Elkton's jail.

Faith.

The memory struck Davis like a sudden, unexpected blow. Everything that had happened in his cabin came flooding back into his brain, sweeping away the pain before it. An aching head was nothing compared to the misery that wrenched at his guts. He curled up against it, vaguely realizing that he was lying on a bunk next to a stone wall. Weak light came through a barred window over his head.

"I'd be sick, too," Abernathy said as he straightened.

"Did . . . did you find him?"

"Who?"

"My brother . . . Andrew Paxton." Davis could barely force the name past his lips. It wanted to cling there like something foul and sticky.

Abernathy snorted. "Didn't have to find him. He found me. Came a-riding in here and said that you'd gone mad and killed your wife."

"No!" Davis cried. "It was him—"

"That's what he told me you'd say." Abernathy

shook his head. His eyes were like stones from the bottom of a stream that had been polished to a high, dead gloss. "Said you came busting into your own cabin shouting like a madman. You beat him, then you ripped her clothes off and shot her even though Paxton tried to stop you. He was too late for that, but he managed to knock you out and tied you up so he could get your poor children away from there and fetch me. That how it all happened, Hallam?"

Davis shuddered, leaned over the edge of the bunk, and retched. Nothing came up except more of the bitter taste that filled his mouth. He lifted a trembling hand, wiped the back of it across his lips. He shook his head.

"No," he said, his voice little more than a whisper. "He did it."

"Why in God's name would your brother kill your wife?"

"He was—"

Davis stopped. He could not bring himself to say the words, could not describe for Abernathy the scene he had found inside the cabin when he got back from Bristow's place. How could he tell this man, this stranger, about that image of Andrew and Faith on the bed, wrapped in the quilts and each other? How could he explain what he had felt then, what he felt now?

"I didn't hurt Faith. I would never have hurt Faith, no matter what she did."

"What about Paxton? He sounded like he was afraid for his life, afraid you'd turn on him next."

"I—"

Again the words lodged in Davis's throat. If he

told Abernathy that he had intended to take his knife to Andrew's face, that would only convince the constable even more that he was insane. And it might not have stopped there, Davis knew. He might have killed Andrew. He had been that angry.

He was able to swing his legs off the bunk and rest his feet on the floor. He sat up, making the jail cell and the rest of the world spin crazily around him for a moment before he put his head in his hands and held on tightly. His stomach lurched again, but he swallowed the bile.

Abernathy went to the heavy wooden door of the cell, which stood open on the other side of the tiny room. There was a small barred window in the door. He said, "There's no point in talking. You can tell your story to the magistrate, and he'll decide what to do with you. But I can tell you now, Hallam, you'll swing for what you did. They might as well start building the gibbet now."

He went out and the door slammed shut behind him. Davis jumped a little at the sound. Then a thought occurred to him and made his head jerk up sharply. He got to his feet, staggered a little, then caught his balance and went to the door. His fingers were slippery with sweat as he wrapped them around the iron bars in the window. "Abernathy!" he shouted. "Abernathy, where are my children?"

No answer came back, and Davis slumped against the door, his grip on the bars the only thing that kept him from collapsing onto the damp, fetid stone floor.

*   *   *

The weak sunlight filtering in through the window gradually faded, leaving the cell in darkness that was relieved only when Constable Abernathy brought in a stub of candle, a cup of water, a chunk of bread, and a thick slice of ham.

"There's your supper," Abernathy told him. "The candle should last until you're finished eating."

"Where are my children?" Davis asked, paying no attention to the food Abernathy handed to him. The bread and ham might as well have been stone for all the interest Davis showed in them.

"You gave up your right to worry about your children when you killed their mother, I'd say."

"I didn't—" Davis stopped. Abernathy had made up his mind about the guilt of his prisoner, and he was not going to be swayed by denials. Instead, Davis said, "Just tell me if they're all right."

"Your brother took them in. He'll see that they're cared for."

Davis closed his eyes and his fingers tightened on the chunk of bread until they dug deeply into it. His children—poor Mary and Laurel and Theodore—were in the hands of the man who had really killed their mother. Andrew had no doubt told them the same lie he had told Abernathy about Davis killing Faith. He would fill their heads with that lie, Davis thought, until there was no room in their minds for the truth.

Would he hurt them? After all, he had killed their mother.

Davis took a deep breath and tried to calm himself. The shot that had killed Faith had been intended for him. Her death had been an accident. The entire incident was engraved indelibly on Davis's brain, and he remembered the look of stunned surprise on Andrew's face as the blood spurted from Faith's throat. Davis had no doubt that Andrew had been trying to kill *him*.

So there was no reason for him to hurt the children, none at all. If anything, it would make him look better and make his story seem more convincing if he took good care of them.

He was a quick one, Andrew was, as quick as a fox. Before Faith had even slumped lifelessly to the floor, Andrew had been plotting and scheming to turn the blame from himself onto his half-brother. But surely somewhere there was someone who would believe him. If he could only talk to the children, he could convince them of his innocence. He was sure of it.

"I want to see them," he said.

Abernathy shook his head. "That wouldn't be a good idea. You've done enough damage, man. Leave those poor motherless little ones alone from now on."

Davis sat down on the bunk and stared up at the constable. "You don't understand," he said. "I have to see them. I have to talk to them."

"No."

For a second Davis thought about leaping up and throwing himself at the man. He could beat some understanding into Abernathy's head. But Abernathy had a short, stout club tucked into his belt, and if Davis attacked him, he wouldn't hesitate to use that club on the prisoner. Davis was sure of that. From the look in Abernathy's cold eyes, he was fairly certain that the constable might well beat him to death and save everyone the trouble of a trial. Abernathy had completely accepted Andrew's story.

Or perhaps that wasn't it, Davis thought suddenly. He said, "How much is Andrew paying you to help protect him and get rid of me?"

He knew that was a mistake as soon as the words were out of his mouth. Abernathy's already grim mouth tightened even more, and he stepped over to the window to set the candle and the cup down on the sill. His long fingers wrapped around the handle of the bludgeon. "You're going to be sorry you said that, Hallam."

Davis saw the blow coming, but he could not get out of the way in time. He dropped the bread and ham onto the bunk and tried to duck, but the cudgel caught him on the shoulder and drove him back against the wall. Pain flared through him, paralyzing him.

Abernathy stepped back. "I'm sworn to uphold the law," he said. "No one pays me except the county. Now, you can eat your supper while that candle is still burning, or you can eat it in the dark. I don't care a whit either way. But you'd best be quiet in here tonight. If there's a lot of shouting or crying, I'll come back and you'll get a taste of this club again, do you understand?"

Davis managed to nod. He clutched at his right shoulder with his left hand, hanging on tightly as if that would somehow make the pain go away. It didn't.

Abernathy went out, locking the door behind him.

Davis huddled on the bunk for several minutes, waiting for the agony in his shoulder and arm to subside. Finally, when it did, he was able to pick up the bread and gnaw off a bite. It was stale and hard and tasteless, and when he tried the ham, the grease that clung to it cloyed in his mouth and almost gagged him. The meat tasted a little rancid, too, but he knew it was all he would get. He forced himself to eat, although he could not think of any reason to do so. The candle flame guttered out about the same time as he swallowed the last bites of the food and washed them down with the water.

He had already found the wooden bucket under the bunk that served as a slops jar for the cell. He dug it out now, relieved himself, and put the bucket in a corner instead of replacing it underneath the bunk. The smell from it only added to the unwholesome stench that filled the air of the cell. The stink of despair, he thought. It had soaked into these stones until they fairly reeked with it. And he was certainly adding his share to it, he added bitterly to himself.

The cell had been cold when Davis first awoke there, but with the coming of night the temperature dropped even more. He couldn't sit back on the bunk and lean against the wall because the stones seemed to suck every bit of warmth from him. The bunk had one thin blanket on it; Davis wrapped up in it as best he could, drawing his feet up off the floor and curling up as tightly as possible. The darkness in the cell was relieved only by what faint starlight filtered in through the barred window. No light came through the window in the door, leading Davis to believe that yet another door shut off the cell block from Abernathy's office.

That night was the longest Davis had ever spent. He could not have said if he ever slept. Surely a few times he dozed off, but when the square opening of the window turned from black to gray and then brightened even more with the approach of dawn, he was wide awake, staring across the little cell at the door without really seeing it.

This time when Abernathy brought food into the cell—a bowl of thin gruel—Davis kept his mouth shut. Abernathy didn't say anything either, and when he was gone Davis ate hungrily. His body still had an appetite despite the stunned condition of his mind.

He was just finishing the gruel when Abernathy unlocked the cell door and stepped inside. "You have a visitor," he said.

Davis looked up in surprise. "A visitor?" he repeated, confused. He couldn't think of anyone who would come to visit him in jail.

Unless . . . unless it was Andrew. Davis's fingers tightened on the bowl in his hands. He had not been given a spoon, probably for fear that he would try to use it as a weapon. Well, that was wise, he decided, because if Andrew stepped through that door and Davis had had a spoon in his hands, he might have used it to dig out what passed for the bastard's heart . . .

Jonas Kirby came into the cell behind Abernathy. Davis's neighbor glowered at him. "How could you do such a thing, Hallam?" he said.

"I didn't."

Abernathy chuckled humorlessly, as dry a sound as a man's boots scuffing through fallen leaves in the autumn. "I told you that's what he'd say, Kirby."

"When I left you after we'd been down to Bristow's, I thought we were starting to be friends— even though you've always been a sour, bitter man, Hallam."

That wasn't true, Davis thought. He was just quiet, the sort of man who pondered before he spoke. Not like most folks who just spouted whatever came to mind.

But Kirby's visit might give him a chance to convince someone of his innocence. Davis stood up, placing the empty bowl on the bunk, and said, "Think about what happened yesterday, Jonas. You were with me right up until the time I went back to my cabin and supposedly killed my wife and attacked my half-brother. Did I seem insane to you when we parted company?"

Kirby hesitated before answering, pulling on his chin whiskers as he thought. Finally, he said, "Well, I reckon not. But I was only a few hundred yards down the road when I heard the most awful shout from back at your place. It sounded like the cry of a madman, right enough."

Davis closed his eyes and took a deep breath. He was going to have to tell them what had really happened, painful though it might be to put the experience into words. He opened his eyes and looked at Abernathy and Kirby and said, "I shouted, all right. You would, too, if you had found your wife in bed with your own brother."

Both men looked shocked and angry. "Don't speak ill of the dead!" Kirby said. "Have you no shame?"

"It was Faith who had no shame," Davis said, pressing on while he still possessed the strength to do so. "I tell you I found them there together, and of course I yelled in anger. I had my knife, and I might have taken it to Andrew after we scuffled a bit, I admit that. I don't know what I might have done. But he had a gun, a little pistol, hidden underneath his breeches. He picked it up and tried to shoot me. Faith got between us just as Andrew fired."

"You mean that Paxton killed your wife, but he was trying to kill you?" Abernathy said.

Davis nodded. "That's right."

"Well, it sounds perfectly logical . . . "

Davis's hopes rose.

"But it's still a damned lie," Abernathy finished.

His hands clenching into fists, Davis stepped forward. Abernathy reached for his club, but when Davis stopped, the constable did not pull the weapon from behind his belt. Abernathy kept hold of it, however.

"Why?" Davis asked. "Why do you believe Andrew and not me? I'm telling the truth."

"It's true that your wife was . . . unclothed," Abernathy said. "But that was only because you ripped her garments from her when you attacked her. Paxton explained all that, and I believe him. Perhaps you only imagined that you saw the two of them together. A man who is losing his mind sometimes sees things that aren't there."

Davis felt his hopes flowing out of him like water. Nothing he said was going to change Abernathy's mind, and Kirby seemed to be just as stubborn in his belief that Davis was guilty of the awful crime.

"You didn't answer my question," Davis said quietly. "Why do you believe Andrew and not me?"

"If Paxton was guilty, he wouldn't have come riding to find me like all the demons of Hades were after him, now would he?" Abernathy said. "Besides, your children have told me how you and your wife had been unhappy with each other and how angry you were at your brother."

"You've been talking to my children about this?" Davis was outraged.

"They saw what you did to their mother. It's a bit late to be worrying about what they know or don't know."

Davis turned away, unable to bear the accusatory stares any longer. He went to the window, raised his hands, and grasped the iron bars in the aperture just above his head. He hung there, leaning against the wall, his weight on his hands, as great shudders shook his body. Despite everything they said, he had not been insane.

But he might be before this was all over.

When he was able to speak again, he asked without turning around, "Will there be a trial?"

"Tomorrow morning," Abernathy said. "Magistrate Symms will preside."

"Perhaps he'll listen to reason. Someone is bound to believe me sooner or later."

"I wouldn't count on it, Hallam," Kirby said.

"Nor would I," Abernathy added. "My guess is that by tomorrow night, you'll be swinging from the gibbet, and deservedly so. We can't have people

going around murdering their wives in fits of mad
rage."

Kirby came closer and laid a hand on Davis's
shoulder. Davis pulled away. "For what it's worth,"
Kirby said, "my wife and I have agreed to take in
your children and care for them as if they were our
own. They're the truly innocent ones in this whole
terrible business."

"I . . . I thought they were with Andrew," Davis
said.

"An unmarried man cannot care for small
children," Kirby said. "If he finds a wife, perhaps
they will go back to live with him and his bride.
Until then, you can rest assured your young ones
will be looked after properly, Hallam."

"By a man who helped condemn their father to
hang."

Kirby moved back to the cell door, his face taut
with anger. "Think what you will. The truth is, I'm
sorry about this, damned sorry—for all of you."

Kirby went out and Abernathy followed him,
closing and locking the door behind them, and
Davis stayed where he was under the window. He
leaned back a little and looked out through the
opening. The sky was a dull, leaden gray again
today, but his mind wasn't really on the weather. A
thought too strong to be denied forced itself into
his brain, intruding its evil image until that was all
Davis could see.

Himself . . . on the end of a hangman's rope.

4

Davis stared down at his hands. They seemed not even to belong to him. They were strange, alien things, the paws of a beast, not a man. He twisted his wrists a little, making the chain connecting the manacles clink slightly.

The iron was cold against his skin, which was nothing unusual. Davis had been cold for a long time now, such a long time that he had trouble recalling what it was like to be warm. Surely more than just two days had passed since the awful afternoon that had changed his life forever. It seemed more like a year at least, he thought, or perhaps two.

"On your feet, Hallam," Peter Abernathy said.

For a moment, the words seemed as foreign to Davis as the sight of his own manacled hands. The constable might as well have been speaking German, like those Hessian mercenaries old George III had brought over to fight for him during the Revolution.

"I said get up." Abernathy's voice was like the

ice on a pond, hard and thin and brittle. He stood in the doorway of the cell, his hand on the polished wooden butt of the pistol tucked behind his wide black belt. He frowned at Davis. "You're not going to give me trouble, are you?"

Davis took a deep breath out of sheer weariness. The stink of the cell filled his lungs, made him want to gag. He swallowed the reflex and put his hands on his knees. With a grunt of effort, he pushed himself to his feet.

Abernathy moved back out of the doorway, still holding his hand on the pistol. "That's good. Come along peacefully, and I won't put the irons on your legs. I never liked putting irons on a man's legs."

Before the shackles had been locked into place around Davis's wrists, Abernathy had allowed him to put on his coat. It would be a chilly walk from the jail to the meeting hall where the trial would take place. Davis had thought that he could jump the constable, knock him unconscious, and escape from the grip of the evil that had closed around him like a giant, callused hand.

But there were three men waiting just outside the cell, all of them armed with muskets. Abernathy had deputized them to serve as guards while he was taking Davis to the trial. The idea of escape had departed Davis's head as quickly as it came.

The three men backed off to give him room to emerge from the cell, just as Abernathy was doing. Abernathy had seen enough tragedy in his life to be able to keep his face expressionless. The same didn't hold true of the three deputies. Their gazes slid over Davis, paused for an instant, then darted quickly away, as if they had accidentally seen something foul.

Murderer. Wife-killer. Those were the names they knew him by now. Davis Hallam was a forgotten man. Only the killer remained.

Once again Davis had to take a deep breath, this time as a shudder passed through him. Perhaps the magistrate, old Albertus Symms, would believe him when he explained what had happened.

Then wings will sprout from my back, Davis thought, *and I will fly over the Shenandoah Valley and far away beyond the Blue Ridge.* That was just about as likely as Symms believing him.

Davis hadn't seen any of this building except the cell he had occupied since his arrest. As he had suspected, there was a corridor outside the cell, with another thick wooden door at the end of it. This door had no window in it. Abernathy moved past him and opened the door.

The constable's office was considerably warmer than the cell. The air was smoky from the burning logs in the stone fireplace on one wall of the room. Heat from the blaze pushed unpleasantly against Davis's face. After two days in the dank cell, this sudden, stifling heat was just as uncomfortable to him as the cold.

The office was dominated by a massive rolltop desk. Davis had to wonder how much it had cost to have that monster freighted over the Blue Ridge in a wagon. A couple of muskets hung on the wall on pegs, and powderhorns and shot pouches dangled from their barrels. Other than that, the room was sparsely furnished. Its usual occupant was a sparse man.

Abernathy opened the front door and gestured curtly. "Outside now."

Sunlight slanted in through the door and stabbed like thorns into Davis's eyes. After the perpetual gloom of the past two days, the brightness was almost unbearable. As unbearable as the thought that the sun was shining down on a world where his wife no longer lived.

He turned to Abernathy and said, "My wife . . . her funeral . . . "

"The services were yesterday," Abernathy said stiffly. "She was laid to rest in the churchyard down the road."

Davis nodded. He was almost thankful at that moment that his story had not been believed. If the sexton had known how Faith had died with the stain of adultery on her soul, he might not have allowed her to be buried in sacred ground. Despite everything that had happened, Davis was glad she had been laid to rest in a decent fashion.

Elkton was a small village of less than a hundred people, but it was the largest settlement in this part of the Shendandoah Valley. As Davis moved out of the constable's office and down three steps to the muddy street, he looked around at the scattering of log structures. A trading post, a blacksmith shop, a church, the meeting hall where Magistrate Symms held court, a dozen cabins. That was the extent of Elkton.

And in front of nearly every building stood small clusters of people watching him. Their heads turned to follow him as he walked down the street toward the meeting hall, trailed by

Abernathy and the deputies. With each step, his boots made an ugly sucking sound as they pulled free of the thick mud left behind when the sun melted the snowfall.

There had been a time when Davis would have found a day like today beautiful. The crisp air moving in a light breeze that ruffled the thatch of brown hair on his bare head, the burnished glow of the sunlight, the deep blue of the sky dotted with white clouds that reminded him of bolls of cotton in the fields of the Tidewater plantations . . .

Memory was like that chain between his wrists, one link leading inexorably to the next. The thought of plantation cotton linked with Faith, who had grown up on just such a vast estate, and the beauty of the day turned to ashes. Davis turned his eyes down to the thick brown mud of the street.

"Keep moving," Abernathy ordered. "Magistrate Symms is waiting."

Davis plodded on toward the meeting hall, feeling the eyes of the watchers, wondering why so many of these people were quick to presume his guilt. Some of them knew him, some didn't, but from what he had seen during that glance along the street, the expressions on the faces of everyone in the settlement had been of condemnation. The mere accusation of killing his wife had been enough to convict him in their eyes.

He reached the broad wooden steps of the meeting hall, and went up them one by one. There was a verandah along the front of the building. Davis crossed it and went through the door Abernathy held open. He wasn't accustomed to

having someone open doors for him. Abernathy
wasn't doing it to be polite, of course.

Davis's steps echoed on the raised puncheon
floor of the meeting hall. The building had no
windows, only narrow slits where rifles could be
fired, relics of the time when this land had belonged
to the Indians and the white settlers had wrested it
away from them. The big, high-ceilinged room was
lit by several lamps and by a fireplace in the back
wall. In front of the fireplace was a long table, and
seated at it, with the flames crackling and leaping
behind him, was Albertus Symms, the magistrate.

He was a thick-bodied man with a red, beefy
face and graying red hair, wearing a dusty black suit
that made him look as much like a minister as a
magistrate. On the table in front of him lay a Bible
and a tricorn hat, the thick black book reinforcing
the image of the man as a preacher. Davis knew that
Symms was hardly a holy man. Symms brewed corn
whiskey and was his own best customer. What was
left over he sold to Herring over at the trading post.
It was rumored that at one time Symms had even
sold whiskey to the Indians, but that had never
been proven and it was long in the past, anyway.
These days he upheld the law, for the most part,
instead of breaking it.

Symms shifted a plug of tobacco from one
cheek to the other, then said to Abernathy, "Is this
the man?"

"Yes, Magistrate," the constable replied. "His
name is Davis Hallam."

Symms nodded. He had met Davis on at least
four occasions, but he had a notoriously bad

memory for names and faces. Davis wasn't sure how Symms had wound up occupying such an important post as magistrate. He knew *he* had never voted for Symms in any sort of election.

"Step forward, Master Hallam," Symms said.

Behind Davis, men were filing into the hall to watch the trial. The womenfolk would have to stay outside; they were allowed to gossip about what was going on in the hall but not actually witness it. Davis heard the happy shout of a child at play as he stepped forward, the sound drifting in through the open door of the hall, and it reminded him so much of his own children that a pang of loss shot through him and made him stumble a bit.

Symms glowered at Abernathy. "Do you allow drinking in your jail now, Constable?"

"No, sir," Abernathy answered quickly. "Hallam's had not a single jot of spirits since I locked him up."

"Perhaps 'twas guilt made him misstep," Symms said. "We'll soon find out. Read the charge, Constable."

Abernathy had no documents in his hands. He simply said, "The sovereign State of Virginia charges Davis Hallam with the crime of murder in the death of his wife, Faith Elizabeth Larrimore Hallam, may God rest her soul. And the sovereign State of Virginia also charges him with the crime of attempted murder in the attack on his brother, Andrew Paxton."

"Half-brother," Davis muttered under his breath.

"Hold your tongue, prisoner," Symms snapped. "You'll have your chance to speak."

Little good that chance would do him, Davis

thought. The magistrate had obviously already made up his mind about the facts of the case, just like everyone else in Elkton.

"Are there witnesses to these heinous crimes?" Symms asked Abernathy.

"Yes, sir."

"Bring 'em forward, then."

Abernathy turned and called out, "Jonas Kirby, step forward."

The tall, rawboned farmer shouldered his way through the crowd and came up to the front of the room. He cast a glance at Davis that was half-regret, half-defiance, then stood and faced Symms, twisting his hat nervously in his hands.

"You're Jonas Kirby, a neighbor of the accused man?" Abernathy asked, strictly for appearance's sake.

"Aye," Kirby said with a nod.

"And you were with Davis Hallam two days ago when he returned to his farm?"

"I was."

"Where had the two of you been?" Abernathy asked.

"Down to the Bristow place. William Bristow has a hurt leg, and me and Hallam been helping him and his family with their chores while he's laid up."

"That seems a neighborly thing to do," Symms said.

Kirby nodded. "Aye. Hallam has always been a good neighbor."

Symms just grunted, as if even that was in doubt. He waved at Abernathy, indicating that the constable should continue with the questioning.

"What happened when the two of you reached Hallam's farm?"

"We parted ways on the lane. Hallam rode to his place, while I went on toward my own."

"And then?"

Kirby turned his head a little, just enough to glance at Davis again. "A couple of minutes later, I heard a shout."

"What sort of shout?"

"An angry one."

"What did you do?"

"I turned my horse around and looked back at Hallam's cabin. I couldn't see anything except his children, playing outside in the snow. Then. . . " Kirby took a deep breath. "Then there was a shot, from inside the cabin. I figured something was wrong, so I rode back as fast as I could."

"What did you find?"

"Before I got there, Andrew Paxton came out of the cabin. He was yelling about how Hallam had killed his wife."

"Hallam's wife, you mean, not Paxton's?"

"Paxton's not married. I meant Hallam's wife. Faith."

Davis closed his eyes and swallowed hard. Kirby's voice, harsh and unyielding as always, softened a bit when he pronounced Faith's name. She had had that effect on people, Davis thought. She had brought beauty and elegance into a hard and unforgiving land, and most folks had loved her for it. Davis certainly had.

And so had Andrew.

"You didn't see Hallam shoot his wife?" Symms asked.

Kirby shook his head. "No, sir, I didn't. But when I looked through the door of the cabin, I could see her there on the floor."

Davis closed his eyes. *Don't say it,* he implored silently. *Don't say that she was lying there as naked as a harlot.*

"She had been shot," Kirby said.

Davis heaved a sigh of relief.

Symms shot him a frown, clearly taking Davis's reaction for something else. Abernathy said, "That will be all, Kirby."

With a nod, Kirby moved back away from the magistrate's table. He faded into the crowd, pushing his way toward the door.

"You have another witness, Constable?" Symms asked.

"Yes, sir, but before I call him, I want to tell you what I discovered from talking to Hallam's children."

Davis's head jerked up and his lips pulled back from his teeth in an angry grimace as he looked at Abernathy. "You've no right to bring them into this!"

"Quiet!" Symms thundered. "I told you you'd have your chance to speak. Go ahead, Constable."

"I don't want to bring innocent children into a court of law," Abernathy said, "so I questioned them at the home of Jonas Kirby and his wife, who are caring for them. Mary Hallam, the oldest child, told me that her mother and father were often angry with each other and that she thought her father hated her uncle Andrew."

"That's not true!" Hallam couldn't stop the outburst. "Faith and I loved each other! We quarreled no more than any married couple."

But he was shading the truth himself, and he knew it. There *had* been serious trouble in their marriage. How could he deny it? If everything had truly been all right, Faith never would have given herself to Andrew that way.

"And what about your brother?" Abernathy snapped. "Can you say that you did not hate him?"

"He . . . he was my brother."

"That's not an answer to the question I asked."

Davis looked down at the floor, studying the grain of the split logs that formed the puncheons. "There were times I . . . hated him," he said quietly, barely recognizing his own voice. "But he was still my brother."

"Proceed, Constable," Symms said. "You've established what Hallam's daughter told you."

Abernathy nodded. "In that case, I call Andrew Paxton forward."

The stir that went through the crowd was a thing with a life of its own. Men stepped aside, and Andrew walked through the gap they left him. Davis turned to look at him, saw the pale, handsome face, the dark eyes, the expensive coat and shirt and breeches. Homespun was not good enough for Andrew. It never had been.

Maybe they were right to have him on trial, Davis thought, because at this moment, he truly wanted to kill Andrew, to wrap his hands around the throat of his half-brother and squeeze until those pleasing features were mottled with blue and his tongue was protruding from his mouth and his eyes were wide and bulging with the horror of death. Davis's fingers trembled with the need.

Abernathy must have been able to read that on Davis's face, because he put his hand on the butt of his pistol again and said, "Step back, Hallam. Step back, by God, or I'll—"

Davis moved aside to give Andrew the room to come forward. Abernathy relaxed slightly, but he still watched Davis closely.

"You're Andrew Paxton, brother of Davis Hallam?" Abernathy said.

"Half-brother," Andrew replied.

"Of course. Mr. Paxton, did you come to the Shenandoah Valley because your half-brother had settled here?"

Andrew looked over at Davis and said, "Naturally. I thought he would welcome me."

"And did he?"

"No, he seemed to . . . resent my presence. I never felt really comfortable in his home, at least not when Davis was there."

"Then you visited your brother's home when he was not there?"

Andrew's shoulders rose and fell in a shrug. "Occasionally. Whenever I rode over, I had no way of knowing if Davis would be home or not, and when he wasn't, I saw no harm in visiting with my sister-in-law and playing with my nieces and nephew. On a cold day, I might share a cup of tea with them."

"And that was all?"

"Of course!"

"There was nothing between you and your sister-in-law?"

Andrew's face hardened into angry lines. "Faith was a married woman, a decent woman. I enjoyed her company, yes, but in a totally innocent manner. We shared some things in common in our background. We had both spent a great deal of our younger years in more, shall we say, civilized surroundings."

The magistrate's face darkened, and Davis knew that Andrew had just slipped a bit in Symms's estimation with his indirectly disparaging remark about the Shenandoah Valley. But the facts of the case were all that really mattered, and Symms still seemed to believe Andrew's version of them.

"What happened on the afternoon of the day before last?" Abernathy asked.

"I rode over to Davis's house, but he wasn't there. Faith said he had gone down to Bristow's place. I wasn't surprised. I thought I would wait there for a bit and see if Davis returned."

"Was there a specific reason you wanted to see your brother?"

"No, not really. It was just a visit."

"What did you and Mrs. Hallam do?"

"We had some tea and talked, while the children played outside; as I mentioned before, that was our custom."

The untruths came so easily from his lips, Davis thought, the words spoken with all the sincerity and conviction of a man who utterly believed everything he was saying. Davis wanted to shout out that he was lying, but he forced himself to remain calm.

"What happened next?" Abernathy asked quietly. The other men in the room were completely silent now, save for the soft sounds of their breathing.

"I . . . I didn't hear Davis ride up," Andrew went on, "but then suddenly he jerked the door of the cabin open and rushed in. He was waving a knife around and shouting. I had no idea what he was so upset about, but after a moment I realized he was calling his wife some vile names."

"Such as?" the constable prompted.

"He called her a . . . trollop. He said she was no better than a harlot, and he accused her of . . . of committing the sin of adultery."

"With whom?"

Andrew's voice was little more than a whisper. "With me."

A groan escaped from Davis's lips. This was wrong, so terribly wrong. Why couldn't anyone see that Andrew was lying?

The intensity of Andrew's story seemed to have shaken even the usually imperturbable Peter Abernathy. He asked, "What did Hallam do then?"

"He grabbed hold of her dress and began to . . . to rip her clothing off her."

"What did you do?"

"I told him to stop, and when he ignored me, I tried to force him to stop by taking hold of his arms."

"What happened next?"

"He threw me aside. I . . . I struck my head against the wall. I was almost knocked senseless."

Abernathy looked over at Davis, then back at Andrew. "But you saw what happened then?"

Andrew swallowed and nodded shakily. "I had taken out my pistol earlier and placed it on the table, not wanting to have it in my pocket while I was sitting and talking with Faith. Davis picked it up, and when Faith came toward him again, trying to get him to stop what he was doing, he . . . he shot her."

The bold, lying accusation rang in Davis's ears like a clap of thunder. He felt a great shudder building inside him, and at the same time, he seemed to be rising up out of his body, so that he could look down and watch what was happening below him. He saw himself lunge toward Andrew, his manacled hands outstretched, the fingers hooked like claws. Oddly detached from it all, he observed as Abernathy moved between him and Andrew. The constable brought up the pistol from his belt, but he didn't fire. Instead he lashed out with the barrel at Davis's head.

Davis's sense of detachment went away abruptly as the heavy iron barrel slammed into the side of his head above the left ear. The impact set off red explosions behind his eyes and dropped him onto his hands and knees. Splinters from the wooden floor dug painfully into his palms as he caught himself. He opened his mouth but no sound came from him.

A second later, strong hands caught hold of his arms and hauled him to his feet. Two of the men Abernathy had deputized held him while the third man stepped in front of him and drove the butt of his musket into Davis's stomach. A spasm of pain and nausea shook him like a tree in a strong wind.

"That's enough!" Abernathy called sharply. "Let him go and stand back!"

Without the support of the deputies, Davis sagged to his knees again and hunkered there, bent

over almost double against the pain flooding
through his midsection. Vaguely, he heard the
excited hubbub of the spectators in the meeting
hall, but the sounds seemed to be coming from far,
far away. He remembered a time as a child when he
and his brothers had been swimming in the creek
near their home, and he had gone under the water.
A current had caught hold of him and tugged him
far beneath the surface. The creek had closed in
around his head, dimming his vision and cutting his
ears off from sounds, and that was the way he felt
now, only he was not underwater. No current had
him in its grasp, save the current of tragic
circumstances that had brought him here today.

He had broken free of that creek long ago. He
would not be able to escape so easily the things
that had hold of him now.

Magistrate Symms was on his feet. "Restrain
that man!" he shouted. "I won't stand for such
behavior in my court! I want the leg irons on him,
Constable."

"Yes, sir," Abernathy said. He might not like
putting irons on a man's legs, but he wasn't going to
disobey Symms's order.

Davis was still sick in his stomach and his legs
were trembling by the time he had been lifted to his
feet once more and the shackles were fastened on
his ankles. He looked around and spotted Andrew
on the edge of the crowd, ready to put the
spectators between himself and Davis if he had to.
Symms summoned him to the front of the room
again, and Andrew came reluctantly, moving each
foot as if he was walking through knee-deep water.

"Finish your statement, Master Paxton," Symms said as the spectators settled down once more to listen.

Andrew leveled an accusing finger at Davis. "You've seen it for yourself! He's lost his mind. He killed Faith, and he tried to kill me. That's all I have to say."

Davis bit back a groan. All he had done by losing control was to make it look even more like Andrew was telling the truth. He had known that giving in to his anger would only hurt his cause, but he hadn't been able to stop himself.

And now he had probably lost his last chance to escape the hangman's noose.

Symms turned watery eyes toward Davis. "Do you have anything to say for yourself, Hallam?"

Davis forced himself to take a deep breath and waited until the hammer blows of his pulse inside his skull had slowed down a little. Then he said, "Am I not entitled to a lawyer?"

"I'm the only attorney in this end of the Shenandoah Valley," Symms said. "If there is someone who will speak for you, call him forth."

Davis looked over at Abernathy. "I told you what really happened," he said. "Can you not find it in yourself to believe even a part of what I told you?"

"I didn't know you or your wife, Hallam," Abernathy said, "but I've spoken to many who did. Your wife was a good, God-fearing woman, and I'll not besmirch her name by repeating the lies you told me about her."

Faith had made a mistake, Davis thought. That

didn't make her any less of a good woman. Anyone could stray, but the Good Book said they deserved forgiveness when they did. No matter how badly Faith had hurt him by betraying him with Andrew, he would have forgiven her. He knew that now.

But he had to think of more than Faith. There were the children to consider, as well as his own life, which was in mortal danger. He looked straight at Symms and said, "My wife was an adulterer. I found her lying with my brother Andrew. I would have been within my rights to kill them both." His voice caught, and he had to force himself to go on. "But I did not kill her. I loved her, and I would have forgiven her once I . . . I got over being so angry. I struggled with Andrew, and *he* is the one who shot her accidentally when he tried to fire his pistol at me."

There. It was done. The truth was told, no matter what happened next. By nightfall, everyone in this part of the valley would know what he had accused Faith of doing. Some of them might even believe it.

Most would not.

Symms certainly didn't. He said, "You have no one to substantiate your claim?"

Davis shook his head. "But neither does my brother."

"The fact that Andrew Paxton sought me out substantiates his story," Abernathy put in. "The testimony of Jonas Kirby, and of Mary Hallam, shows the state of mind Davis Hallam was in when he went into that cabin. I believe he shot his own wife in the heat of passion and would have murdered Andrew Paxton as well if he had had the chance."

"As do I," Symms said. "I declare Davis Hallam guilty of the crimes of murder and attempted murder and sentence him to be hanged by the neck until dead. The sentence will be carried out tomorrow morning at ten o'clock."

Just like that, he was condemned to death. Davis felt numb in both mind and body, and it was a moment before he realized that Symms had given him longer than he had really expected to have if he was found guilty. He would not be hanged until the next morning, instead of this afternoon.

That was a small favor for which to be thankful, to be wrongly executed a bit later than one would have anticipated. Davis fought down the impulse to laugh madly at the absurdity of it all.

"Do you have anything else to say?" Symms asked him.

For a moment, Davis considered demanding that he be tried again before a jury. But the result would be the same, he knew. He had no friends here, no one who would take his word over that of Andrew's. His quiet nature that most took for aloofness or even arrogance was now going to cost him his life, because no one here—no one!—knew him well enough to know that he was telling the truth.

"I have nothing to say," Davis rasped in a husky whisper.

"Then may God have more mercy on your soul than you showed your late wife." Symms stood up, taking the Bible in his hand. The black leather binding had cracked in places, revealing red streaks underneath. The magistrate gestured with his free hand. "Take him away."

One of the deputies took hold of Davis's shoulder and jerked him around. Abernathy's gun was still in his hand. He pointed it in Davis's general direction as he said, "Let's go back to the jail."

Davis didn't argue. He shuffled through the parting crowd, out the door, and down the steps to the street. The leg irons made walking in the thick mud even more difficult, but Davis paid no attention to that. His mind was filled with other things.

Faith. Poor, dead Faith.

And the fact that each step brought him that much closer to his own grave.

5

"I'll have no man say that a prisoner of mine was mistreated," Abernathy declared as he brought a tray of food into the cell.

Davis didn't look up. He sat on the bunk, hands hanging between his knees, and stared at the floor. He had been doing a great deal of that lately, he realized, but for all of his studying the hard stone, it gave him no answers. It was as mute as his own heart.

He had deadened as much of himself as he could, trying to think about nothing, feel nothing. In the morning when he was marched to the gallows, only an empty shell of a man would be hanged. The part of him that had been truly living would have long since departed.

At least, that was Davis's hope. He saw no other choices he could make. Faith was gone, he would never be with his children again, and any reason he might have had for living had melted away like the snowfall under a warm sun.

Yet, even now, there were shady patches where thin layers of dirt-smudged whiteness remained, places where the sun seldom if ever reached.

Davis felt a coldness touch him, as if he had stretched his hand down and plunged it into one of those lingering patches of snow. He lifted his head and looked at Abernathy, at the tray of food in the constable's hands. He saw a thick slice of roast beef, cooked with wild onions, and a chunk of bread, and suddenly he was hungry.

"Here," Abernathy said. He handed the tray to Davis, who took it and rested it on his knees. Abernathy left the cell and came back with a jug. "This won't hurt, either," he said as he placed it on the floor just inside the door of the cell.

"A last meal for the condemned man," Davis said in a hollow voice.

"You'll get your supper, and breakfast in the morning if you want it," Abernathy snapped. "Like I said, I won't have anyone claiming that I mistreated a prisoner."

"You're a humane jailer."

"Of course I am."

"Yet you'd take me out of here in the morning—after giving me breakfast—and see me hanged for something I didn't do."

"The verdict of the court is that you're guilty, Hallam," Abernathy said stiffly. "I carry out the sentence, that's all."

Davis lifted the bread to his mouth, bit off a large piece of it, and began to chew. Around the bread, he said, "Go away, Abernathy."

"Aye, that I will." The constable stepped ou

into the corridor, slammed the door shut, and rattled the key in the lock.

Davis ate quickly, almost savagely, as the coldness within him grew. He stood up and fetched the jug Abernathy had left behind. When he pulled the cork and tilted the mouth of the jug to his lips, he was a little surprised to find that it contained wine. He had expected some of Magistrate Symms's corn squeezings. The wine was thin and sour, and the faint warmth it generated in his belly did nothing to mitigate the chill he felt inside.

He finished the food, drank the last of the wine, then rubbed the back of his hand across his mouth. *Nothing to live for*, he thought. That was what he had believed. But he knew now it wasn't true. There was one thing to which he could cling, one very important reason that he should live.

His hatred for Andrew Paxton, who had stolen everything else from him.

All during that long afternoon, feeling seeped back into the numbed mind and heart of Davis Hallam. He wasn't sure what he was going to do, but he knew now that he could not simply resign himself to his own death. If he was ever to have his revenge on Andrew, he would have to get out of this jail somehow.

Despite the seething activity that was going on inside him, Davis remained stoic on the outside. He said nothing to Abernathy when the constable came into the cell to retrieve the tray and the empty jug. Davis stayed where he was on the bunk, seemingly looking at nothing.

But in reality, he was studying Abernathy, assessing the way the constable was paying less attention to him now. Davis didn't know if any of Abernathy's prisoners had ever been hanged before, but Abernathy seemed to find Davis's defeated attitude normal. Perhaps most prisoners awaiting execution retreated into themselves the way Davis had been on the verge of doing. Davis didn't know, didn't care. It was enough that Abernathy was showing signs of growing careless.

The afternoon edged by, and the light in the window faded. Davis climbed to his feet and looked out, saw that the clouds which had been white earlier in the day were now mottled shades of orange and purple. They looked like clusters of bruised fruit hanging in the sky.

This might be the last dusk he would ever see, Davis thought. Might be . . . but not if he could do anything to prevent it.

He moved over to the door and put his ear close to the small, barred window. He heard faint sounds coming from Abernathy's office: the scrape of a chair leg, a drawer opening and closing in the rolltop desk, a cough. The sounds of one man, Davis judged. No one spoke. Abernathy must have sent home the men he had deputized, now that the trial was over and the prisoner was safely locked up. The deputies would be back in the morning, ready to accompany Davis on his last walk to the gibbet.

Abernathy scraped the chair again, then a moment later the front door of the building opened and closed. Davis put his face close to the window in the cell door and angled his eyes toward the office as much as he could. The candle glow he saw told him that the connecting door was open. He turned his head and looked through the bars at the sky again. The colors he had seen in the clouds earlier were gone. Everything was gray now.

Time for his supper.

Abernathy would probably go over to the trading post to get it. Herring's wife sold meals to travelers when they passed through Elkton, so it made sense that she would also provide food for any prisoners locked up in the jail across the street. The constable probably wouldn't be gone long.

Sure enough, not more than five minutes had passed when Davis heard the sound of the front door again. He waited at the cell door until he was certain that the footsteps of only one man had entered the building. When those footsteps started down the corridor toward the cell, he moved quickly back to the bunk and slumped down on it in the same posture of despair he had exhibited before.

The light in the corridor grew brighter. Abernathy was bringing a candle with him again, just as he had done the previous two nights. Davis heard a clatter outside the door, then the key turned in the lock.

He let his head fall forward dispiritedly. The door swung open, and the glow from the candle washed into the cell. Davis had his eyes squinted almost shut so that the light wouldn't blind him. He didn't look up as Abernathy stepped into the cell.

"Here's your supper, Hallam," the constable said. "Are you awake?"

A touch of worry edged into Abernathy's voice,

as if he was really concerned that Davis might be dead instead of sleeping. Davis lifted his head slowly, letting his eyes adjust to the yellow glare of the candle flame. He said in a husky voice, "Did you bring another jug?"

He saw the faint smirk that appeared on Abernathy's lips for a moment. He saw as well that the constable was not armed except for the stout club he usually carried in the jail. The pistol that had been tucked behind Abernathy's wide black belt earlier was nowhere to be seen.

"Don't you want your food?"

"Just the jug will do," Davis said.

Abernathy shrugged. "Whatever pleases you." He had the candle in his right hand, a plate of food in his left. Without setting down the plate, he bent and scooped up the jug from the floor next to the door of the cell, hooking a finger through the curved earthenware handle. He straightened and took a step toward Davis.

Davis came off the bunk in a diving lunge that carried him under Abernathy's arms. The constable had time to yell once in surprise and alarm before Davis slammed into his thighs and drove him backward.

Davis felt the jolt shiver through Abernathy's body as the man's back crashed against the jamb of the door. Abernathy cried out again. Davis went to his knees, his arms still wrapped around Abernathy's legs. The plate of food made an unholy clatter as it fell to the floor, and the jug burst open with a sound like a muffled gunshot when it landed on the stones an instant later. The sickly sweet smell of the wine rose from the floor like an ascending soul. Davis didn't know what had happened to the candle, but the cell had gone dim and shadowy again.

All he knew was that he had to put Abernathy out of the fight quickly, before the constable got his hands on that bludgeon he carried. Davis remembered all too well how a blow from the club had made splinters of agony shoot through his shoulder and deadened his whole arm a couple of nights earlier. He let go of Abernathy's thighs with his right arm and brought that fist up as hard as he could into the man's groin.

Davis had never been much of a brawler. Like any man, there had been times in his life when he had been forced to fight. He had been in the Continental Army during the last year of the Revolution and had seen action in several battles against the British. But that hadn't been hand to hand combat like he was experiencing now. Days and weeks and months of hard work, of swinging an ax and wrestling a plow behind a mule, had hardened his muscles and packed a great deal of strength into their flat, corded lengths.

He felt a surprisingly strong surge of satisfaction as his punch landed and Abernathy screamed. Davis got his feet underneath him and pushed himself upward, butting Abernathy in the stomach and slamming him into the door jamb again as he did so.

Davis smelled the constable's sweat and the acrid tang of beer. Abernathy must have gotten a mug of the brew over at the trading post when he picked up Davis's supper. Davis's hands went to Abernathy's waist and searched frantically for the handle of the club. His fingers slid over the smooth wood, then closed around it. Davis jerked the club free.

Instead of using it on Abernathy, he flung it behind him and heard it rattle against the rear wall of the cell. He had no wish to kill Abernathy, but he knew that he would if he had to in order to get out of here and find Andrew. Best to remove the temptation to use the club to smash Abernathy's skull.

Davis got hold of Abernathy's coat and used it to steady himself as he straightened. Abernathy hit him once in the chest, but the blow didn't have much power behind it. Abernathy was still stunned from Davis's unexpected attack.

Davis hit him in the face with his right fist, then hit him again. Abernathy's head rocked back each time. He tried to throw another punch at Davis, but it was easily blocked. Davis grabbed the lapels of Abernathy's coat, swung him around, and hit him again, this time with a left. The blow sent Abernathy crashing back against the bunk. Davis heard a sharp snap, and Abernathy gave a high, thin cry of agony as he fell to the floor.

Davis didn't know what he had done, but he knew he couldn't leave Abernathy free behind him to raise the alarm. He stepped closer to the constable and saw that Abernathy's left arm was bent at a strange angle beneath him. The arm was broken, Davis realized.

Then he stopped in his tracks and sniffed the

air in the cell. Something was burning. Suddenly, he felt heat on his back. He hadn't even noticed it before. With a grimace, he whipped off his coat and saw that it was on fire.

Melted wax from the candle must have splattered on it when he tackled Abernathy, Davis thought, setting the fabric to smoldering and finally blazing. He threw the burning coat to the floor and started stomping on it with his boots to put out the flames.

While he was doing that, something suddenly attached itself to his leg and pulled hard. Davis wasn't ready for that. He grunted in surprise as he fell. In the light from the still burning coat he saw Peter Abernathy struggling with him. Abernathy had managed somehow to get his hand on the club Davis had taken away from him earlier. He drew back his good arm, ready to strike with the bludgeon.

Davis didn't stop to think about what he was doing. He just kicked Abernathy's broken arm as hard as he could.

Abernathy didn't scream this time. The pain must have been too great for that. His eyes just rolled back in his head, and he fell away from Davis, out cold from the agony that had shot through him.

The sleeves of Davis's shirt were smoldering from where he had landed beside the burning coat. He slapped out the little fires, then clambered to his feet and finished stamping out the coat. His chest was heaving, and the lungfuls of air he gulped down were bitter with the mixture of smoke, spilled wine, and the cell's usual stench. The blood was roaring in his head.

After a moment, he forced some coherent thoughts through his brain. He had no idea how long Abernathy would be unconscious, but it wasn't likely to be long. Davis picked up the remnants of the coat, ripped off and balled up a piece of the fabric, and shoved it into Abernathy's mouth. He used another strip of cloth from the ruined coat to bind the makeshift gag in place. Then he tied the constable's good arm to one leg of the bunk.

That ought to hold him for a while, Davis thought. Long enough to get away from the settlement, anyway. He wiped the back of his hand across his face and stumbled out of the cell.

Abernathy had yelled enough during the fight that he might have attracted the attention of someone in the settlement. His movements still somewhat awkward, Davis moved to the desk and picked up the pistol he saw lying there. After he had shoved the weapon behind his belt, he turned to the wall and lifted one of the muskets down from its pegs. He took the powderhorn and shot pouch that had been hanging with the gun, as well as the horn and pouch from the other musket, and slung them all over his shoulder by their straps. He would have liked to have a knife as well, but there was no time to rummage around the office looking for one. He was already well armed.

He went to the door and eased it open, peering through the narrow crack at the gathering night. Seeing no one, he pushed the door open a little more. The trading post across the road came into view. The big log building was brightly lit, but no one was on the porch. It was still too cold at night to sit outside. Herring, his wife, and any customers would be inside, close by the stove.

Davis moved out of the constable's office, not hurrying as he went down the steps, and turned toward the corner of the building. Haste would just draw attention to him. But he didn't lag about. He walked like a man who knew where he was going and had every right to be going there.

When he reached the corner of the jail building, he turned around it, relaxing slightly as he put himself out of sight of the trading post and the other businesses and cabins. The woods grew close to the back of the jail, and Davis headed straight for them, eager to lose himself in their thick, clinging shadows. It would have simplified matters if he'd had a horse, but the only way to get one here in Elkton would be to steal one. He wasn't going to do that.

No matter what else might be said about him, Davis Hallam was no thief.

But he was a man who had been terribly wronged, and he swore that by the time this night was over, he would have his vengeance on Andrew Paxton.

It was a long walk to Andrew's farm, but Davis felt little of it. His hatred urged him on like a hand tugging at him, a tiny voice imploring him to keep moving. Yet he could not totally ignore the blisters that formed on his feet, even through the thick socks he wore. Work boots were not meant for walking more than ten miles. By the time he was halfway to his destination, prickles of pain shot through Davis's feet with each step.

He told himself he felt nothing, and he kept his eyes on the stars overhead much of the time, steering by their brilliant points of light. The sky was clear; the clouds that were there earlier in the evening had been blown away by the cold wind that cut through Davis's shirt and numbed his ears. There was no moon, but he could see the road by the light of the stars.

Few people would be abroad at this time of night, and Davis was thankful for that. In fact, he had not seen a single soul since circling around the settlement and reaching the road that ran through the center of the valley. Numb or not, he used his ears diligently, listening for the slightest sound of pursuit behind him. If he heard anything, he planned to leave the road and hide in the woods on either side. His nervousness increased every time he reached an area of fields, where there was little place to hide.

Davis's plans were vague. He wasn't sure what he would do when he reached Andrew's cabin. He had never thought of himself as a killer. That was one reason it had been so shocking to be accused of Faith's murder. He was a peaceful man.

Yet he knew now that he *was* capable of taking the life of someone else. He would have gladly killed Andrew there in the meeting hall during that travesty of a trial. He might yet kill Andrew.

But if he did, everyone in the Shenandoah Valley would know who was responsible. He would spend the rest of his life as a fugitive, running from judgment . . .

Which was exactly what he already was, he told himself. If he was going to be a fugitive anyway, better to be running from something he had actually done, rather than something he hadn't.

If he didn't kill Andrew, though . . . if he could take his brother back to Elkton and somehow force him to confess . . . then Davis's name would be cleared and he wouldn't have to live his life on the run from the law. He would be reunited with his children and could return to his existence on the farm. True, Faith would no longer be there, and he would have all the bitter memories to contend with, but he was confident that he and Mary and Laurel and Theodore could still make a decent life for themselves. If that proved to be too difficult to do here in the Shenandoah Valley, they could move on elsewhere. They could head west.

There was a whole country out there for the taking, after all.

Davis used those thoughts to distract himself from the blisters on his feet and the dull, throbbing ache in his legs. The stars wheeled in their heavenly courses overhead, and the hours passed. It had to be after midnight by now. Davis wondered if Constable Abernathy had gotten loose yet, or if anyone had found him tied up there in the cell. It was possible he was still lying there helplessly on the cold stone floor, and Davis felt a little bad about that. But only a little, because he had not forgotten Abernathy's unbending attitude of disbelief, nor how his arm and shoulder had hurt from that blow with the club. Abernathy was a hard, cheerless man.

Of course, some had accused Davis of being the same thing . . .

He shook his head, trying not to think about some of the harsh words Faith had spoken to him in the past. Dwelling on that would do no one any good, least of all him. And he had to look out for himself, because no one else would now.

Dawn was still several hours off, he judged, when he reached the lane leading from the road to Andrew's farm. He turned onto the narrower path and increased his pace. The tug on him was even stronger now. His hands tightened on the musket he had taken from Abernathy's office, and despite the coldness of the night, he felt tiny beads of sweat break out on his forehead to be almost instantly dried by the wind. That just made the chill inside him deeper, more numbing.

No lights shone in the windows of the cabin as he approached. That came as no surprise. Andrew was probably asleep. Davis wondered if his dreams were haunted by nightmares of what he had done. Probably not, he decided. Anyone who could stand before a magistrate and lie the way Andrew had lied would probably sleep soundly—no matter what else he might have done.

No dogs barked as Davis came up to the cabin. Andrew didn't keep any, claiming they were too much trouble. Davis was thankful for that. He looked around the place, seeing the fallen pole fences, the rocks and stumps still in the fields that should have been cleared, the way the barn leaned to one side like a tired old man. Those were all things that Andrew should have taken care of before now if he planned to make a success of this farm.

But that was just it, Davis realized. Andrew had never planned to make a go of it. That would involve too much hard work. No, Andrew would have been content to keep things just as they had been. Davis would have helped him, would have fed him and taken him in if necessary. Davis wouldn't have liked it, but Andrew was family, after all. Where a man's family was concerned, you sometimes did things whether you really wanted to or not.

Andrew had stepped over a line that could not be crossed when he persuaded Faith to take him into her bed. Davis had no doubt that the whole thing had been Andrew's idea. Faith had given in to temptation, but it had been Andrew who had placed it before her. And so far, Andrew was the only one who had not been punished for his transgression.

That was about to end, Davis told himself.

His booted foot crashed against the door of the cabin, knocking it open. His thumb was curled around the hammer of the musket, ready to cock the weapon and fire it if he needed to. "Andrew!" he bellowed as he lunged into the one-room cabin. "Your judgment is upon you, Andrew!"

Not much starlight penetrated the interior of the cabin, but Davis's eyes were open wide to take advantage of what illumination there was. He swung the barrel of the musket from side to side, alert for any movement in the shadows, any sound that would give away Andrew's position.

There was nothing. Nothing.

Davis stood there, his breath harsh in his throat. He was holding so tightly to the gun that his arms began to tremble. "Andrew?" he said.

No answer but silence.

Outside the wind whispered in the trees. Inside the cabin, Davis lowered the musket and felt around in the darkness until he located the fireplace. He knelt in front of it, found some slivers of wood for kindling, and took out his flint and steel and tinder, which Abernathy had left him. He struck a spark and soon had a small fire going. There were only a few half-burned twigs left in the fireplace.

Their light was enough to tell him that the cabin was empty. Everything was gone—not that Andrew had had much in the way of furnishings. He'd had more clothes than anything else, Davis recalled. He had been proud of his wardrobe, along with a silver-headed walking stick and a knife with a silver knob on the end of its handle, both of which he had bought in Philadelphia, he'd said.

Davis took a deep, ragged breath. He had come all this way for nothing. Andrew was gone, almost as if he had never been here. All he had left behind him was the wreckage of several lives.

Leaving the little fire burning, Davis stalked out of the cabin and quickly checked the barn, but the results of the search were what he expected. Andrew's horse was missing, too, and so was the brace of mules he had bought. He must have used the mules as pack animals when he left, Davis thought. The beasts could have easily carried away Andrew's few belongings.

Davis stood on the threshold of the cabin and

tiredly scrubbed a hand over his face. He had not shaved in several days, and the beard stubble on his cheeks and chin was thick and bristly. Faith would have hated it and claimed that he was trying to scrape her raw if he had kissed her looking like this. Davis's eyes felt wet and hot at that thought.

There was nothing he could do here. He had been cheated of his vengeance. And yet, he wasn't ready to just walk away from the place. Instead, he went inside and took the stopper from the mouth of one of the powderhorns. With a flicking motion of his wrist, he scattered some of the black powder around the room, then laid a trail of it to the door. He capped the powderhorn again, then went to the fireplace, where the blaze had burned down to almost nothing. Flames still flickered along the length of one of the twigs, however. He picked it up by the end that wasn't burning and walked back to the door, holding the twig in front of him.

He turned, took another deep breath, then bent to hold the burning twig to the trail of powder that snaked across the room. The powder caught with a sudden hiss and flared up brightly. Davis dropped the twig and stepped back quickly. He moved away from the cabin, watching the spreading flames through the open doorway as he did so.

Within a matter of seconds, or so it seemed, the whole cabin was ablaze, throwing out great waves of light and heat that broke around him. The flames glittered in Davis's eyes, and the crackling of the dry wood as it burned filled his ears.

So much so, in fact, that he didn't hear the thunder of hoofbeats until it was almost too late.

He spun around so that the inferno seared the fine hairs on the back of his neck and saw the horsemen coming down the lane toward him. They were still a good distance away, but the light from the fire reached far enough for him to see the face of Peter Abernathy. The constable rode at the head of the group, his broken arm splinted and wrapped and held in a sling. His features were contorted with rage, and he was shouting something. Davis couldn't hear the words, but that didn't matter. He knew what Abernathy was saying.

He was telling the men with him to shoot down Davis Hallam like a mad dog.

Davis threw himself to the side as orange muzzle flashes sparked in the night. He couldn't hear the lead balls thudding into the burning walls of the cabin, but he was certain they were. He scrambled around the corner of the blazing structure, unsure if he was hit or not.

Somehow, his exhausted body found the strength to run. He was beyond the barn by the time the riders reached the cabin. A glance back over his shoulder told him that some of the men were stopping, perhaps to see if they could determine whether or not Andrew was inside the cabin, but several others came on at a gallop.

Across the field behind the barn was a dark line that Davis knew to be a thick stretch of woods. If he could get in there, the men couldn't pursue him on horseback because of the undergrowth. He would have a chance of slipping away from Abernathy and the others, but only if he made it to the forest first.

Firing on innocent men went against every instinct he had except one.

Self-preservation.

He stopped, swung around, and lifted the musket to his shoulder. As he settled the sights on the onrushing figures on horseback, he cocked the weapon and curled his finger around the trigger. At the last instant, he altered his aim slightly, firing just above their heads.

The boom of the musket and the tongue of flame that licked from its muzzle was enough to make the riders veer to one side. Davis turned and ran again, and the trees drew steadily closer in front of him. Something whined past his ear, and he knew it had been a ball from a flintlock. He lurched from side to side as he ran, making it more difficult for anyone to draw a bead on him.

Then suddenly he was among the trees and the brush, and he heard the angry shouts from across the field. Davis plunged deeper into the undergrowth, ignoring the way the branches caught at him and cut his face and hands and tore his clothes. By the time he emerged from this thicket, he might be stripped naked and bleeding from a thousand scratches, but he would come out a free man.

Or die trying.

6

The trading post was a busy place. Wagons hitched to teams of massive, stolid-looking oxen were parked in front of the big log building. A dozen or more horses and pack mules had their reins tied to the railing along the edge of the long porch. Women and children bustled in and out through the open double doors, the women wearing homespun gray or brown dresses and bonnets, the girls in similar dresses, the boys in wool pants and linsey-woolsey shirts. The men were wearing everything from buckskins decorated with beads and fringes in the Indian fashion to town clothes bought back east in Boston or Philadelphia; they stood along the porch smoking pipes, sharing drinks from jugs that were passed around, talking solemnly about politics, or laughing raucously at some tall tale. Every stripe of frontier humanity was here, Davis Hallam thought as he trudged up the path that led to the trading post. He wondered if he was the only one who was wanted by the law on murder charges. Probably not, he decided.

The wilderness was big enough for just about everybody.

Three weeks had passed since the night he had fled from the burning cabin of his half-brother, with pursuers dogging his heels. Most of the cuts and scrapes he had gotten that night had healed by now, but they had left quite a few new scars. Not to mention the scars that no one could see, such as knowing that his wife was dead and he would probably never see his children again. And knowing, as well, that justice had been forever denied.

He had gotten away from Abernathy and the other men by the skin of his teeth. Some of his pursuers had come into the forest after him, while others had tried to ride around it and catch up with him on the other side. There were some stretches of woods in the Shenandoah Valley that ran for miles, however, and that was one of them. By the time the riders reached the far side of the thick growth, Davis was long gone.

It had been trickier eluding the men who came after him on foot. He could have stopped and waited to ambush them, and he probably could have killed several of them before he was finally captured or killed. But he had no wish to cause them harm, so he had pushed on, listening to the crash of brush behind him, using that noise as a goad to urge him on whenever he felt like giving up.

By the next morning, he had been miles from where he had started, and the sounds of pursuit had faded and finally disappeared. He was safe, at least for the moment.

The worst part of it was that he had had no

chance to pick up Andrew's trail. He had no idea which direction his half-brother had gone when he left the farm. And of a certainty, Davis could never return to that place, or even to the vicinity. To do so would be to risk capture and hanging. His own farm was forfeit, just as his life had nearly been.

Over the past three weeks, he had come to terms with that as best he could. His life had utterly changed, and there was no going back. Might as well try to grasp and hold the wind as to try to get back what he had lost. It would be as easy a task.

During that time he had traveled mostly at night, hiding by day in thick woods or brush-choked gullies. Luckily, there was plenty of game about, and no one on the frontier wondered too much about an occasional shot in the distance. Nearly everyone supplemented what they could grow by hunting. Davis didn't go hungry too often.

The blisters on his feet broke and healed. New ones formed and broke. Still he kept walking at night, heading in a generally southwest direction, paralleling the Blue Ridge to the east and the Shenandoah Mountains to the west. In time he left the valley entirely, unsure of where he was going, knowing only that he had to put as much distance as possible between him and everything that was now behind him.

The weather had grown warmer, and he was thankful for that. With no coat, a hard winter storm might have done him in. The worst of this season's storms appeared to be over. By next winter, he had thought to himself one day, he would have a good coat again.

That day was special, he realized later, because for the first time since his life had fallen apart around him so unexpectedly, he was thinking in terms of the future once more. When he was locked up in that cell, his life had been measured in hours. Now it stretched in front of him indefinitely, like a road that dwindles into the distance.

He was going to travel down that road as far as it would take him.

Today it had taken him to a settlement called the Block House, after the massive, two-story, stone and wood structure around which it had grown. He was in the far southwestern reaches of Virginia, he thought, although he couldn't be sure of that. Borders didn't mean a lot out here. Several trails from Pennsylvania, Carolina, and eastern Virginia came together here. In the distance rose the Cumberland Mountains, green and hazy like the water in a pond, and beyond them was the land known by some as Kaintuck, by others as Kentucky.

Davis stopped between the trading post and the Block House, which had served as protection for the settlers during times of Indian raids since its construction in 1777, and stared toward the mountains. He could see the narrow, winding trail that started toward them, but he soon lost sight of its twists and turns in the thick forests. He didn't have to see it to know where it led, however.

He stood at the beginning of the Wilderness Road.

A hand fell on his shoulder and he stiffened, muscles tensing in case he had to fight. As he jerked his head around, however, he saw a friendly grin on the face of the man standing next to him.

"I seen ya lookin' at the Cumberlands," the man said. "Got a mighty powerful lure to 'em, don't they? Makes ya want to see what's on the other side."

Davis relaxed a little. Evidently this frontiersman was just talkative. The man wore greasy buckskins which were stretched tight across his massive shoulders. He had a bushy black beard shot through with gray; his hat, with a drooping brim and a feather stuck in the band, perched on a tangled thatch of dark hair. Some accident had befallen the man's left eye in the past, leaving a white scar above and below the socket. The eye itself was milky and seemed to wander of its own accord. In the man's other hand was a long-barreled flintlock rifle, and the butt of the weapon rested on the ground at his moccasined feet.

Davis nodded at the trail that wound toward the mountains. "That's the Wilderness Road, isn't it?"

"Oh, aye, 'tis indeed. And a fittin' name it is, too. There was nothin' but wilderness out there when me an' Dan'l Boone started carvin' it out fifteen year ago."

"You were with Daniel Boone?" Davis asked, trying not to sound too skeptical. He figured that most old-timers in these parts probably claimed to have been through the Cumberland Gap with Boone, whether they really had been or not.

"Aye, Dan'l an' me was the first white men to see Kaintuck, I reckon." The man took his hand off Davis's shoulder and extended it toward him. "I'm Titus Gilworth."

Davis hesitated. Even now, this far away from

where his old life had ended, he hesitated to give his real name. "Call me Dave," he said.

"All right, Dave. Thinkin' 'bout goin' to Kaintuck, are ya?"

Davis nodded. "Thinking about it."

"Good time to go, and get paid to boot. Colonel's over at the tradin' post, signin' up men for a chore."

That caught Davis's interest. "What sort of chore?"

"Choppin' down trees, makin' the road wider. Ain't nothin' but a trail now, you understand. Can't get no wagons through there without a heap o' trouble, only two-wheeled carts. Gov'ment wants to make it easier for folks to get to Kaintuck so's it'll get settled faster, so they figger to improve the road." Titus Gilworth spat on the ground at his feet. "You ask me, the place is already gettin' settled too damn fast. Can't hardly find a place where you ain't crowded no more. Last time I was over there, I heard other folks shootin' once, twice a week. I can't take all that uproar."

Davis enjoyed listening to the garrulous old man, but what Gilworth had said about some colonel hiring men to widen the Wilderness Road intrigued him too much for him to stand there and let Gilworth ramble on. He inclined his head toward the trading post and said, "I think I'll go talk to that colonel you mentioned."

"Good idea, son. Tell him ol' Titus sent ya."

Davis didn't intend to do that, but he nodded anyway. As he turned to head for the trading post, he asked, "Are you signing on?"

Gilworth shook his head. "Nope. I'm too old for such shenanigans." He sighed. "I got a cousin named Ulysses who settled up in Ohio country a while back, durin' that war against the redcoats. He wants me to come yonder an' live with him, and I'm thinkin' on it. Don't know if I'll be able to stand so damned much civilization . . . but hell, a man ought to try just about ever'thin' once, don't you think?"

Davis nodded and smiled, then waved a hand as he started toward the trading post. He was glad he had decided to alter his pattern of traveling at night and avoiding settlements. This trip to the Block House might turn out to be fortunate if he was able to sign on with the group heading across the mountains to Kentucky.

Over there in that far, wild land, the law would never catch up to him.

He went up the steps onto the porch, then moved into the dim interior of the trading post. It was cluttered with goods, and the aisles were full of customers. Davis was taller than most of them, so he was able to look over their heads and see the group of men standing at a table set up in front of the rear counter, near the barrels of pickles and crackers. Davis made his way toward the table and joined the line of men waiting there. Most of them had a rugged look about them, and they were all armed. Some carried only a rifle, but others had pistols and knives tucked behind their belts as well. They looked like bad men to cross. Davis wondered if he gave that impression to people as well.

After several minutes, he had moved close enough to the table to see the two men who were sitting there. Both of them seemed to be in robust middle age, but that was where the resemblance ended. The one on the left wore a dark brown suit and had graying sandy hair that was pulled straight back from his high forehead. His companion was dressed in buckskins and a cap made from the hide of a raccoon, with the animal's head still attached. Raven-black hair fell loosely to the man's shoulders, where it had evidently been hacked off squarely with a knife. His features were lean and dark, as opposed to the other man's broad, florid face.

The man in the brown suit had a book open in front of him, an inkwell beside it. After talking to each of the men lined up in front of him, he used the quill pen in his hand to write something in the book, Davis noted. This man had to be the colonel Titus Gilworth had mentioned, and likely what he was writing in the book were the names of the men he hired for the work crew. Davis hoped his name would soon be in that book.

When his turn came, he stepped up in front of the man in the suit and nodded. The man looked at him and asked, "Name?"

Instead of answering right away, Davis asked a question of his own. "Are you the man who's hiring workers to widen the Wilderness Road?"

"That's right. I'm Colonel Tobias Welles. And you are?"

"Name's Davis." He thought quickly. "Hal Davis."

"All right, Mr. Davis," Welles said. "Are you a fugitive from the law?"

The question took Davis by surprise, but he tried to control his reaction. "Of course not," he said.

"I have to ask that, you understand," Welles commented as he began to scribble the false name Davis had given him in the book. "We want only law-abiding men on our crew. This is Conn Powell, my foreman for this job."

The man in buckskins nodded curtly to Davis, who returned the greeting in similar fashion. Powell's eyes seemed narrow and suspicious, but maybe that was how he looked at everyone, Davis thought. He couldn't remember seeing a different expression on Powell's face since entering the trading post.

"We'll feed you along the way, and the wages are twenty dollars, payable when we reach Logan's Fort at the other end of the Road. Is that acceptable?"

Davis nodded. Twenty dollars was more money than he had seen in some years, when he was trying to make a go of the farm. To make that much money for a few weeks of work chopping trees seemed astounding to him. Of course, in addition to the labor involved in this task, there would also be the danger from Indians and bandits to consider.

He was more than willing to run the risk. After everything he had gone through, such things didn't seem quite so bad.

"Very good," Welles said. "We'll be setting out tomorrow. I'll have a full crew by then. Be ready to leave at dawn."

Davis nodded and turned away from the table, as he had seen the other men do before him. Conn Powell stopped him by saying, "Davis."

Looking back at him, Davis waited in silence for whatever the buckskinned man had to say.

"I'll be keepin' an eye on you. Something about you rubs me the wrong way, mister."

Welles said to his foreman, "If you'd rather I mark out his name . . . "

Powell shook his head. "That ain't necessary. I just want this fella to know I'm goin' to be watchin' him."

Davis swallowed the bitter taste of anger that welled up in his throat. "Go ahead and watch," he said. "I'll do my job and give you an honest day's work for an honest day's pay."

"I'm sure you will," Welles said. Evidently he wanted to head off any further confrontation between Davis and Powell, because he hurried on, "Next man, please."

Davis walked back to the front of the trading post, his pulse hard and his jaw clenched. What was it about him that had put Powell on edge? he wondered. Perhaps it had been just an instinctive dislike, the kind that had no rhyme or reason to it.

Whatever had caused it, the incident had taken away some of the anticipation Davis felt for this job. Still, he was confident that he could force himself to get along with Powell for however long it took to reach Kentucky.

And once he was there, he would lose himself on the frontier, spending the rest of his life in the isolation he craved.

Davis had some venison in his pouch from a kill he had made a few days earlier. He had smoked the meat as best he could, and it was still edible. Sitting cross-legged under a tree near the trading post, he gnawed on the tough flesh and watched the comings and goings in the little settlement. If there were this many people here now, what would it be like once the Wilderness Road had been improved enough to make travel over the Cumberland Gap into Kentucky much easier? If old-timers like Titus Gilworth thought the frontier was already getting too crowded, they really wouldn't like what they saw over the next few years, Davis sensed.

He didn't waste much time thinking about such things. To him, the future was something to be endured in loneliness. He could hope that someday he would feel differently, but for now, that was all it was—a hope, as fragile and insubstantial as the mist that curled around the trunks of trees in the early morning light.

As dusk began to settle down around the Block House and the trading post and the other buildings, a figure shambled toward Davis. He recognized the man in the gathering shadows as Titus Gilworth. The old frontiersman had a jug dangling from his hand, and his steps were a little unsteady. He stopped in front of Davis and said, "Evenin', Dave. Want a nip from this here jug?"

Davis hesitated before answering. He had never been much of a drinking man, and the last time he had touched liquor had been when he drank the wine that Constable Abernathy brought him in the Elkton jail. Ever since then, while he was on the run, he had avoided spirits, knowing that if he allowed himself to get drunk, he might retreat into the oblivion it brought and never sober up again.

But Titus was just trying to be friendly, and it seemed like an eternity since Davis had been able to call anyone friend. He had been convinced that he didn't *want* any friends. Without pondering the decision any more, he reached up to take the jug Titus was extending toward him. "Much obliged," he said, then he tipped the neck of the jug to his mouth and took a long swallow.

The liquor burned like the flames of hell as it slid down his throat and landed hard in his belly. Davis couldn't suppress the little shudder that went through him. Titus must have noticed it, because he chuckled and said, "Mighty fine, ain't it?"

Davis lowered the jug and swiped the back of his hand across his mouth. "Aye," he said.

Without waiting for a formal invitation, Titus sank down onto the ground beside Davis and put his back against the broad bole of the tree. "Signed up t' go over the Road, did ye?"

Davis nodded. "Yes, Colonel Welles hired me."

"Colonel ain't a bad sort. Some kind o' engineer, he claims to be. Don't know much about the frontier, but he's good at buildin' roads, I reckon."

Giving in to curiosity, Davis asked, "What do you know about Conn Powell?"

Titus looked over at him owlishly. "Used to be a long hunter. Don't know him very well, but I know he's still got the hide on. He's bossin' the job for the colonel, ain't he?"

"That's right. I don't think he likes me much, but he told Welles to go ahead and hire me."

Titus grunted and said, "Ain't nobody Powell

likes overmuch. Try to stay downwind of him, son. Don't let him get your scent."

Davis wasn't sure exactly what Titus meant by that, but he nodded anyway. He didn't plan on crossing Powell. He didn't want to draw any attention to himself, and causing trouble with the foreman of the timber-cutting crew would only accomplish that very thing.

He handed the jug back to Titus, having taken just the one drink. That was enough to be sociable, Davis told himself. He shook his head when Titus took another swig, then offered him the jug again.

"You sure?" Titus asked.

"I'm sure," Davis replied.

"You got somethin' to hide? That the reason you don't want to get drunk?"

Davis frowned. Despite Titus's inebriated condition, the old man had made a shrewd guess. Davis didn't want to admit that, of course. Instead, he said, "I'm just not much of a drinker."

Titus shrugged his brawny shoulders. "Whatever you say." His tone made it clear that he didn't really believe Davis.

It was a good thing, Davis thought, that Titus Gilworth was going to live with his cousin in Ohio, rather than traveling back over the Wilderness Road with Colonel Welles and the others. Titus was just canny enough to have caused problems for Davis before the journey was over.

Several of the travelers who had stopped at the settlement had cooking fires blazing near their wagons, and the flames provided enough illumination for Davis to see fairly well even though night had fallen. He noticed three men walking past the tree where he and Titus were sitting, but he didn't recognize any of them. From the looks of them, they were probably part of the crew that would widen the Wilderness Road. One wore buckskins while the other two were in rough homespun.

Just as the men walked past, Titus gave a mighty yawn and stretched his long legs out in front of him. That put his feet directly in the path of the buckskin-clad man, and he tripped over them, barely catching his balance before he sprawled headlong on the ground. His long-barreled flintlock rifle slipped from his grasp and thudded to the dirt.

"What the hell!" the man roared as he swung around to face Davis and Titus.

Titus was blinking rapidly and frowning, as if he was just as surprised as the man he had nearly tripped. He tilted his head back and said, "Better watch where you're goin', son. You could hurt somebody, trompin' 'em like that."

"Watch where I'm—" the man began, then stopped to give out a string of curses. "You almost made me fall down, you mossbacked old bastard!" he added. "You did make me drop my rifle." He bent over to pick up the weapon.

The confrontation was drawing the attention of several people who were camped nearby, and Davis felt his nerves start to crawl like worms as he sensed all the eyes turned in his direction. He realized they weren't looking at *him*. Their attention was focused on Titus and the angry man who was yelling at the old frontiersman. But in the past few weeks, Davis's aversion to too much attention had become as ingrained as a lifelong habit. He felt uncomfortably edgy.

"I'm sure Titus didn't mean anything—" Davis started to say, but an angry exclamation from the buckskinned man cut him off.

"I don't give a damn what he meant. You'd better stay out of this, mister. It's between me and the old man."

That was excellent advice, Davis thought. He had never met Titus Gilworth until today, and he had no business defending him. True, Titus had been friendly toward him, but Davis hadn't asked for that.

The buckskinned man sneered at Titus and kicked the bottom of his foot. "Get up, old man," he ordered. "I want an apology."

"Oh, it's an apology you're wantin', is it?" Titus asked. He pulled himself shakily to his feet, still holding the nearly empty jug. "Well, you won't be gettin' it from me. It ain't my fault you're near as blind as a bat."

"Teach the old sot a lesson," one of the other men said.

"Aye." The man in buckskins clenched his hands into fists. "That's just what I'm going to do." He took a step toward Titus.

Stay out of it. The words hammered a drumbeat in Davis's head. *Stay out of it.*

Titus didn't wait for the man to reach him. With a yell, he flung the whiskey jug at the man's head and then reached for the butt of the pistol stuck behind his belt.

Once again, just like that awful day back in the

cabin, Davis was struck by the way the seconds seemed to sometimes slow down at a moment of extreme violence. He saw the jug tumble through the air toward the man's head, saw droplets of whiskey fly from its open neck like a shower of amber rain, watched as the man flung up an arm and batted the jug aside before it could do any harm. Davis turned his head toward Titus and opened his mouth to shout something, but no words came out. They froze in his throat as he saw how Titus was struggling to draw the pistol. The barrel had hung on something, and Titus was tugging frantically at the weapon.

Davis's gaze flicked back to the man in buckskins. The man had his own pistol drawn, the barrel lifting inexorably as his thumb looped around the hammer and drew it back. Davis's eyes widened and he reached for Titus, intending to shove the old man out of the way, but before he could do so, the roar of exploding gunpowder slammed against Davis's ears. He seemed to see every grain of burning powder that spewed from the muzzle of the pistol in the man's hand, followed by a cloud of thick black smoke. The thud of the heavy lead ball striking flesh blended with Titus's grunt of pain and Davis's shout of "No!"

He had finally managed to say something, but as usual, it was too late.

Titus was thrown back against the tree. Davis felt a warm wet splatter on his cheek. For a second that seemed much longer, Titus hung there, more blood welling between the fingers of the hand he had pressed to his chest. The blood was thick and black in the garish glow of the firelight. Then Titus began to slide down the trunk until he was sitting again. His head lolled forward limply, and his arm fell to the side.

Davis looked at the man in buckskins and saw that tendrils of smoke were still curling from the barrel of the pistol. Barely aware of what he was doing, Davis came up off the ground and launched himself in a dive at the man who had just killed Titus.

7

Davis's attack took the man by surprise. He slammed into the man, driving him backward. Both of them went down, landing hard on the ground. Davis heard the loud *whoof!* as the man's breath was driven out of his body by the impact.

Several people were shouting. Davis heard them but ignored the noise. He concentrated on the man squirming underneath him. The man slashed at Davis's head with the empty pistol, but Davis saw the blow coming and was able to jerk back out of the way. He lifted his arm and brought his fist down like a mallet in the middle of the man's face.

The next instant, something crashed into his left shoulder and knocked him to the side. He cried out at the agony that shot through him, but he had the presence of mind to roll over rapidly, taking him away from whoever had hit him. He looked up and saw one of the other men looming over him, booted foot upraised and ready to stomp down at him. Davis threw his hands up and managed to catch the

man's ankle. A sudden heave sent the man
staggering back, arms flailing.

Shouting seemed to fill the whole settlement by
now. Nothing broke up the monotony of frontier life
like a fight. The shot would have drawn the
attention of everyone in the vicinity, too. In the
midst of the commotion, Davis tried to scramble
back to his feet. He wished he hadn't gotten mixed
up in this, but now he had no choice except to
defend himself.

The third man came at him swinging
roundhouse blows. Davis warded off a couple of
them, but then the man's knobby fist cracked
against Davis's chin, rocking his head back and
making him see stars that put the ones in the
heavens to shame. Davis stumbled over something
and glanced down, realizing to his horror that it was
Titus's corpse he had bumped against. That
distracted him, and his opponent hit him again,
knocking him against the tree this time. Davis could
barely stay on his feet.

"He's mine!" The furious shout came from the
first man, the one who had shot Titus. He had
gotten back to his feet and now came at Davis with
a murderous rage twisting his face. His nose was
bloody and grotesquely flattened and swollen
where Davis had hit him. He had picked up his rifle
and was holding it by the barrel. He slashed at
Davis with the stock, hitting him across the
midsection with it. Davis doubled over and slumped
to his knees next to Titus. Above him, the man lifted
the rifle again, ready to bring it down in a blow that
would probably crush Davis's skull.

Davis's fingers closed around the hilt of the knife sheathed at Titus's waist. He brought the blade up and rested the point on the crotch of the man's buckskin trousers. All it would take was a shove to send the blade slicing into his groin. The man froze where he was, the rifle lifted above his head.

"If I . . . see your arms start to come down . . . I'm pushing on this knife," Davis said through teeth clenched against the pain.

"Be careful, Hedge," one of the other men said. "I think the bastard's daft enough to do it!"

The man called Hedge looked down at Davis, eyes wide and lips pulled back from his teeth. "Somebody shoot him!" he said.

"There'll be no more shooting here," a new voice barked. From the corner of his eye, Davis saw Colonel Welles and Conn Powell come striding up to the scene of the fight.

"Put that knife down, Davis," Powell growled.

"And let him bash in my skull?" Davis asked.

"Nobody is going to continue this battle," Welles said. "I want everyone to lay down their weapons." The tone of command in his voice was unexpectedly strong.

Stubbornly, Davis waited until Hedge had lowered the flintlock and was holding it loosely in one hand. Then he took the point of the knife away from the man's groin. Hedge seemed to be suppressing a sigh of relief, not altogether successfully.

Davis pulled himself to his feet. His whole body was a mass of aches and pains, but he stood straight and stiff as he glared at Hedge and the other two men. Then he looked down at Titus's body, and something twisted inside him. He had only been acquainted with the old man for a few hours and really knew very little about him. But he was certain that Titus had deserved a better end than this, shot down callously by Hedge.

"What happened here?" Welles demanded.

"That old man tried to shoot Hedge," one of the men in homespun said, pointing at Titus's body. "Then the other one went mad when Hedge defended himself and shot the old bastard."

"That's not how it happened," Davis said.

Powell's dark eyes swung over to Davis. "Then you tell us how it did happen," he said coldly.

"This man here, the one called Hedge, was going to give Titus a beating."

"He deserved it!" Hedge said. "He tried to trip me, the sot, and then he threw a whiskey jug at me. He's the one who reached for his pistol first!"

"What about that, Davis?" Welles asked.

Davis hesitated. He had already lied to the colonel twice, about his name and about not being a fugitive from the law. He didn't want to add a third lie to that list, especially one that could probably be proven false quite easily. There were enough people around so that some of them must have seen the fight start.

"Gilworth reached for his pistol first," Davis finally said after a moment. "But I'm sure he felt justified. There were three of these men bullying him, and they were a lot younger than him. They might have beaten him badly."

Powell gestured at Titus's body. "His gun's still behind his belt. What happened?"

"It got caught on something. He wasn't able to draw it in time."

"He was trying to," Hedge said. "That's all that matters."

Powell shrugged. "Seems to me like Hedge is right, Colonel. Looks like self-defense."

"Three against one?" Davis said angrily. "You call that self-defense?"

"Three against two, I'd say, the way you jumped into the fracas, Davis," Powell snapped. "Those aren't such bad odds."

Welles held his hands up, the palms spread. "That's enough," he said. "I'll have no more arguing. This man's death is unfortunate, but I don't see that there was any crime here. Hedge, you and Clade and Johnson go on about your business. Davis, I expect you to do the same. We have many miles in front of us, and we must work together in order to complete our mission."

Davis swallowed the bile of resentment in the back of his throat. Welles was right, and on top of that, Davis didn't want to draw any more attention to himself. He nodded and said, "That's all right with me."

Hedge made no such gesture. He just turned on his heel and stalked off, followed by the other two men—Clade and Johnson, Welles had called them. Davis watched them go and knew that they wouldn't soon forget what had happened tonight.

Welles looked down at Titus and said, "This man wasn't one of us, but I'll see that he gets a proper burial."

Davis wanted to say that he would do that, but he merely nodded in acceptance of the colonel's decision. It would be better for him to withdraw into the background as much as possible.

Welles motioned for several of the men who were standing around to pick up the body, and as Titus was carried off, Conn Powell sidled over closer to Davis and said in a low voice, "You made yourself some enemies tonight, mister. Hedge and his friends will remember what happened."

Davis had just been thinking the same thing. He said, "I don't want any trouble."

"Sometimes it comes callin' on us, whether we're lookin' for it or not."

Davis didn't waste any breath explaining to Powell how well aware he was of that very fact . . .

During the weeks he had been on the run, Davis had stopped a few times at isolated farms and done a day of chores in return for food and a place to sleep out of the weather. At one of the farms, the farmer's wife had insisted that Davis take a blanket with him when he left, as part of his pay. He was glad he had the blanket tonight, because a spring cold snap came through, dropping the temperature almost to freezing. Davis wrapped up in the blanket and huddled near the base of the tree, trying not to think about how Titus Gilworth's blood had soaked into the ground beside him.

Someone ought to write to the old man's relatives and let them know what had happened to him, Davis mused as he tried to fall asleep. But all he knew for sure was that Titus had a cousin somewhere in Ohio. It would be difficult if not impossible to find the man with only such sketchy information to go on.

Still, Davis would keep it in mind, and if he ever ran into anyone else named Gilworth, he would tell them about the fate that had befallen Titus.

Not surprisingly, his sleep was uneasy that night. He didn't doze off for a long time, and when slumber finally claimed him, it brought dreams of blood and death. Davis was grateful the next morning that he could recall none of the details. All he knew for certain was that his sleep had been filled with red-tinged horrors.

His brain felt like insects had built a nest in it. He sat up, leaned against the tree trunk, and shook his head. The smell of meat cooking drifted to his nose, reminding him that he was hungry. The colonel had said that he would be fed while he was working for the government. Davis hoped that started this morning, as his venison was gone.

Dawn was still a ways off. The sun had barely begun to send red feelers into the black night sky, like the shoots of a tender young plant poking up through the soil. Most of the men camped around the trading post were up and about despite the early hour. Welles had said they would leave at dawn, and evidently the men had believed him.

Davis heard his name being called and looked up to see the colonel himself striding toward him. Welles was alone for a change, rather than being accompanied by the dark-faced Conn Powell. He held a sheathed knife in his hands.

"Good morning, Davis," Welles said. "I'm glad to see you took me at my word. Anyone not ready to start at dawn will be left behind."

"Didn't have any reason to doubt what you told me," Davis replied.

"No, I suppose not." Without any more preliminaries, Welles extended the knife toward Davis. "Here. I think you should have this."

For a second, Davis was confused. There was something familiar about the knife and the fringed sheath, but . . .

"That was Titus Gilworth's knife, wasn't it?" he said, suddenly realizing where he had seen the weapon before.

"The rest of his belongings went to pay off the bill he left behind at the trading post," Welles explained. "But I thought since you were his friend, you ought to have something of his."

Davis reached out and took the sheathed knife, turned it over in his hands. "I barely knew the man."

"Keep the knife anyway. I notice you don't have one."

"No. I don't." Davis remembered how he had run out of the jail in Elkton without taking the time to search for his own knife.

The knife he would have used on Andrew, if he'd had half a chance.

"Thanks," he grunted. The sheath had a loop on it so that it could be hung from a belt. Davis placed it on his left hip.

"About the fight last night," Welles went on. "I don't want anything like that to happen again."

"Neither do I," Davis said honestly. "I won't start any trouble, Colonel."

"That's fair enough. I intend to have this same talk with Hedge and his friends. If you have any problems with them, come see me or Conn."

Davis doubted that Conn Powell would go a step out of his way to help him, but he kept the thought to himself. Obviously, Welles placed quite a bit of faith in Powell, and Davis would just get himself even more on the colonel's bad side if he complained about Powell.

"Breakfast in ten minutes," Welles said as he started to turn away. "Afterwards, you'll be issued an ax. You don't already have one, do you?"

Davis shook his head. "Not even a tomahawk."

"Well, we'll see that you're outfitted properly." Welles took a deep breath. "It's going to be a glorious adventure, isn't it?"

"Whatever you say, Colonel."

But Davis doubted if there would be anything glorious about it at all.

He was right. He had just thought he knew what backbreaking labor was all about. The Wilderness Road taught him differently.

It began with the men, forty of them all told, assembling for breakfast at the trading post. The food was plain fare, johnnycake and fried ham, but good and filling. Then three wagons had pulled up, loaded with supplies. Axes were taken from one of them and passed out, and the workers were told to put their rifles in the wagon for safekeeping, since they couldn't very well swing an ax and carry a flintlock at the same time.

The ax was long and heavy, with a thick, double-bladed head. Davis remembered using one just like it back in the Shendandoah Valley. It had been in his barn the last time he saw it. He wondered where it was now, then pushed that thought out of his head. The ties of memory could stretch only so far before they snapped, he told himself. Better to cut them now, so they wouldn't hold him back.

The work started only a few yards from the Block House itself, where the trail began. The men spread out along either side of the path and began felling the trees that grew along the edge of the road. Davis's breath plumed in front of his face like smoke from a pipe in the dawn light as he lifted the ax and drew back his arms. He felt the pull of the tool's weight on his muscles. Then he swung it forward, hearing the faint hiss of its passage through the air, punctuated first by his own grunt of effort and then the dull *thunk!* as the blade bit deep into the wood of the tree. One-handed, he wrenched the blade free and saw the juices of the tree glistening on the brightly honed metal. Then he slid his right hand up the smooth wood of the handle, got a good grip with his left hand, and drew the ax back again for the next strike. All around him, the cold air was filled with the sound of axes. He swung again . . .

And again, and again.

As the trees fell, they were dragged to the side

by men using mules and heavy ropes. The path widened before the eyes of the men as they chopped down tree after tree. A persistent ache spread through Davis's body, muscle by muscle. His legs began to tremble a little, and his hands stung from the blisters that popped up on his palms. Years of work on the farm had hardened him, but for the past few weeks he had done nothing but walk and sleep. He had gone soft.

The Road would toughen him up, he thought. Either that or kill him. He didn't much care which, most of the time.

The morning seemed like it would never end, but it finally did. The men were out of sight of the trading post, but Davis could tell they really hadn't covered much distance. It was some two hundred miles to Logan's Fort, at the other end of the Wilderness Road, and Colonel Welles expected to cover that distance in three weeks. That was a highly optimistic estimate, Davis decided. There was no way the work party was going to cover nearly ten miles a day. They'd be lucky to make half that distance.

Not that it mattered, he told himself as he slumped against a rear wheel on one of the wagons and drew a deep, shuddery breath. He was in no hurry. There was no place he had to be by a certain time.

As a matter of fact, there was no place he had to be, period, and that thought filled him with an unutterable sadness.

Biscuits and molasses and strips of smoked venison were handed out from one of the wagons.

Davis was almost too tired to eat, but he forced himself to dip a biscuit in the thick black molasses and followed it by gnawing on a piece of the venison. The meat was tough and made his teeth hurt, but what was one more ache considering how he already felt? When he was finished eating, he drank a dipperful of water from one of the barrels attached to the side of a wagon. He decided that he actually felt a little better. The food had helped him regain some of his strength.

He had eaten alone and in silence. Most of the men had formed into small groups, and some of them got out their pipes and tobacco pouches when they were finished. Davis heard the talk and laughter eddying around him, but he took no part in it, nor did anyone approach him.

When he turned away from the water barrel, he saw someone watching him, however. The man called Hedge stood several yards away, regarding him with a cold, intense stare. Clade and Johnson weren't with him for a change, but Davis was sure they were somewhere close by. Hedge's nose was still swollen and somewhat crooked-looking, as if it had been clumsily wrenched back into place after Davis broke it. An ugly purple bruise covered the center of Hedge's face.

Hedge turned away, but not before Davis saw the hate in the man's eyes. He would have to sleep lightly from now on, Davis told himself. But then, these days he always slept lightly anyway.

When everyone had finished eating, Powell strode up and down through the group and said loudly, "All right, back on your feet! We won't get this road cut through by sittin' around and lollygaggin' all day!"

There were a few groans of complaint as the men pushed themselves to their feet and took up their axes again. Davis was almost glad to start working once more. If he had sat there much longer, his muscles would have stiffened up and it would have been even more painful to move again.

The afternoon proceeded as the morning had, with Davis's exhaustion growing deeper and deeper. Progress was slow. The men worked until dusk was settling in around them. Finally, Colonel Welles trotted along the road on his big chestnut horse and called a halt to the day's work. "I'm well pleased," he told them, "at least for a first day. We need to cover more ground tomorrow, though. We can't be falling behind schedule so early on."

Davis sensed the undercurrent of resentment that went through the men. Talk like that wouldn't do Welles any good. But no one said anything in reply, because Conn Powell was riding along right behind the colonel, and the fierce glower on his face cast a pall of silence over the group.

The night's rations were somewhat better than what had been served in the middle of the day. There were biscuits and molasses again, but with them this time was a big pot of stew rich in salt pork and wild onions. Davis ate hungrily, replenishing his body after the day's labor had drained it. He sat well back from the big roaring campfire built in the center of the small circle of wagons. That blaze would be visible for miles around, he thought, and he wondered how much trouble folks in these parts had with bandits and Indians. He put the distance between himself and the fire, however, not out of any sense of caution, but simply because he still didn't feel a part of this group. He might be with them, but he was still alone.

He had been ever since the day Faith died.

After a while, some of the men began to sing. They must have been sailors at some time in their lives, because they lifted their voices in sea chanties that spoke of rolling waves and faraway ports and sweethearts left behind. Davis found the songs moving, even though he had never seen any body of water larger than the Shenandoah River. Some of the other men took up the singing, launching into ballads that Davis knew, but still he took no part, preferring to just sit and listen. He found himself dozing off as he leaned against the trunk of a small tree.

Everyone was tired, and the singing didn't last long. The fire began to burn down as the men rolled themselves in their blankets for the night. Davis did likewise, and he was so worn out that sleep claimed him easily this time.

Despite the ease with which he fell asleep, his dreams were troubled again. If anything, they were even more vivid than the night before. Instead of reliving Faith's death, he saw his children this time. They were standing on a raft in the middle of a river, and they were calling frantically for him. The raft was drifting into a fast current, its speed picking up with each passing second. They were getting farther and farther away from Davis, and there was nothing he could do about it, no way he could reach them. Finally, the raft was carried around a bend in the river, disappearing from Davis's sight.

Mary . . . Laurel . . . little Theodore . . . all of them gone from him forever. He would never see any of them again.

He woke up, far into the night, with his face wet from tears, and spent the rest of the time until the camp roused an hour before dawn staring into the darkness.

The days crept forward, just as did the widening of the Wilderness Road. The work grew more difficult, as it came to be more than a matter of simply felling trees. Now the undergrowth was thicker and had to be cleared away as well. The men worked with shovels and hoes and heavy knives as much as they did with axes. Davis recalled clearing a bramble thicket from his own land, not long after he and Faith had come there from the Tidewater. This work was a lot like that, and despite the thick sleeves of his shirt and the gloves he wore, his hands and forearms were badly scratched at the end of each day.

Just as he had thought, his muscles had soon regained their lean, corded strength, and now he could swing an ax or chop at brush all day without waking up in such pain the next morning. He was still exhausted at the end of each day, however, because Colonel Welles and Conn Powell pushed the men unmercifully. Even under the more arduous circumstances, the group was covering close to five miles a day, which was still only half of what Welles had estimated.

One evening, a week into the journey, Welles and Powell had a long conversation, then Powell tapped into a barrel on one of the wagons that brought up the rear each day. He filled a jug, then began passing it around. A cheer went up from the men. When the jug came to Davis, he tipped it to his mouth and took a long swallow of rum. He passed the jug along as the warmth of the liquor flooded through him.

Welles climbed onto the wagon and lifted his hands, calling out for the group's attention. "You'll get a drink of rum every night from now on," he told the men, "providing that we make at least five miles that day. What do you say to that, boys?"

Another cheer welled up. Davis didn't join in it any more than he took part in the singing that still went on around the campfire nearly every night, but he was grateful to Welles anyway. Maybe the rum would deaden his brain enough for him to sleep soundly, unbothered by phantoms from the past.

Phantoms . . . that was what his wife and children were to him now, he mused. And insistent ones at that. No matter how much he wanted to get on with his life, to face the future instead of the past, memories of Faith and the youngsters insisted on reminding him of what he had lost instead.

He would have given his soul—dry, shriveled thing that it was—for the feel of Theodore's arms around his neck in a hug or the softness of his daughters' hair brushing his face as they leaned over to give him a kiss on the cheek.

When the refilled jug came around one more time, Davis seized it eagerly and took an even longer swallow of the rum. In his misery, he had forgotten all about Hedge.

Later that night, he shifted restlessly in his sleep, and his eyelids flickered open. Something had disturbed him, but he wasn't sure if it had been the hard ground underneath him, the far-off howl of a wolf, or something else. Davis started to lift his head and look around.

A hand grabbed his hair and jerked his head back painfully, pulling the skin of his neck taut. Davis's eyes widened in shock and horror as he saw the light from the embers of the fire glowing redly on the blade of the knife that was about to slit his throat.

8

Instinct took over. Davis's arm shot up, his fingers clamping onto the wrist of the hand wielding the knife. Someone else grabbed at him, but it was too late. He had a death grip on the would-be killer's wrist.

At the same time, Davis twisted on the ground, kicking free of the blanket and bringing his legs around toward another shape that loomed between him and the glow of the fire. He drove the heels of his feet into the middle of that shape and heard a satisfying grunt of pain and surprise.

"Get him!" a voice hissed. "Hang on to him, damn it!"

Davis thought he knew who the voice belonged to, but he didn't waste any time thinking about that. It didn't really matter *who* was trying to kill him. The only important thing was stopping them.

He reached up with his left hand, groping for the man who had grabbed him from behind. His fingers touched beard-stubbled cheeks, then found the man's eyes. Davis dug in hard. A scream of agony ripped through the night, and the hand tangled in his hair suddenly released him and went away.

He pulled his knee up, slammed the arm he was holding down across it. There was a sharp crack and another scream. The knife fell from nerveless fingers.

Some sort of club crashed into Davis's side. He gasped in pain but managed to hold on to the man whose wrist he had grabbed. He rolled over, hauling the man on top of him and then underneath him. Davis's knee jammed into the man's groin. There was a lot of shouting going on in the camp now, but Davis paid no attention to it.

The club hit him again, this time clipping him on the side of the head hard enough to make him dizzy and knock him off the first man. He tumbled onto the ground, rolled over a couple of times, and came up in a crouch, trying to shake off the effects of the blow. Two of the men who had attacked him were down, but the third one was still on his feet, swinging the ax handle he had used as a bludgeon. Someone had thrown some more wood on the fire, and it caught with a crackle and hiss, sending a wider circle of light around the camp along with a shower of sparks that ascended into the night sky. The red glow was bright enough for Davis to see that the third and final attacker was the man called Clade. Hedge and Johnson were both sprawled on the ground where Davis had left them.

Clade came at him with a yell, bringing the ax handle down in a murderous sweep. The heavy length of wood might have crushed Davis's skull if he hadn't dodged aside. He hit Clade in the small of the back, then darted away before Clade could bring the ax handle around in a vicious backhand.

The rest of the crew had them pretty much surrounded, Davis saw from the corner of his eye. They were shouting encouragement to the fighters. Most of them seemed to be supporting Clade, but to his surprise, Davis heard his own name called out several times. He had thought he had no friends among these men. That might well be true, but there were at least some of them who obviously didn't want to see his brains leaking out of his head.

Clade rushed him again, and once more Davis managed to get out of the way. His legs felt like lead by now, however, and his head was still spinning. It was only a matter of time until that ax handle connected with him, and then the fight would be over. His life might well be finished, too.

The unexpected roar of a pistol shot made silence fall heavily over the camp. The ring of men parted, and Conn Powell strode through the gap. He had a pistol in each hand. Powdersmoke drifted from the barrel of the gun in his left hand, but the one in his right was still cocked and primed, and it was aimed right at Clade's chest.

"Drop that ax handle," Powell grated.

Clade hesitated, then lowered the ax handle and let it fall at his feet. Powell came closer to him and glanced past him at the sprawled bodies of Hedge and Johnson. His lean, dark face was unreadable.

Davis's chest heaved as he tried to catch his breath. His pulse thundered in his temples, and his scalp hurt where Hedge had practically pulled out handfuls of hair. He knew from the way Hedge's right arm was bent at an unnatural angle between the elbow and the wrist that Hedge was the one who had tried to cut his throat, the one whose arm Davis had broken across his knee. Hedge seemed to have passed out. Johnson was still conscious, but he was curled up in a ball, clutching his belly where Davis had kicked him. A man could die from a hard enough kick in the stomach, Davis knew. At the moment, he didn't much care whether that fate befell Johnson or not. Nor did he feel any sympathy for Hedge's broken arm.

"I think it's pretty obvious what happened here," Powell said. "Hedge just couldn't let it go, could he?"

Clade pointed a shaking finger at Davis. "It's all his fault! He—"

"Shut up!" Powell snapped. "You think I'm a fool, Clade? I know what's goin' on. I know you and Hedge and Johnson been plottin' to kill Davis." Powell shook his head grimly. "If you hadn't been so damned clumsy, we'd've only lost one man from the crew, 'stead of three. I'm mighty disappointed in you."

Davis thought he heard an edge of bleak humor in Powell's voice. It had been surprising enough that Powell had defended him from Clade. What the foreman said next surprised Davis even more.

"You and your friends get out of here," Powell went on. "I don't care where you go, but I don't want to see you around here anymore."

"You . . . you're kickin' us out of camp?" Clade was as taken aback as Davis was.

"That's right. You're leavin' tonight. I'll give you half an hour, no more."

"But . . . but where'll we go?" A whine crept in Clade's voice.

"Told you, I don't care. Back along the Road to the Block House, or ahead to the Gap and Kaintuck. As long as you're out of my sight."

"But there's Indians, and bandits—"

"That's your look-out, not mine." Powell's tone was cold and merciless.

Clade took a deep breath, then, as if realizing the futility of arguing, turned and went over to Johnson. He took hold of the other man's shoulder and hauled him to his feet. "Come on," he grunted. "We got to help Hedge."

Powell turned to Davis. "You all right?"

"I think so."

"Good. Bad enough we'll be short-handed by three men. If you hadn't been able to work, this night really would have turned out bad."

Powell started to turn away, but Davis stopped him with a hand on his arm. "Why did you help me?" Davis asked. "I thought you didn't trust me."

Pointedly, Powell looked down at the hand on his arm, and Davis took it away. "I don't trust you. But that doesn't mean I'm goin' to let those three kill you."

"You as much as said that if they had gotten away with it, you wouldn't have done anything to them."

Powell shrugged. "If they'd gotten away with it, I wouldn't have had any proof. Since it wound up all out in the open, I didn't have any choice. Got to maintain discipline around here." He heaved a sigh. "But I sure do hate to be short-handed."

This time when he turned away, Davis let him go. Despite what Powell had done to help him, Davis sensed that he hadn't made a friend of the man tonight.

But on the other hand, he was still alive, and there was something to be said for that. The emotions he felt as that thought went through his brain surprised him almost as much as the fact that Powell had helped him.

Once again, he was forced to confront the idea that, no matter what had happened in the past, he still wanted to live. He had fought with the desperation of a man who wanted to cling to life for as long as possible, who wanted every last second that he had been allotted.

Davis was going to have to think about that, think long and hard.

He slept fitfully the rest of the night. Between almost being murdered and the realization that he wasn't ready to give up on life after all, his mind was whirling.

When he dragged himself out of his bedroll the next morning and walked stiffly over to the wagons for breakfast, one of the men surprised him by offering him a cup of tea. "I reckon you probably need it," the man said with a grin. "You look a mite haggard this morning, Davis."

"Thanks," Davis grunted as he took the cup. "I didn't sleep very well."

"I can understand why." The man extended a big, callused hand toward him. "Name's Grimsby, Bill Grimsby."

Davis's hesitation lasted only an instant, then he shook hands with the man. "Pleased to meet you, Grimsby." It struck him as odd that he had worked beside this man before but was only now learning his name. But that was the way you wanted it, he told himself. He hadn't wanted to make any friends.

"Mighty glad Hedge and those two cronies of his didn't kill you last night," Grimsby went on. "I was yellin' for you durin' the fight."

"Thanks," Davis said. "I'm pretty glad myself that I didn't get killed."

Grimsby smiled. "There's more of us than you might think who were happy to see those three go. It'll be more work for us now without 'em, I suppose, but good riddance, I say. Their kind never does anything except stir up trouble."

"Powell probably thinks *I'm* the one causing trouble, after what happened back at the Block House and then last night."

Grimsby waved off that comment and said, "Don't you pay him any mind. Powell's just a naturally sour son of a bitch—and if you tell him I said so, I'll deny it. Get yourself some johnnycake there and come along with me."

Davis took a hunk of the johnnycake from a pan on the tailgate of a wagon and followed Grimsby over to a small group gathered underneath a tree at the edge of the road. The other men greeted Grimsby in a friendly fashion, then looked at Davis and waited until Grimsby said, "This here is Hal Davis, boys. I reckon you all know him."

Most of the men just nodded noncommittally, but a few of them smiled. "Aye, we know him, Bill," one of them said. "'Tis not every day that one man holds off Hedge *and* Clade *and* Johnson, and not only that but does considerable damage to a couple of 'em." The man held out his hand to Davis. "McIntosh is me name, Davis. It's pleased I am to meet you."

Several of the other men shook hands and introduced themselves as well, and while Davis could still feel the barrier of unfamiliarity between them and him, there was a new sense of camaraderie. New to him, at least. The other men had already formed rough friendships during the week since leaving the Block House.

It would still be more than a month until they reached the end of the Wilderness Road, he told himself. Now that Hedge and the other two had left camp, the danger might be over, but the boredom and the arduous labor would continue. The weeks might pass more quickly if he had some friends among these men. The concept was still somewhat foreign to him, but he thought he could adapt.

He ate breakfast with them without talking much, but he enjoyed listening to their conversation. The eastern sky was gray and the men were about to head for the wagons to claim their axes for the day when Colonel Welles came riding up.

Immediately, the colonel singled out Davis and called his name. He swung down from the big chestnut and walked up to Davis, leading the horse.

"I'm aware that there was more trouble last night," he said without preamble.

Davis nodded warily. "Some." His old habit of being close-mouthed was still with him, especially at times like this.

"Conn told me that you severely injured Hedge and Johnson."

"I was defending myself."

Bill Grimsby put in, "That's right, Colonel. I saw most of the ruckus myself."

Welles silenced him with a look. "Thank you, Mr. Grimsby, but this is between Davis and myself."

"I didn't do anything wrong," Davis said. His chin lifted slightly in defiance.

"No, I suppose not," Welles admitted. "And Conn was right to expel those three troublemakers from our midst. Still, that leaves us woefully lacking in numbers, and we weren't making satisfactory progress even with a full crew."

"We'll all work harder, Colonel," McIntosh said. "Those lads Conn Powell ran off were loafers anyway. One of us can do as much work as the whole three of them."

"I hope you're right, Mr. McIntosh. I sincerely hope you're right."

Davis didn't like the sound of that, but he didn't say anything. He didn't want to make a bad situation any worse.

Welles looked at him again and went on, "I'll have no more trouble on this job, is that understood?"

"Yes, sir," Davis said. "But if anybody else tries to slit my throat, I'm damned sure going to try to stop him."

Welles's eyes narrowed at the blunt reply, but then his glare eased a bit and he nodded. "That's certainly fair enough, I suppose." He put his foot in the stirrup and stepped up into the chestnut's military saddle. "I hope you men are ready to work today."

With that, he wheeled the horse and rode toward the spot where the head of the work crew would be. Powell was already there waiting for him on horseback.

The pace they set that day was harder than ever before. Davis worked gladly, however, relieved that Hedge and the others were gone. He worried briefly that one of them might stalk the group and try to shoot him from a distance, but that seemed unlikely. If anything happened to him, everyone would know who was responsible. Besides, the three men had headed east when they set out from camp the night before, after Hedge's broken arm had been crudely splinted. They were probably well on their way to the Block House by now, since they could travel much faster along the already widened trail.

Two days later, with Welles and Powell still pushing hard, the men crossed a stream that, according to Bill Grimsby, was called the Powell River. Davis wondered if it was named for the foreman or perhaps one of his relatives, but he didn't ask. Powell hadn't spoken a word to him since the night of the murder attempt, and he seemed as dour and suspicious as ever.

The water in the stream was running fast, but there was a good ford and the men and wagons had no trouble crossing. As Davis felt the tug of the current around his boots, he wondered what it would be like to follow this river and see where it led. The thought made him smile faintly. He had never known that he possessed such a wanderlust. But now, when he lifted his eyes to the mountains in the distance and found the notch of the Cumberland Gap, he felt a deep sense of anticipation that in a few days he would see what was on the other side.

Later in the afternoon, as he finished felling a tree, Davis rested his ax on the ground and leaned on it for a moment, staring off at the blue-green heights. Bill Grimsby came up beside him and grinned. "Ever been over there, Davis?" he asked.

Davis shook his head. "No, this is the farthest west I've ever traveled."

"Where do you hail from?"

"The Shenandoah Valley, lately. Before that—" Davis stopped abruptly, realizing that he had let his guard down. He didn't need to be talking about the past with anyone, even someone like Grimsby who seemed to be totally harmless.

Grimsby noticed the reaction but misunderstood it. "Never you mind about that," he said quickly. "Out here on the frontier, it doesn't really matter where a man's from or what he did there. It's what you do in the here and now that counts." He paused, then added, "Got any plans for when this job's over?"

"I was thinking about staying on in Kentucky," Davis admitted.

"It's a fine land," Grimsby said, enthusiasm creeping into his voice. "I was there once. Signed on with some freighters who were taking goods over

the Gap in hand carts. It was a long hard walk
pullin' that load, let me tell you. But when I got there
and saw the mountains, and the forests, and those
fields full of the prettiest grass you ever saw . . .
well, I told myself then and there that I'd come back
someday and settle there myself. I figure to look for
some land near Logan's Station or Harrodsburg.
Might even push on as far as Boonesborough."

"Sounds like a fair plan."

Grimsby's grin widened. "Might even look to
find me a wife. A man needs himself a woman, if he's
goin' to make anything worth keepin'. You got a wife
waitin' for you back in Virginia, Davis?"

The question made Davis feel as hollow as some
of the logs they had seen, as if insects had gotten
inside him and gnawed him clean.

"Naw, of course not, since you were talkin'
about settlin' in Kentucky yourself," Grimsby went
on before Davis even had a chance to answer.
"'Less'n you're plannin' on bringin' her out after
you've got yourself situated."

Davis shook his head. "No," he said, and he was
surprised at how normal his voice sounded. "I don't
have a wife."

"Maybe you'll get yourself one. Not a lot of
unmarried ladies out there in the wilderness, of
course. But some of the families have daughters,
and there are some widow women who didn't want
to go back wherever they came from." Grimsby
laughed. "Maybe we'll both be fortunate and find
somebody."

"Maybe," Davis said, although the discussion
meant little or nothing to him at that moment. He

was just agreeing with Grimsby so that perhaps the
man would shut up, rather than peeling away any
more layers of the wall that Davis had thrown up
between himself and his pain.

Conn Powell chose that moment to ride by and
notice both men standing there, leaning on their
axes. "Get back to work, you two," the foreman
snapped. "You're not bein' paid to dream."

"Aye, sir," Grimsby said. He cast a quick,
conspiratorial glance at Davis, then shouldered his
ax and headed for the nearest tree.

Davis picked out another tree as well and began
swinging his ax. After a moment, he noticed that his
strokes had even more force behind them than
usual, and it was difficult to wrench the head of his
ax out of the wood after each one. Grimsby's talk of
wives had upset him, had stirred up too many still-
raw memories.

And yet, there was something to what the man
had said, some truth in his garrulousness. A man
needed a woman to be complete. Davis had always
believed that. But he had also believed that Faith
was the only woman for him. He had been
convinced that Faith felt the same way . . . until
Andrew had shown up and the world had slowly
begun to fall apart around Davis.

Perhaps someday he would love again. Right
now, that seemed impossible—but he had seen with
his own eyes how people could change, how things
that had seemed utterly inconceivable might
become all too real. If they could change for the
worse, maybe they could also change for the better.

Davis hoped that was true. But for now, he

swung his ax and tried to tell himself that this was his world: hard work, tree after tree to be felled, a road to widen so that other people, other families, could find a new home for themselves.

The men pushed on, reaching the Cumberland Gap four days later. Davis paused while standing in the Gap itself, looking at the steep, thickly wooded slopes that rose on each side of the passage. The route of the Wilderness Road was an old Indian trail discovered by Daniel Boone, Bill Grimsby had told him, and Davis could easily imagine red-hued woodsmen trotting along this path. Some evenings, Faith had read aloud to the children from the pamphlets put out by the promoter John Filson, so Davis knew all about Boone and his adventures with the Indians and wild game of Kentucky. Some of the stories were probably exaggerated, of course, but there was bound to be a grain of truth in them. After all, Davis thought, he was standing in the Wilderness Road, wasn't he?

Colonel Welles rode up alongside him, and Davis tensed, expecting the engineer to scold him for woolgathering. But Welles just smiled and said, "It doesn't look like much, does it? Just a pass between some mountains."

"It's not the pass," Davis said. "It's what's on the other side."

"Ah, indeed. Very perceptive, Mr. Davis." Welles heeled his horse into a trot that carried him on toward the front of the work crew, but he gave Davis a friendly wave as he rode off.

Davis had never considered himself a perceptive or even an overly thoughtful man. The words had just come to him, striking home with their rightness.

On the other side of the Cumberland Gap was safety, he told himself. He was already more than a hundred miles away from his former home, and with each mile that the crew put behind them, he knew he was that much more isolated from the law. More than likely, it would never be safe for him to return to the Shenandoah Valley, or anywhere else in Virginia. But here in Kentucky he could live out the rest of his life in peace. He was confident that no one would ever come this far to look for him.

With a rare smile on his face, he picked out a tree on the edge of the trail and began chopping it down. Tonight, if the men sang around the campfire, he might just join in.

9

Peter Abernathy stood up from his desk with a grunt and walked over to the small stove in the corner of the office. Despite the fact that it was spring, the weather could still turn raw and damp and nasty, as it was today. Abernathy picked up several pieces of wood from the wood box and placed them carefully on the embers in the stove. He grimaced as he felt a twinge in his left arm. Sometimes he forgot and used the arm as if it had never been injured, and he always paid for that forgetfulness in coin of pain.

It had only been a little over a month, he told himself as he went back to the desk and lowered himself into the chair. The local physician had set and splinted Abernathy's arm, but he had warned the constable that it would take a long time for the arm to regain its full strength, if indeed it ever did. There was nothing unusual about the ache that he felt in it. With time, the injury to his arm would heal.

The injury to his pride never would.

Abernathy scowled and tried to force his mind

onto other topics. He knew from bitter experience
not to dwell too long on Davis Hallam. When he did,
the anger and hatred rose up inside him until
sometimes he found himself trembling from the
depth of the emotions gripping him. He was a good
Christian, he told himself when that happened. He
shouldn't allow himself to become consumed with
such feelings.

And yet, he could not deny that he would have
cheerfully killed Hallam himself, or at least watched
him kick his life away at the end of a hangman's
rope.

The front door of the office was closed, but
Abernathy heard the steady thud of hoofbeats and
the creaking of wheels anyway. He looked up and
frowned when the noises came to an abrupt halt in
front of the building that housed Elkton's jail and
the constable's office. A moment later, footsteps
thumped on the porch outside, and the door
opened.

The man who came into the office was medium-
sized, but he carried himself with the bearing of
someone larger. Confidence, even arrogance, was
etched in every line of his face and figure. He wore a
dark gray suit over a stiff white shirt that was
buttoned to the neck. A black tricorn hat sat on his
head, and underneath it was thick, crisp white hair.
The man's face was ruddy and clean-shaven, his
cheeks trenched by lines of hard-won experience.
His high-topped black boots were spotted with mud
from the road outside, but that was the only thing
about him that was less than immaculate. In his left
hand he carried a piece of paper, but Abernathy

couldn't tell what it was. He had never seen the man before.

"You're Constable Peter Abernathy?" the stranger asked in a deep, resonant voice.

Abernathy came to his feet and nodded. "That's right. What can I do for you, sir?"

The man slapped the paper down on the desk. "Then you're the man responsible for sending out these."

Abernathy looked down and saw the face of Davis Hallam staring back up at him. Actually, a crude drawing of Hallam's features, and underneath the picture was the word *FUGITIVE*. The lettering went on to explain that Hallam was wanted on a charge of murder and had taken flight from the settlement of Elkton, Virginia. Anyone with information concerning Hallam was requested to correspond with Constable Peter Abernathy, also of Elkton.

"Aye, those papers are my work," Abernathy said as he looked back up at his visitor. "Have you seen this man?"

"Not for more than ten years." The stranger's jaw clenched, one of the muscles jerking as he tried to control what was evidently a deep, disturbing emotion. He went on, "I wish to God I had never seen him at all. I wish my daughter had never seen him."

Abernathy felt himself tense. "And you are . . . ?"

"Hammond Larrimore is my name. My daughter was Faith Larrimore. Faith Hallam." Larrimore's mouth twisted bitterly as he spoke his daughter's married name.

Abernathy took a deep breath. "I'm sorry, Mr. Larrimore. I had no way of knowing—"

Larrimore shook his head and waved off Abernathy's apology. "Your words can't hurt me, Constable. I've gone far beyond that." He pointed at the paper. "I saw that in a settlement back up the trail."

Abernathy nodded and said, "Yes, I sent out quite a few of them."

"Have you had any success at catching the murderer? Has he been executed?"

Reluctantly, Abernathy shook his head. He didn't want to add to Larrimore's pain, nor was he pleased at the prospect of admitting his own failure. Yet there was no denying it. "So far, Davis Hallam has escaped justice," he said heavily.

Both of Hammond Larrimore's large, knobby-knuckled hands closed into tight fists for a moment, then he nodded. "I feared as much."

"I know that . . . in tragic circumstances such as these . . . my protestations mean little to you, sir. But I swear to you that I regret allowing Hallam to escape his punishment." Abernathy's right hand went to his left arm, and he rubbed the place where the bone had been broken, almost taking pleasure now in the pain. It was a release of sorts. "I promise you, no one wants to see Hallam brought back and hanged more than myself."

"I believe you, sir. And your words do have some value."

"I take it you received Magistrate Symms's letter advising you of your daughter's . . . death?"

Larrimore nodded. "He said that Davis Hallam

attempted to kill you, too, and that you were injured when he escaped."

Abernathy touched his arm again. "A broken bone. But it's mending now."

"Some injuries never mend," Larrimore said, echoing the same thought that frequently passed through Abernathy's mind.

After a moment of silence, Abernathy said, "I wish I could tell you that I have high hopes of Hallam being captured. But after so much time has passed . . . the man could be anywhere."

"Do you know which direction he was going when he fled?"

"West," Abernathy said. "Toward the Kentucky frontier. It's quite a large country out there, Mr. Larrimore. Plenty of places for a man to hide."

"I suppose so. I've never visited that area. Spent most of my life in the Tidewater."

Abernathy recalled that Hammond Larrimore owned a tobacco plantation in Virginia's coastal lowlands. Larrimore was a wealthy, powerful man. Abernathy wondered how the daughter of such a man had wound up married to someone like Davis Hallam, but he kept the question to himself. Larrimore didn't need anything else to add to his pain right now.

The visitor drew in a deep, ragged breath. "Faith is buried here in Elkton, is she not?"

Abernathy nodded. "Aye. Down in our churchyard. For what it's worth, Mr. Larrimore, I can assure you that she got a good Christian burial."

"And my grandchildren?"

"They're living with a man named Jonas Kirby and his wife. Fine folks, the Kirbys, and they've taken good care of the children. I've made sure of that."

"You have my thanks for that, sir. But the youngsters won't have to depend on the care of strangers any longer."

"You'll be taking them back with you, then?"

"Of course." Larrimore frowned slightly. "Surely the law will have no objection."

"You'll have to talk to Magistrate Symms, but I imagine there will be no problem. After all, you're blood kin."

"My wife and I will care for them as if they were our own," Larrimore said solemnly. "Now, if you would be kind enough to show us our daughter's grave?"

"Us?" Abernathy repeated. "Mrs. Larrimore is with you?"

"We set out from the plantation as soon as we received the magistrate's letter. My good wife would not hear of being left behind."

It surprised Abernathy somewhat that a fine lady such as Mrs. Larrimore would make the rugged journey from her home to a settlement on the edge of civilization such as Elkton. And yet, he knew little of what motivated a parent, since he had no children himself; he had never been married to anything but his work. But he decided that if he had a daughter, and if that daughter had been murdered, he would probably be willing to make a long journey to visit her grave, too.

"Let me get my coat," he said to Hammond Larrimore. "Then we'll go down to the church."

"Thank you, Constable." Larrimore hesitated, then added, "I can see it in your face, sir. I believe you hate Davis Hallam almost as much as do I."

Abernathy nodded slowly. "Almost," he admitted.

Perhaps even more, he added to himself. He had not lost a child at the hands of Davis Hallam. But he had lost something just as important to him.

Elizabeth Larrimore was a handsome, middle-aged woman with graying brown hair. Abernathy had not known the Hallam family well, but his memory of Faith Hallam was clear enough so that he was convinced she had gotten her good looks from her mother.

A closed coach was waiting outside the jail when Abernathy and Larrimore emerged into the blustery wind. The coach's driver sat with his shoulders hunched and his hat pulled low against the wind. It was fairly comfortable inside the coach, though, and that was where Mrs. Larrimore was waiting.

Abernathy gave the driver directions to the church while Larrimore opened the door of the coach. Instructions weren't really necessary, Abernathy thought, since Elkton was small, little more than a village, and the church was sitting there in plain sight only two hundred yards away. But he spoke to the driver anyway, out of a sense of formality. Likewise, even though he could have easily walked to their destination, he climbed inside the coach with the Larrimores. The planter introduced Abernathy to his wife, and Abernathy put his most solemn expression on his face as he nodded to the woman.

"My sincere regrets on the loss of your daughter, madam," he said.

Mrs. Larrimore returned his nod. Her face was so pale, her blue eyes so wispy, that she was barely there, Abernathy thought. Obviously, the death of her daughter had been a terrible blow to her.

"Thank you, Constable," she said, her voice as fragile as her features. "We would never have been able to endure this ordeal without the kindness of compassionate people such as yourself."

That was all she said to him during the brief ride to the church. She lifted a lace handkerchief to her face and kept it there, withdrawing behind it as if the gossamer lace was as thick and sturdy as a stone wall.

Larrimore was silent, too, and Abernathy remained so as well. Let them think their own thoughts, the constable told himself. Surely there had been much to sort through during the long trip from the Tidewater.

When the coach reached the church and came to a stop, Abernathy opened the door and stepped out first, holding it for the Larrimores against the wind that threatened to catch it and slam it. Larrimore emerged from the vehicle and reached up to assist his wife. When they were both on the ground, Abernathy closed the door softly and ushered them toward the church, which was built of whitewashed planks that had been freighted inland all the way from Richmond. To one side of the church was the cemetery, surrounded by a fence made of sturdy posts. Hammond Larrimore and his wife walked directly to the churchyard, bypassing the sanctuary itself.

Abernathy opened the gate in the fence, then stepped back to give the grieving couple their privacy. Mrs. Larrimore stumbled a bit, but her husband was there beside her to take her arm and steady her. Abernathy was unable to tell if her misstep had been because of the roughness of the ground, or the sorrow that filled her eyes with tears and left no room for anything else inside her.

In a small settlement such as Elkton, word of anything unusual got around quickly, and the arrival of a fancy coach bearing two strangers certainly qualified as news. Abernathy heard voices and looked over his shoulder to see several of the town's wives coming out of their cabins, pulling shawls around their shoulders and chattering among themselves. The men who generally loafed on the porch of the trading post had taken an interest in the new arrivals and left their benches to amble toward the church. Abernathy turned to face them squarely, folded his arms across his chest, and shook his head as he directed a firm glare toward the townspeople. Everyone interpreted the look correctly, and since no one wanted to cross Abernathy, they backed off to allow the Larrimores to mourn in peace.

Once he was satisfied that the visitors to Elkton would not be disturbed, Abernathy turned toward the churchyard again. He saw the two of them standing in front of the gravestone. Elizabeth Larrimore reached out, tentatively at first, and placed her hand on the stone. A shudder went through her, as if the coldness of the grave was traveling directly from the stone into her body through her hand and leeching the last vestiges of warmth and humanity from her. Her husband put his arm around her shoulders and held her tightly. He leaned his head close to hers and spoke, the words much too quiet for Abernathy to hear them. That was all right. Whatever was being said, it was between husband and wife, mother and father, and he had no right to be privy to the conversation.

After a few minutes, Larrimore seemed to be trying gently to urge his wife away from the grave of their daughter. Elizabeth wasn't budging, though. Larrimore spoke to her again, then his shoulders rose and fell in a heavy sigh. He patted her on the back and turned away, coming toward the churchyard gate with slow steps.

"My wife wants a few minutes more with Faith," Larrimore said quietly as he joined Abernathy outside the fence. "This has been very . . . difficult for her."

"Of course," Abernathy murmured.

"If only Davis Hallam had never come to the Tidewater."

"What was he doing there?" Abernathy asked, thinking that it might do Larrimore some good to talk about it while his wife was grieving. He was genuinely curious, too. "I didn't know the man well, but I thought he was simply a farmer."

"That's all he ever was," Larrimore said. "I was acquainted with his stepfather, a man named Henry Paxton who has a shipping concern. Evidently

Hallam was a bit of an embarrassment to Paxton, who gave him a letter of introduction to me in hopes that I would find a place on my plantation for him. I made him an assistant overseer."

Abernathy shook his head. "Hard to imagine Hallam as an overseer. He was a quiet man. Almost too quiet."

"Indeed. As I said, he was a farmer at heart, and he might have made a good overseer, given time. But he wasn't content to merely do his job and see that the slaves did the work. He went into the fields with them! Said that he needed the dirt on his hands, that he could judge the tobacco better if he helped plant it and care for it himself. Utter nonsense, of course. I couldn't have such a thing. I told him he would have to leave."

Larrimore winced, as if he had just felt a physical pain. "But it was too late. By that time Faith was smitten with him, and he with her. He had a dream of having his own farm, and he had convinced her to share that dream. I did everything I could to discourage the match—" Again Larrimore's hands clenched into fists. "No words of mine could reach her. She was determined to marry Hallam and come with him to this backwoods valley . . . I beg your pardon, Constable. I meant no offense to your home."

"That's quite all right, sir. I understand completely."

Larrimore sighed, as he had done in the churchyard. "So she came with him and bore his children and . . . and now she lies there cold in the ground because of him. By God, if I had Davis

Hallam here before me, I wouldn't wait for the hangman! I'd choke the life out of that blackhearted devil myself!"

Since Abernathy had experienced that same feeling many times himself over the past few weeks, he couldn't blame Hammond Larrimore for the outburst. He simply nodded and said nothing, and after a moment, Larrimore went on in a more controlled voice, "Is there suitable lodging for the night here in Elkton?"

"There's an inn," Abernathy told him. "Nothing fancy, mind you, just some rooms on the second floor over Perry's tavern. But the place is fairly clean, and I'll speak to Jeremiah Perry myself, to insure that you and Mrs. Larrimore will not be disturbed."

Larrimore nodded in appreciation. "That's very kind of you, Constable." He looked intently at Abernathy, his eyes narrowed in thought. "I'd like to speak to you later. I have a feeling you regard Davis Hallam in much the same light as do I."

"I can come down to Perry's place," Abernathy offered.

"No, I'll pay a visit to you in your office, if I may. After supper, perhaps."

Abernathy nodded. "That will be fine. Whatever you wish, Mr. Larrimore."

"I wish my daughter were still alive," Larrimore said. "But oftentimes, we don't get what we wish for, do we, Constable?"

Abernathy thought about the way Davis Hallam had escaped. "No, sir, we don't," he said. "We certainly do not."

*   *   *

Larrimore was finally able to persuade his wife to leave Faith's grave. Abernathy had been growing concerned that Mrs. Larrimore would have to be physically removed from the churchyard, which probably would have required his assistance. He was grateful such an unpleasant scene had been avoided.

After taking the Larrimores to the inn and making sure Jeremiah Perry understood how they were to be treated, Abernathy returned to his office. It was late afternoon, and he could have gone to the small cabin behind the building, where he was allowed to live since he was the constable. But the visit to the churchyard had taken away whatever appetite he might have had, and besides, Larrimore had mentioned that he would come to the office to see him later. So Abernathy poured himself a cup of wine and sat behind the desk, brooding. From time to time he distractedly massaged his left arm, where the mending bone still ached.

He wasn't really aware of the grayness outside turning into the black of night, but when the door opened later and Abernathy looked up, he saw that darkness had indeed fallen. The wind had picked up even more, and its cold fingers curled around him. Hammond Larrimore stepped into the office, his normally ruddy face even more flushed than it had been earlier, and pushed the door closed behind him against the wind. Abernathy stood up to greet him.

Larrimore waved the constable back into the

chair. "Do you have another cup?" he asked, nodding toward the jug of wine sitting on the desk.

"Of course," Abernathy said, taking a cup from the drawer and filling it with wine. He pushed it across to Larrimore, who settled down in the room's other chair.

Larrimore took a healthy swallow of the wine, then inhaled deeply. "My wife has gone to sleep," he said. "Thank God for that. I feared that the visit to Faith's grave would keep her up all night."

"Your daughter's death was a dreadful thing," Abernathy murmured. "Just dreadful."

"We lost three children in infancy," Larrimore said. "Faith was the only one who survived. She was a grown woman, she lived her life, she made her own choices that led to her death. That should make it . . . easier somehow. Easier than putting those helpless little ones in the ground. But it's not." He shuddered. "Dear God, it's not."

A couple of moments passed in silence. Abernathy did not know what to say to this man to comfort him. Such things had never come easily to him.

"Well, Constable," Larrimore finally said. "I came down here to ask you what was done about finding Davis Hallam."

"We trailed him as best we could the night he escaped. It was a dark night, though, and we were unable to keep up with him. Nor could we find him the next day." Abernathy poured more wine into his cup. "I had men looking for him for the next week, but he was gone, of course. Far and away, I would imagine. We have a journeyman printer here, and I had him make up those posters you saw. I sent them

to all the settlements in the area." His shoulders
rose and fell in a shrug. "That was all I could do. I'm
sorry, Mr. Larrimore."

"I understand. You were injured," Larrimore
said gruffly. "But what about since then?"

"My duties keep me here. I'm Elkton's constable.
I have a responsibility to the town."

"Because the townspeople pay your wages, give
you a place to live."

"Well . . . yes."

"Then I suggest," Larrimore said, "that it's time
you change employers, Constable."

Abernathy frowned. "Just what do you mean by
that, sir?"

Larrimore reached inside his coat and brought out
a small leather pouch. He set it down on Abernathy's
desk, hard enough so that the clink of coins from
within was clearly heard. "I mean that I will pay you
handsomely to track down Davis Hallam and bring
him to justice, Constable Abernathy," he said.

Abernathy looked from the planter's grim
features to the bag of coins, and his gaze lingered
there for a long moment. When he lifted his eyes to
Larrimore's face again, he asked, "You're saying that
I should give up my job here and work for you?"

"Exactly."

"And you'll pay me for finding and capturing
Hallam?"

"Naturally."

"Or for killing him?"

"Whatever is necessary to bring about justice
for my daughter's death," Larrimore said, his voice
flat and cold.

Abernathy took a deep breath. "I see."

Larrimore untied the string at the top of the pouch and upended it so that the gold coins within poured out onto the desk. "*Now* you see," he said.

For a second, Abernathy felt insulted. Larrimore was obviously accustomed to getting whatever he wanted just because he had money and power. Neither of those things had helped, though, when his daughter had decided to marry Davis Hallam and come with him to the Shenandoah Valley. Nor could they ever bring Faith back to life. But it was clear that Larrimore still thought justice could be bought.

And perhaps he was right . . .

Abernathy took a deep breath. "I've served this settlement well—" he began.

"I know that," Larrimore said. "I talked to people who know you, or know of your reputation, before Mrs. Larrimore and I ever came here. I decided that you were the man to track down Hallam. I'm convinced that no one else can do it."

"There are other men, long hunters, who know the frontier lands better than I."

"None of them had Hallam escape from their jail. None of them had their arm broken by the man."

A thin, humorless smile touched Abernathy's lips. "So you think that because my pride was wounded, I would pursue Hallam more diligently than anyone else?"

Larrimore returned the smile, but his eyes were just as cold as the constable's. "Isn't that the case?"

After a couple of seconds, Abernathy nodded abruptly. "I suppose it is."

"Then take the job," Larrimore urged. "Resign your position as constable. Magistrate Symms can find someone else to take over. I need *you*, Abernathy. My daughter demands justice."

"All right," Abernathy said, although the words sounded to him as if they were coming from someone else's mouth. "I'll do it."

Larrimore sat back in his chair, sipped his wine, and said smugly, "Good. I knew you'd see things my way."

Abernathy reached out, scooped the coins back into the pouch, and pulled the cord tight, closing it. He dropped it in the drawer of his desk. "When do you want me to start?"

"As soon as possible."

"Tomorrow," Abernathy said. "I'll speak to the magistrate in the morning."

"Excellent." Larrimore looked as if a thought had occurred to him. "If I remember correctly from Symms's letter, Hallam's brother was involved somehow in all of this."

"Half-brother," Abernathy corrected. "His name was Andrew Paxton. Did you know him?"

Larrimore shook his head. "No, I can't say that I ever met the lad, though I may have heard Henry mention him from time to time. What happened to him?"

"He disappeared the same night Hallam escaped. It was at Paxton's cabin, in fact, that we almost caught up to Hallam."

Larrimore frowned. "Do you think Hallam killed him, too?"

"There was no sign of a body, no indication of

violence in the cabin," Abernathy replied with a shake of his head. He hesitated, then asked, "How much do you know of the actual events of the case?"

Larrimore sat forward in his chair. "The magistrate was very discreet in his letter. And sympathetic, of course."

"Then it falls to me to be blunt, sir. Davis Hallam claimed that your daughter was involved with his half-brother. He said that he found the two of them . . . together . . . and that Andrew Paxton was really the one who killed her. Hallam claimed the death was accidental, that Paxton was actually trying to shoot him."

Larrimore's face had reddened even more as Abernathy spoke, and a thunderous frown creased his forehead. "Impossible!" he exclaimed. "Faith was a good Christian woman. She would never be an . . . an adulteress!"

Abernathy nodded. "That was my feeling as well, Mr. Larrimore, and all the evidence supported that conclusion. Andrew Paxton was devastated by Mrs. Hallam's death and by his brother's wild accusations. I believe that, when the trial was over, he simply decided to leave the area and put the whole tragic affair behind him. It's entirely possible he doesn't even know that Hallam escaped."

Larrimore settled back. "Then there's no chance this Andrew Paxton might have helped Hallam, hidden him or anything like that?"

"Absolutely none. Hallam's lunacy made the two of them bitter enemies."

Larrimore sighed and said, "Well, then, there's no help there."

"Don't worry, Mr. Larrimore. I'll find Hallam."

"You sound convinced of that."

"I am." Abernathy grasped his left arm, rubbed at the aching bone. "He'll not escape me again."

Larrimore lifted his cup of wine. "Let us drink, then, to justice."

"To justice," Abernathy echoed as he raised his own cup.

But both men knew what they were really drinking to, and it wasn't justice at all.

It was revenge. And it was going to be sweet . . .

10

Two days after passing the Cumberland Gap, the group was working in a particularly thick stretch of woods on either side of the trail. The weather had turned quite warm and humid, with a strong breeze that swayed the tops of the trees but did little to relieve the discomfort of the men on the ground. Davis was sweating as he swung his ax at the thick trunk of a tree. Winter, though only recently over, was already beginning to seem almost like a memory.

The thud of hoofbeats made Davis pause in his work and look back along the trail. He knew that both Colonel Welles and Conn Powell were farther along the road, and no one else was mounted. The pace of the approaching rider made it clear that it was one man on horseback, not the wagons that brought up the rear of the party every day.

Sure enough, a man on a big bay horse rounded a bend in the trail and rode toward the workers. He was wearing buckskins and a broad-brimmed hat.

Most of the men stopped working to watch him as he trotted up to them and reined in.

"Hello, boys," he said in a hearty voice. "I'm lookin' for a fella named Welles, supposed to be in charge of this outfit."

Bill Grimsby pointed along the trail toward the west. "You'll find him up thataway, 'bout half a mile or so, scoutin' out our work for tomorrow."

The stranger grinned. "Scoutin' is what I'm doin', too. Name's Mather. I'm guidin' the wagon train that's comin' up the trail behind you."

That statement brought several excited questions from the men. Davis's interest perked up, too. He hadn't known anything about a wagon train following along behind them on the Wilderness Road. And yet, that was why they were widening the trail, wasn't it? So that immigrant wagons could get through more easily and carry more and more settlers into the land of Kentucky? Obviously, the people in the caravan being led by Mather wanted to be the first ones to take advantage of the improved route.

The men in the work party weren't thinking about that, however, Davis figured. They were thinking that after several weeks in the wilderness, it was going to be good to see other people again— including the women who were no doubt with the wagon train.

As for himself, he hadn't minded the isolation. He had welcomed it, in fact. The friendships he was beginning to form with some of the men were all well and good, but Davis had no desire to be in a crowd of people again. He had always liked having some distance around him, which was why his farm hadn't been close to any of the others back in the Shenandoah Valley.

"The wagons ought to be catchin' up to you late this afternoon," Mather went on, "seein' as how even oxen can move faster than you boys when you have to stop every few feet and cut down some trees or clean out a mess of underbrush."

"You'll have to wait on us, though," Grimsby said. "The trail's too narrow up ahead for full-sized wagons. It'll be that way until we widen it out."

Mather nodded. "I know that, and so do the folks with the wagons. I just want to let your boss know that we'll be right behind you the rest of the way."

Davis saw several of the men exchange grins. They obviously liked that prospect.

Davis wasn't sure that he did. He had come out here to get away from people, especially people who might know that he was wanted by the law. But it was pretty unlikely anybody in that wagon train would know anything about what had happened back in the Shenandoah Valley, he decided. None of them would recognize him.

But still, he felt uneasiness prickling along his nerves.

Mather rode on, leaving the men talking animatedly among themselves about the prospect of company. Davis didn't join in the conversation. Instead, he turned back to the tree he had been chopping down, and once again his ax began to thud into the wood in a steady rhythm. His example reminded the other men of the work they still had to do, and gradually they got back to it. The atmosphere of the group had changed, however, and Davis sensed that there would be no going back to the way it had been.

A little later, Mather, Colonel Welles, and Conn Powell appeared, heading east. The three men paused and Welles looked around at the workers before saying, "Lads, I'm going to speak to the leaders of the wagon train Mr. Mather is guiding, then I'll want to address you when I get back. But for the time being, just continue working as you have been. This won't change anything."

It would be nice if that was true, Davis thought, but he certainly doubted it.

Welles and Powell were gone for almost an hour. When they returned, bringing the group's supply wagons with them, the men had moved a couple of hundred yards along the trail. Powell waved them all together, and then Welles spoke to them from horseback.

"As you know, a wagon train of settlers will soon be coming along behind us," the colonel began. "It's a good-sized caravan, almost fifty wagons."

Most of the men grinned at that news. The more settlers there were, the better the odds that some of them would be unmarried women. Bill Grimsby was standing next to Davis, and he leaned over to say quietly, "Maybe I'll find me a wife before we even get to the end of the Road."

Welles frowned for a second at the murmuring that went through the group, then, as things quieted down again, went on, "I've spoken to Captain Harding, who's in charge of the expedition. We are in agreement that although some interaction between his group and ours is unavoidable, for the most part we should stay to ourselves."

A groan went up from the men, but it was quickly silenced by a glare from Conn Powell. No one wanted the foreman angry at them.

"This is for the benefit of everyone," Welles continued, raising his voice slightly. "We don't want to be distracted from our work, and the people on the wagon train—"

"Don't want to be bothered with roughnecks like us, is that it?" McIntosh called out.

Powell edged his horse forward a little. "Damn right that's it," he said. "Those settlers are respectable folks."

"And we're not respectable?" Grimsby asked angrily.

Welles held up his hands, palms out. "No one said that. Other than the men who have already left our party, I've been very pleased with all of you. You've worked hard, and you've done everything that Conn and I asked of you. Now we're asking you to cooperate again and honor our wishes."

This was going to be trouble, Davis thought. The men were still grumbling, and they were going to go along with what Welles was asking of them only reluctantly. But he could understand why the colonel and Powell felt as they did. Men who were busy courting wouldn't be chopping down trees or clearing away brush.

"Just consider that wagon train forbidden to you," Powell said bluntly. "That's the way it's going to be."

Welles cast a worried glance at his second-in-command, as if he was concerned that Powell's declaration might spark a full-scale mutiny. But, gradually, the men began to nod in acceptance. They might not like the situation, but none of them was willing to cross Powell openly, either.

"Well, now that we all understand each other," Welles said, "you can get back to work. I think there's at least another hour of good light remaining."

Davis was the first one to lift his ax from his shoulder and turn back to the trees at the edge of the trail. Powell sat on his horse, regarding the men coldly as they followed Davis's lead one by one. Soon the woods were full of the sound of ax against wood again.

That lasted perhaps half an hour. Then, one of the men looked back down the road to the east and froze with his ax drawn back for another swing. "There they come!" he shouted, and immediately all the attention of the workers shifted to the sight of a team of oxen lumbering around a bend in the trail, pulling a wagon with a tall canvas cover over the vehicle's bed. In the late afternoon shadows, the canvas stood out whitely.

As the men lowered their axes, another wagon followed the first one, then another and another, rolling toward the workers at the plodding pace their teams of oxen could maintain for mile after grueling mile. Even Davis stopped working to watch as the trail filled with wagons.

The thunder of hoofbeats made him turn his head. Conn Powell came galloping along the trail, and the foreman's face was dark with fury. "Damn it, get back to work!" he shouted. "Those wagons aren't even here yet, and you're already slackin' off!"

Colonel Welles approached at a slower pace, adding, "Do as you're told, men." He followed Powell toward the wagon train, and they were met by two men who rode out ahead of the caravan. Davis recognized one of them as the guide, Mather, and the other one was likely Captain Harding, who was in charge of the immigrants. After a moment of animated discussion with Welles and Powell, the one Davis took to be Harding raised his hand and signaled for the wagons to halt.

Davis turned back to his work, hoping the others would do likewise. If they angered Powell too much, that anger would be liable to spill over and be directed at every man in the group, not just the ones who were loafing. Powell already had little enough liking for him, Davis thought. No need to make it worse.

Gradually, the men returned to their tasks, and the wagons stayed where they were, parked along the trail. Even though he told himself he wasn't interested in the settlers at all, from time to time Davis found his eyes straying toward the big, canvas-topped vehicles. He saw women and children moving around them, and his chest tightened abruptly. He had experienced the same reaction when he saw other families back at the trading post where he had signed on with this crew. The sight was an all too poignant reminder of everything he had lost.

For the first time in quite a while, he found himself thinking about Andrew. Davis knew he would never see *him* again, either, which meant that true justice would be forever denied. His breath hissed between clenched teeth as he swung the ax and felt the blade cut into the tree in front of him. In his mind's eye, that tree seemed to become Andrew, and his blows with the ax fell harder and harder.

"Here now!" Bill Grimsby said from beside him, startling him. "What are you tryin' to do, Davis, chop through what's left of that tree with one stroke?"

Davis lowered his ax, blinked, shook his head. The tree was just a tree again. Andrew Paxton was nowhere to be seen.

"I sure hope the colonel thinks twice about lettin' us visit with those folks from the wagon train," Grimsby went on quietly.

"Maybe he will," Davis said. It didn't matter to him one way or the other. Even if Colonel Welles allowed the men from the crew to go over to the wagon train, Davis didn't intend to do so. He didn't need any more reminders of what he had lost.

He swung his ax again, feeling the satisfying shiver of impact go up his arms. Damn the world for not leaving him alone, he thought. And damn the past for not staying where it belonged.

As dusk fell, the immigrants made camp along the trail while the workers moved along to their own camp, which was set up about a quarter of a mile farther on. That distance was not enough to keep either group out of sight of the other, however, or even completely out of earshot. Davis could hear firewood being chopped in the other camp, heard as well an occasional loud voice or the high, shrill laugh of a child. He tried to ignore that sound as much as possible, even though it carved slivers off his heart like an old man whittling a block of wood.

An air of sullenness hung over the men as they gathered around their own wagons and campfire for supper. The usual talk was subdued tonight, and no one laughed. It went without saying that there would be no singing.

That wasn't the case in the other camp. Voices were raised in song, and Davis found his gaze drawn to the wagon train, just like every other man in the group. Their main cooking fire was large, and scattered around it were quite a few smaller fires. Silhouettes small and large moved against the glow of the flames.

The cook had prepared stew again tonight, probably at the orders of Colonel Welles. Normally, it would have been several more nights before the men would have enjoyed such a meal instead of johnnycake and salt pork. There was even fresh deer meat in the stew, and Davis wondered where the cook had gotten it. Conn Powell had ridden out a short time before dark, he remembered, then come back into the camp as night was falling. He must have brought the venison with him.

Welles didn't wait until after supper to tap the keg of rum, either. He began passing the jug around while the men were still eating. Obviously, he wanted to take their minds off the settlers so close by.

But if that was the plan, it wasn't working. One of the men, whom Davis knew only as Asa, refused the jug of rum when it came to him. "I don't want it," he said in a loud, angry voice as he suddenly came to his feet. "I don't want this damned stew, either. It'll take more than a jot of rum and a bowl of stew to make me forget there's women right over there!"

Several calls of agreement came from the men. A couple of them stood up to join Asa. Davis stayed where he was, sitting cross-legged on the ground next to one of the wagons.

That was the wagon Conn Powell chose to stand on, stepping up onto the lowered tailgate. "Shut up!" he snapped at Asa. "We'll not be havin' any of that kind of talk! You've been told that you're to stay away from that wagon train, and that's all there is to it."

Bill Grimsby spoke up. "Why can't we go over there? What harm will it do just to visit?"

Powell's lips pulled back from his teeth in what Davis supposed was a sarcastic smile, but the expression was a hideous one. "So, a little innocent visit is all you've got in mind, is it?"

"What else?" Grimsby demanded.

"You wouldn't be plannin' on courtin' any of those immigrant women, or maybe tryin' to find an old man to play a tune on his fiddle so that you can dance with 'em?"

Grimsby smiled. "Well, now that you mention it, boss, that don't sound like such a bad idea. How's about a dance, boys?"

This time the men cheered enthusiastically, and Powell responded by putting his hand on the butt of the pistol tucked behind his belt. That gesture made most of the men fall silent.

But not all of them. Asa lifted a clenched fist and shook it at the foreman. "Ye can't threaten me,

Conn Powell!" he shouted. "I may take orders from you durin' the day, but damned if I will at night! I'm goin' visitin'."

With that, he turned, pushed through the crowd of men around him, and started walking down the trail toward the immigrant camp.

"Hold it, you son of a bitch!" Powell jerked the pistol free and leveled it at Asa's retreating back. His thumb looped around the hammer.

Davis was holding his breath, and he wasn't the only one. Tense anticipation gripped the entire camp. If Powell shot down Asa, murdered him in cold blood simply because Asa had disobeyed an order that all of the men considered unjust, there would be trouble, bad trouble. The men might riot, violence feeding on violence. More of them would likely die.

Powell's face was as hard as stone, and in the firelight, his finger whitened on the trigger of the pistol. Asa never looked back, never broke stride.

"Conn! No!"

The words, practically shouted in an urgent voice, came from Colonel Welles. He came hurrying up to the wagon where Powell stood. Davis didn't know where the colonel had been—probably hoping that the situation would resolve itself or at least not get this bad—but he had waited almost too late to take a hand. Powell had come within a whisker of shooting Asa in the back.

But he hadn't, and now, with a muscle twitching in his jaw, the foreman eased off on the trigger. He glanced down at Welles and said, "You're goin' to have trouble, Colonel, if you don't put a stop to this now."

"I'll have more trouble if you kill that man, Conn."
Welles sighed. "Perhaps we made a mistake. Come
down from there and put that gun away. If the men
want something that badly, we can't stop them, short
of killing all of them. I doubt if they'd stand by while
we did that." A bleak smile touched the colonel's
face. "Besides, even if we did, then we'd have to
finish widening the road by ourselves. I think that's a
bigger job than either of us can handle."

Powell didn't like it. His grimace made that
plain. But he lowered the hammer of the pistol
carefully and slid it behind his belt again. "You're in
charge, Colonel," he said. His tone made it clear he
considered that unfortunate.

Welles ignored that and turned to face the
workers. "All right, men," he said. "You've made
your point. I suppose it wouldn't hurt for you to pay
a visit to the wagon train. But I expect you to be on
your best behavior. If there's any trouble . . . any
trouble at all . . . I won't stop Mr. Powell the next
time when he wants to take discipline into his own
hands."

Asa had stopped on the edge of the camp to
listen to what Welles had to say. Now he lifted a fist
into the air and called out, "Three cheers for the
colonel, boys!"

Most of the men cheered, but it was rather
perfunctory. They were too busy getting on their
feet, straightening and brushing off their clothes,
and swiping their palms over tangles of unruly hair
to put too much enthusiasm in their cheers for the
colonel. The group swept eagerly toward the other
camp.

Davis stayed where he was, watching them go.

Bill Grimsby noticed him and hung back for a moment. "Come on, Davis," he said. "Aren't you going?"

Davis shook his head. "You go on," he said. "I'd just as soon stay here."

Grimsby frowned at him for a moment, then shrugged. "Suit yourself. Me, I'm not goin' to pass up the chance to dance with a pretty woman—or even an ugly one!"

He hurried after the others, and Davis turned his attention back to the bowl of stew in his hands. He used a piece of johnnycake to sop up the last of the stew, then reached out to snag the jug of rum someone had left sitting on a nearby stump. He took a bracing swallow of the fiery liquor.

Colonel Welles strode past him, along with Powell. "I'd better go over there and make sure Captain Harding doesn't try to turn the men back. That could cause an ugly scene, too," the colonel said to his second-in-command.

"I'll go with you," Powell said, his voice still taut with anger. Davis couldn't decide who Powell was more angry with: the men, for disobeying orders, or Welles, for allowing them to get away with it.

Davis stayed where he was, not really ready to head for his bedroll yet, but unwilling to join the other men in the immigrant camp. He had the place to himself after a bit. Even the cook and the wagon drivers from the work crew ambled over to the other camp. Davis allowed his thoughts to drift.

His mind went back, unbidden, to the early days of his marriage to Faith. They had been so happy then, or at least that was the way he remembered it. In truth, he supposed, not everything had been so rosy. Although Faith had been adamant about marrying him over her father's objections and moving with him to the Shenandoah Valley, Davis knew there were times when she missed her family. She had probably wondered if she had made the worst mistake of her life.

It had certainly turned out that way, he mused.

But in those first weeks and months . . . even years . . . of their life on the farm, Faith had seemed happy. She had been loving and cheerful most of the time, and no one could have asked for a better mother to the children who had come along one after the other. Davis had been convinced that things would always stay the way they were.

Ah, but that was when he should have begun to worry, he realized now. The good things that happened to a man had only a limited span of life, like the wildflowers that pushed their way up through the soil every spring to bloom in lush beauty for a few weeks before they withered and died. That was what happiness was—a wildflower quick to blossom, quicker to fade.

But at least a wildflower sowed its seeds before it died, so that the beauty would return the next spring. And a flower didn't have the capacity to hate the ones that came before it.

As his children probably hated him now, having been filled with the lies about their mother's death and his part in it . . .

His forearms were resting on his upraised knees, and his hands clenched into fists as his head dropped forward in his pain. Sitting here alone and brooding had been a mistake, he told himself. Better he had gone over to the immigrant camp with the other men, uncomfortable though it might have been for him. In seeking to avoid the painful reminders of what he had lost, he had simply found an even deeper grief.

Perhaps it wasn't too late. He lifted his head, forced his hands to relax, and put one of them on the ground beside him to balance himself as he got to his feet. He could still visit the other camp, where everyone seemed to be having a good time. The sounds of energetic fiddle music and the clapping of hands floated through the night air. He wouldn't dance, Davis decided, but it wouldn't do any harm for him to watch the others enjoying themselves. He brushed his hands off and started walking toward the wagon train.

He had gone only a few steps when the darkness was split by a gunshot, and a woman's scream, harsh and shrill.

11

D avis stopped in his tracks, shocked at what he had heard. Angry shouts broke out in the immigrant camp. Davis saw several figures struggling against the light of the campfires. Without thinking about what he was doing, he broke into a run toward the site of the trouble.

There hadn't been any more gunshots since the first one, but the night was still filled with the uproar coming from the wagon train. As Davis pounded up to the edge of the camp, a stranger— obviously one of the immigrants—turned to face him, yelled a curse, and swung a fist at Davis's head.

Even knowing that some sort of ruckus was going on in the camp, the attack took Davis by surprise. The man's fist caught him flush on the jaw and knocked him backward. His feet tangled with each other, and his balance deserted him. He sat down hard on the ground.

The man who had attacked him came after him, trying to kick him in the head. Instinct took over, and Davis was able to throw up his hands in time to block the kick and grab the man's boot. He yanked on it as hard as he could and upended the settler, who fell with an angry howl. Davis started scrambling to his feet, saying, "Hold on a minute!"

The man paid no attention to him. Instead, the settler rolled over, came up on his knees, and launched himself into a dive at Davis. His arms wrapped around Davis's waist, and the power of his lunge sent both of them sprawling to the ground again.

There were similar battles going on all around them, but Davis had no time to pay any attention to them. He was too concerned with his own opponent, who managed to wind up on top of him, his fingers locked around Davis's throat. Davis arched his back up from the ground, trying to throw the man off, but that didn't work. He hooked a punch to the immigrant's midsection, but the man just grunted in pain and squeezed that much harder on Davis's neck. There was a red haze swimming in front of Davis's eyes, and blood was thundering inside his skull. He knew that if he didn't dislodge his attacker's hands from his throat soon, he would pass out—and then the man would probably go ahead and choke him to death.

Davis reached up with his left hand and got his fingers on the man's face, clawing for his eyes. At the same time he swung his right hand toward the man's head, cupping the palm as it slapped sharply against the immigrant's left ear. The man cried out in pain and flinched back, and his grip on Davis's throat loosened. Davis heaved his body up from the ground again, and this time the man went flying off of him.

Davis went after him. At the moment, he wasn't worried about who had started the fighting or the wrong and right of it. He just wanted to make sure the man who had jumped him wouldn't continue the battle.

Landing on top of the man, Davis pounded a couple of blows into his midsection, then grabbed his shoulders, jerked him up, and shoved him down so that his head bounced on the hard-packed dirt of the Wilderness Road. The man's eyes were glassy in the firelight now, and his struggles were feeble. All the fight had been knocked out of him. Slowly, Davis lowered the fist he had cocked for another blow.

Another shot boomed. Davis's head jerked around. He saw quickly that this time, the shot had been meant to stop the fight, rather than starting one. Captain Harding had a pistol in his hand, smoke curling from the barrel, which was pointed straight up into the night sky. With him stood the guide, Mather, as well as Colonel Welles and Conn Powell. All four men were grim-faced.

"Stop it!" Harding bellowed. "Here now! Stop fighting, you men!"

The explosion of the shot, followed by the shouted commands, penetrated the brains of the brawlers. Men stopped what they were doing, fists still upraised, enemies still clutched in angry hands.

"All of my men, step back!" Welles called. "Now!"

"Do as the colonel says, damn it!" Powell added.

Gradually, the workers stepped away from the men with whom they had been struggling only moments earlier. Davis pushed himself to his feet and moved to join them, but as he did so, a young woman suddenly appeared in front of him. "You're bleeding," she said, pressing a piece of cloth into his hand.

He was so startled that he took the cloth, but he didn't do anything with it. He just stood there dumbly, holding it. The woman smiled a little at him and lifted her hand to her own jaw. Davis realized that he could feel something warm and wet oozing from a scratch on his face in the same place. He held the cloth there, then took it away and saw the red smear on it. The woman was still smiling at him.

Now that he had gotten a better look at her, he could see that she wasn't quite as young as he had first thought. Twenty-two or twenty-three, perhaps, instead of seventeen or eighteen. There were a few lines on her face, faint but definitely there. They didn't detract from her attractiveness. Her features were strong, not beautiful perhaps, but certainly pretty. Light brown hair framed her face. In the firelight, it was difficult to tell what color her eyes were, but Davis thought they were blue.

"Emily!" a man's angry voice exclaimed from behind Davis. "What in blazes are you doing, girl?"

Davis looked over his shoulder and saw Captain Harding standing there glaring at him.

"This man is bleeding, Father," the young woman said.

"So are a dozen other men in this camp, maybe more," Harding said. "And it was him and his kind who started the trouble in the first place!"

"I started no trouble," Davis said, making an effort to stay calm. "I was in our camp when the fight broke out."

Harding gestured at the cut on Davis's face. "How'd you get that, then?"

"I made the mistake of coming over here to see what was going on after that gunshot," Davis replied, allowing a little bitterness to creep into his voice. "One of your immigrants jumped me with no warning and no provocation and tried to kill me, Captain."

"No provocation?" Harding echoed. "I'd say we had all the provocation in the world! What do you call it when some damn woodsman makes improper advances to a respectable married woman?"

Welles, Powell, and Mather came up behind Harding. The colonel said, "My man has already explained that he didn't know the woman was married, Captain. It was an honest mistake, and he meant no harm. The woman's husband had no call to shoot at him."

"Mighty lucky that fella's a poor shot," Powell added dryly. "If he'd killed our boy, there really would've been hell to pay."

"I ain't so sure the whole thing was accidental," Harding said stubbornly. He glanced once more at the young woman . . . Emily, he had called her, Davis remembered. "You get on back to the wagon, girl."

She looked like she was about to protest being ordered around like that, but before she could speak, Davis handed the blood-stained cloth back to her and said, "Much obliged, ma'am. I hope I didn't ruin that."

"It's just a rag," she told him. "It wouldn't matter if you did." Her father was still glowering at her, so she added, "I'm glad I could help," then turned away quickly.

Powell caught Davis's eye and jerked a thumb toward the rest of the crew. "Get over there with the others." Grimsby, McIntosh, Asa, and the rest of the men were still standing on the edge of the wagon train camp, looking sullen.

Davis joined them, but not before noticing which of the wagons Emily was walking toward. A stern-faced woman and several children of younger years stood there waiting for her. She glanced back over her shoulder, and if he had been closer to her, Davis thought, their eyes might have met. As it was, though, the distance between them was too great.

As Davis came up to the other men, Grimsby said fervently, "I swear, I thought the lady was unmarried. I didn't mean to cause a ruckus."

McIntosh spat on the ground. "She had a weddin' ring on her finger. What more d' ye need?"

"She could've been a widow!"

Davis didn't join in the argument. His jaw throbbed where the immigrant's punch had landed, his throat hurt from the choking, and he had a pounding ache in his skull. Despite that, his eyes were drawn to the wagon where he had last seen Emily. She must have climbed into the vehicle, because there was no sign of her around the wagon.

Welles, Powell, Harding, and Mather were deep in discussion again. While that was going on, the immigrants and the workers stood on opposite sides of the camp, glaring at each other. The immigrants outnumbered them ten to one, Davis judged, perhaps even more, so he hoped that no more fighting broke out.

He could make out some parts of the conversation—argument was more like it—going on between the leaders of the two groups. "—mutiny on my hands!" Welles was saying.

"—troublemakers!" Harding responded. "I'll not have—"

The discussion went on in that vein for several minutes before the men finally began to nod grudgingly. Finally, Harding climbed onto a stump so that he could address both groups at the same time.

"We have several weeks of travel in front of us before we reach the settlements in Kaintuck," the wagon train captain began. "We can't get through unless the trail is widened, so I reckon we're going to have to learn to get along with these government men, folks."

"We can widen the road ourselves!" one man shouted from the group of immigrants.

"Aye, we could, but Colonel Welles and his men know what they're doin'. It ain't just for us the road's bein' improved, you know. It's for all those folks who come after us, as well." Harding's words were a little forced, but there was no denying the truth of them.

"So we have to let these . . . these scoundrels do as they please?" another man asked indignantly.

"Not at all," Harding replied. "Colonel Welles and I have reached an agreement. His men will be allowed to visit our camp, but no more than five of them at a time." He shrugged. "Seems to me there's mighty little harm five men can do."

There was grumbling from both sides at the announcement of the agreement, but what Harding had said made sense to Davis. No one could expect the men from the work crew to ignore the presence of the wagon train right behind them, but neither could the immigrants be expected to put up with anyone bothering their women and starting fights. The situation had to be controlled somehow, and the proposed solution seemed like the best one. The fact that it really satisfied no one was beside the point.

Harding stepped down from the stump, and Welles took his place. "You men go on back to camp," he told his workers. "There'll be no more dancing—or fighting—tonight."

Again there were mutters of complaint, but after a moment the men turned and walked back toward their own camp. Davis went with them, glad things hadn't gotten any worse. With such hot tempers involved, someone could have easily been killed. Welles and Powell followed the men to make sure no one turned back.

Davis headed for the jug of rum, but he didn't drink any of it. He poured a little into the palm of his hand instead and rubbed it on the scratch on his face. The liquor stung like blazes, sending even more needles of pain through his head, but he didn't want the injury to fester. Liquor, he knew, was good for such things.

When he had done that, he spread his blanket for the night and rolled up in it, his head pillowed on his pack. Sleep was a long time in coming, but it wasn't from his aches and pains.

He was thinking, instead, about a young woman with light brown hair and eyes he thought were blue.

*   *   *

In the morning, Davis's head still hurt, and he was angry with himself. He should have stayed where he was the night before, he told himself, and not gotten mixed up in the brawl in the immigrant camp. If he had done that, he wouldn't have gotten hit.

And he wouldn't have seen that young woman called Emily and had all those thoughts about her.

Faith was less than six months dead. It was nothing short of an utter betrayal of her for him to have even noticed Emily's hair, or her eyes, or the way she looked when she smiled. Davis was ashamed of himself. The fact that Faith had betrayed him with Andrew was of no consequence in this matter. *He* still had a responsibility, no matter what she had done when she was alive.

But she was no longer alive, a part of his brain reminded him, and the marriage vows he had sworn bound him to Faith only so long as they both lived.

He gave a short, savage shake of his head that made the ache in his temples pound even worse. *No.* No, that was too easy. He wouldn't be trapped into that kind of thinking.

He wasn't the only one in a bad mood this morning. Most of the men were still upset from the night before. The colonel and Powell didn't give them much of a chance to brood, however, nor to spend a lot of time looking back down the trail toward the immigrant camp. They hurried the crew through breakfast and then got them to work, setting a hard pace all through the morning.

Davis welcomed the distraction, even if most of the other men didn't. He knew from experience how exhaustion could drive most things out of a man's mind, so he threw himself wholeheartedly into the work, chopping and clearing and helping dig up some of the more stubborn stumps.

Still, with each swing of the ax, Emily Harding's face lurked in the back of his mind.

The wagon train stayed where it was, not moving as the work crew moved on along the road and went out of sight by mid-morning. It wouldn't take long for the wagons to catch up once they started rolling. Since the caravan could only travel as far each day as the distance the crew covered, it made sense to rest the oxen and the mules . . . and the people as well. Davis figured they would get started again after the noon meal. That would allow them to close the gap during the afternoon.

That was the way it turned out, and that day set the pattern for the days to come. For a week, both groups pushed on, the workers starting at dawn, as usual, the wagon train following them later in the day. Each night, five men were allowed to visit the immigrant camp, and although tensions were high the first couple of nights, they soon eased as everyone got used to each other. A stern warning to Bill Grimsby from Welles and Powell to steer clear of married women probably helped matters, too.

Davis didn't visit the camp. That was the last thing he wanted. He hadn't seen Emily since that first night, and that was best for everyone concerned, he decided. He stayed in the workers' camp and either played cards or turned in early each night.

That was the way things stood until one evening after supper when Conn Powell came over to where Davis was sitting with his back against a tree.

Powell used a booted foot to nudge one of Davis's outstretched legs.

"What do you want?" Davis asked coldly, not taking very kindly to Powell's action.

"On your feet, Davis," Powell said. "You're goin' over to that immigrant camp."

Davis frowned. He hadn't been sure what to expect from Powell, but a statement such as that certainly wasn't it. "I'd rather not," he said.

"I ain't askin'. It's an order, Davis. Everybody in the crew's been over there 'cept you, and the colonel wants you to go tonight. Bill Grimsby's been makin' a pest of himself, so you're takin' his place."

Davis knew that Grimsby had managed to be among the five men chosen nearly every night. That had been fine with Davis, because he figured that Grimsby was just taking his turn. Obviously, he wasn't the only one who had noticed that, however.

"I don't want to go," he said stubbornly, thinking about Emily Harding. If he visited the immigrant camp, he was bound to see her. She might even try to talk to him again, if her father wasn't hovering over her too closely.

"Like I said, it's an order. Now get on your feet."

Davis sighed in resignation. He knew Powell pretty well by this time. If he defied the foreman, Powell would seize the excuse to demonstrate his authority. He might even try to force Davis over to the wagon train at gunpoint, which would look completely ridiculous to everyone concerned. Davis wasn't going to allow Powell to make a laughingstock of him.

"All right," he said as he pushed himself to his feet. "I'll go."

Powell grinned humorlessly. "That's more like it. Who knows, Davis, you might even enjoy yourself."

That, Davis realized, was exactly what he was afraid of.

The other four men had already gone over to the wagon train camp. Davis followed, his pace reluctant. As he trudged along the now-widened path, he thought about how he had no right to get any pleasure out of this visit. His wife was dead, his children were forever out of his reach, and he was a fugitive convicted of murder. *That* was his life, not talking and laughing and dancing with a pretty girl.

Now, how in the hell had *that* image popped into his head? he asked himself.

With a grimace, he forced the thought out of his mind and continued on toward the camp. When he got there, several men gave him friendly nods, and he was glad to see that not everyone was hostile to his presence. The immigrants were obviously making an effort to get along.

So were the men from the work crew. Davis saw a couple of them sitting next to a fire with one of the immigrant families, laughing and talking. Another man had borrowed a fiddle and was scraping the bow across the strings while his companion danced with an older woman, probably the grandmother of one of the families. That was innocent enough not to cause hard feelings, Davis thought. As for himself, he intended to wander around the camp for a few minutes, just long enough to satisfy Powell's order, then head back to his bedroll.

His ambling pace was interrupted abruptly by the figure who appeared in front of him. Emily

Harding smiled up at him and said, "Well, Mr. Davis, it's good to see you again. I was wondering when you'd come over to visit us."

He stiffened, feeling the sudden urge to turn and run. That would be impolite, however, and he didn't want to offend Emily. He managed to nod and said, "Good evening to you, Miss Harding. How are you?"

"Why, I'm just fine. I see that cut on your face is healing up all right."

"It was just a scratch," Davis said. "But I appreciate your concern."

"Come over to the wagon and have some tea with us," Emily said. "Have you had supper?"

"Yes, ma'am, but I thank you anyway, Miss Harding."

"No need to be so formal," she said with a laugh. "Call me Emily. And I should call you . . . ?"

"Davis."

A slight frown appeared on her face. "But I thought that was your last name."

He took a deep breath. Something inside him was unwilling to lie to this young woman, despite the habit he had developed over the past few months of keeping his real identity a secret. "My name is Davis Hallam," he said, "but the other men don't know me as that."

There. Maybe that hint of mystery would scare her off. Surely she had enough sense to realize that there was something unsavory in his past, otherwise he wouldn't be using a false name. He had seen the keen intelligence in her eyes and knew she would figure that out.

But if she did, it didn't seem to matter to her,

because she said, "Oh. All right. I'll remember that. Now, come along, and we'll have that tea."

She was nothing if not persistent, Davis thought. He would humor her for the time being and still make this visit as brief as possible. He was reasonably certain that Captain Harding would welcome him only grudgingly to the family fire.

Emily led him across the camp to the first wagon. A small fire burned nearby, and Captain Harding sat beside it on an overturned crate. He had a tin cup in his hand, and when he looked up at Davis, his eyes narrowed in suspicion. "I remember you," he said without any other greeting. "You were part of that brawl the first night."

"Not through any choice of my own," Davis said. Harding just grunted in acknowledgment of the comment.

"Don't be unpleasant to our guest, Father," Emily said sternly to him. "I've offered Mr. Davis a cup of tea, and I intend to see that he shall have it."

"Go ahead," Harding said with a wave of his free hand. "I'll not have anyone say that Linus Harding is an inhospitable man."

That reminded Davis of what Peter Abernathy had said back in the jail in Elkton. Harding was about as friendly as Abernathy had been, too. But at least the wagon train captain didn't want to string him up from a gallows, Davis thought.

Not yet, anyway.

Emily brought another crate from the wagon and placed it on the ground, on the other side of the fire from her father. Not only intelligent, Davis thought, but wise, too. "Please, sit down," Emily said. "I'll get your tea."

She fetched a tin cup from the wagon and used a piece of leather to protect her hand as she picked up the pot sitting in the edge of the fire. After pouring tea into the cup, she handed it gingerly to Davis, adding, "Careful, it's hot."

Indeed it was. Hot and good, he discovered as he sipped the brew. Strong, just as he liked it. He took another sip.

Emily had gone back to the wagon, and when she returned to the fire, she wasn't alone. She brought with her an older woman and three children—two boys and a girl. "Mr. Davis," she said, "I'd like for you to meet my mother and my brothers and sister."

Davis stood up, nodding politely to the older woman. "I'm pleased to meet you, ma'am," he said, but as he spoke, his mind was racing back to the day he had first met Faith's parents.

There was no reason for this to remind him of that, he cautioned himself. This was completely different.

"This is Tom and Joel," Emily went on, touching each of the boys on the head as she spoke his name. "And Sarah Anne," she added, placing her hand on the shoulder of the little girl, who peered up at Davis with awestruck eyes.

Davis gravely shook hands with Tom and Joel Harding, who appeared to be around twelve and ten, respectively. Sarah Anne was about eight, he judged. The gap between Tom's age and Emily's suggested that the Hardings had had several other children who had likely died young. That was all too common. Life was hard anywhere, and more so the farther one went from civilization.

"Where are you from, Mr. Davis?" Mrs. Harding asked.

"Virginia, ma'am," he replied, figuring that was a vague enough answer.

"We're from Pennsylvania ourselves," the older woman said. "We had a farm near Pittsburgh. But Linus wanted to move on, and he'd heard stories about this land of Kaintuck. Have you ever been there?"

"No, ma'am, but I hear it's a mighty fine place."

"Thinking about settling there yourself, are you?"

"Yes, ma'am," Davis replied honestly. "I've given it some thought."

"Perhaps you can claim some land near ours," Emily said. "It would be nice to have good neighbors."

Davis swallowed hard. Evidently Emily didn't notice, or didn't care, that she was being rather bold. "I'm sure you and your neighbors will get along just fine, ma'am," he managed to say.

The children were allowed to go back to the wagon, and Mrs. Harding settled down next to her husband, perching on a corner of the crate. Davis hoped fervently that Emily wouldn't try to follow her mother's example. There would be room on the crate for her, but just barely, and her hip and thigh would have to be pressed up against his . . .

With a force like a striking hammer, the realization that he wanted Emily Harding went through Davis. He had not thought about a woman like that in months . . . or perhaps he had just denied it to himself. He had figured that in the future, if his needs became too overwhelming, he could satisfy them with a trollop from some tavern. The subject really hadn't occupied much of his thoughts.

But this was different. Emily was no trollop, and he had no right to think lustful thoughts about her. She was a respectable young woman, and the only way he could even entertain such fancies concerning her would be to start thinking about marriage as well—

Abruptly, he lifted the cup to his lips and drank down the rest of the tea, ignoring the fact that it was still hot enough to burn his mouth slightly. "I have to be going," he said as he came to his feet. He couldn't afford to worry any longer about being polite. He had to get out of here—*now*.

"What—" Emily began, but Davis stopped her by pressing the empty cup into her hands.

"Much obliged for the tea, ma'am. It was good." He nodded across the fire to Harding and his wife. "Good night, Captain. Good night, ma'am. Thank you for your hospitality."

Then he turned and walked quickly away from the wagon, not daring to look back. He was afraid that if he did, he would see the confusion and hurt on Emily's face. He knew that expression had to be there after the way he had acted, and he regretted it more than he could say.

But he'd had no choice. He had strayed far too easily onto forbidden ground. He had his pain and loneliness to live with.

And as he walked into the night, he embraced them both.

12

For several days after that, Davis brooded as he worked, wishing he had never allowed Conn Powell to browbeat him into visiting the immigrant camp in the first place. If he had only stayed away, as he had intended to do all along, he never would have gotten to know Emily better. And if he had not known her better, he would not have allowed such thoughts about her to enter his head.

It would have been easier, though, to make all the trees that had been felled by the work crew spring back to life than to ignore the feelings that had taken hold of him. No matter what his intentions had been, the image of Emily Harding haunted him practically every waking moment.

He decided that even though he couldn't banish her from his mind, he could stay away from her. No matter what Powell or anybody else said, he wasn't going near that immigrant camp again, and nothing could force him to visit it.

As usual, he was wrong.

fear that Emily might be in danger and it was taking him so damned long to get there.

He rounded a couple of bends in the road and saw the scene he had feared spread out before him. The wagon train was stalled in a long straightaway between two bluffs that crowded in closely on both sides. A deadly rain of gunfire was pouring down from the bluffs. The oxen pulling the first few wagons had dropped in their harnesses, felled by the rifle fire, and that had effectively blocked the road. Even after the work done by the colonel's crew, the Wilderness Road still was not wide enough for more than one wagon to pass.

Not only had some of the oxen been killed, but the bodies of several men were sprawled on the ground alongside the wagons. Davis slowed in his run, stunned by the horror of what he was seeing. Men were working their way down through the trees on the slopes, firing as they came, and more bandits were attacking from the rear of the wagon train, these on horseback.

Davis had no doubt that they were bandits. He got a good look at several of the ambushers and recognized them as white men. As one of the raiders paused to draw a bead on a target, Davis came to a stop as well and flung his flintlock to his shoulder. He cocked the rifle, settled the weapon's sight on the chest of the bandit, and pulled the trigger at the same time as the man fired. Both rifles belched smoke and flame.

Davis had no idea if the bandit had hit what he was aiming at, but through the haze of powdersmoke, he saw his own shot strike home.

The bandit was flung backward by the heavy lead ball slamming into his chest. He fell in a twisted heap and didn't move.

Acting on instinct, Davis was already reloading. He dropped to one knee as he did so. The other men from the work crew dashed up to join him, and as he rammed home another ball and charge of powder, he called to them, "Bandits on the bluffs!" More rifles boomed around him as the men took a hand in the fight.

Davis saw Conn Powell racing along the wagon train, the reins of his horse in his mouth, a pistol in each hand. The foreman veered his mount toward a pair of bandits who had just reached the bottom of the slope on that side of the wagons. Powell fired the brace of pistols, the shots coming so close together that they sounded like one. Both bandits were blown backward.

A grim smile touched Davis's lips for an instant. Conn Powell might be a dyed-in-the-wool bastard, but he was a fighting man. You had to give him that.

Then Davis had the butt of the flintlock socketed firmly against his shoulder again, and he fired at another bandit he had glimpsed through the trees. The man stumbled, fell, and rolled down the slope, crashing through the underbrush.

Davis loaded the flintlock again, then surged to his feet and broke into a run once more. He knew that the Harding wagon was the first one in the train, and he wanted to reach Emily's side. No matter how many bandits swarmed the wagons, he would protect her, keep her from harm.

Just like he had kept Faith from harm . . .

The thought slithered through his brain like a snake. He gritted his teeth and forced the image of his dying wife out of his mind. That was the past. There was plenty of danger in the here and now.

He saw Linus Harding crouched beside the lead wagon, firing an old blunderbuss of some sort toward the raiders. The weapon lacked the accuracy of the newer flintlocks, but it packed plenty of power in its shots. Harding began reloading, then suddenly slumped backward against a wagon wheel, dropping his gun and clutching his shoulder. His wife cried out, "Linus!", and reached down toward him from just behind the seat of the wagon.

Harding motioned for her to get back under cover, then awkwardly started pulling himself upright again. Davis spotted one of the bandits drawing a bead on the wagon train captain and fired hastily at the man. The shot missed, but it came close enough to make the bandit duck back behind some bushes, and that gave the wounded Harding time to scramble into the wagon.

Davis hoped fervently that Emily and the children were staying low inside the wagon. The thick sideboards of the vehicle would stop most of the rifle balls.

Since the bandits were attacking from three sides, the only places to take cover were inside and underneath the wagons. Davis reached the Harding wagon, threw himself down, and scrambled underneath it. The wheels would offer him some protection, and the body of the vehicle shielded him from the gunmen who were higher on the slopes. He reloaded his rifle and crawled to one side, peering out in search of a fresh target.

The next few minutes were a nightmare of gunfire, screams, and shouted curses. Clouds of acrid powdersmoke stung Davis's nose and burned his eyes. He was deafened by the continual roar of shots. His brain was numb, his actions all instinctive as he loaded and fired, loaded and fired. Horses thundered past the wagon, their hooves churning up the dirt only inches from Davis's face and making him draw back to blink away the grit that clogged his vision. But even in the midst of the hellish action, he wondered about Emily, wished that he could know if she was all right.

From what he had seen of the bandits, there were several dozen of them, a big enough group to attack even a large wagon train such as this one. The ambush had been planned almost like a military operation. Davis had known there were well-organized gangs of highwaymen along the Wilderness Road, but he had been convinced they wouldn't strike at such a large, well-armed caravan. Obviously, he had been wrong.

Finally, the shooting began to die away. When it stopped entirely, the silence that descended on the scene was eerie. All the birds and animals of the surrounding forest had been frightened away by the battle, and for a moment, as his ears adjusted to the quiet, Davis heard absolutely nothing. Then, as more of his hearing returned, he became aware of sobbing. It seemed to come from all along the line of wagons and was punctuated by an occasional heartfelt curse or a desperate calling

of a loved one's name. Davis knew even before he
crawled out from under the Harding wagon that
people had died in this raid, probably quite a few of
them.

On hands and knees, he moved out from under
the wagon and stood up. He was unhurt, somehow
untouched by all the lead that had been flying through
the air. He took a deep breath and looked around. The
bandits were gone, just as he had thought.

Stepping up to the front of the wagon, he looked
anxiously inside, beneath the arching canvas cover.
He saw Mrs. Harding kneeling beside her husband,
apparently unharmed. She was winding a bandage
around Harding's shoulder, where he had been
struck by one of the bandits' shots. Clustered around
Mrs. Harding were the three younger children.

Davis didn't see Emily anywhere in the wagon.

"Captain Harding," he said urgently, "are you all
right?"

"I will be," Harding replied in a voice drawn taut
by agony. "Damned musket ball smashed my
shoulder." His pain-dimmed vision seemed to clear
a little, and he went on, "Davis? Is that you? What
are you doing here?"

"All of us from the crew came to help when we
heard the shooting," Davis explained. Impatience
and worry were growing rapidly inside him, and he
hurried on, "Where's Emily? Is she all right?"

It was Mrs. Harding who answered without
looking up from her grim work of bandaging her
husband's shoulder. "We don't know. She was back
with one of the other families, visiting friends, when
we were attacked."

Davis's hands tightened convulsively on his rifle. "How far back? Which wagon?"

"She was with the Fletchers," Harding said. "Six wagons back."

Davis didn't linger any longer. He turned and ran as hard as he could toward the Fletcher wagon.

Counting off the vehicles as he ran, he found the one he was looking for. The canvas cover had been torn loose on one side, and it was flapping in the gusty wind that had sprung up in the past few minutes. The inside of the wagon was revealed. Davis saw a woman kneeling there over the body of a man. Great shuddering sobs wracked her as she lay against his bloody, unmoving chest. Davis came to a stop and stood there watching helplessly. He didn't see Emily anywhere, but he could tell that the sobbing woman wasn't her, although they seemed to be about the same age. This woman had bright red hair underneath her bonnet.

Finally, several of the other women from the wagon train climbed into the wagon and gently pulled the woman away from the man's body. Davis guessed that he was her husband, and obviously he had been killed fighting the bandits. But, despite the sympathy Davis felt for the redheaded woman, he still had to find out what had happened to Emily.

He stepped forward and held out a hand, saying, "Excuse me," to the women who were helping the grieving widow. "Is that Mrs. Fletcher?"

"Who're you?" one of the immigrant women asked.

"I'm from the crew that was working up ahead,"

Davis said. "I came back to help drive off the bandits. But now I'm looking for Emily Harding, and her mother said she was on the Fletcher wagon."

His words must have penetrated to the stunned brain of the red-haired woman. She let out a wail and turned her haggard, tear-streaked face toward him. "Em—Emily was here," she managed to gasp out. "But they . . . they got her!"

Davis restrained the impulse to reach out and grab the woman by the arms. He leaned forward, trembling from the intensity of the emotions that gripped him. "What do you mean, they got her?"

"One of those men . . . he rode by and tore the cover loose from the wagon . . . then another one reached inside and . . . and grabbed Emily! He rode off with her! And then they shot . . . shot Andy . . . !" More sobs doubled the poor woman over.

Davis stood there, too shocked and horrified to move. The bandits had kidnapped Emily. She was out there now, somewhere in the wilderness, in the hands of men brutal and ruthless and bold enough to attack an entire wagon train. Either that, or she was already dead.

God help them all, Davis didn't know which possibility was worse.

The one thing that burned in Davis's mind was pursuit. He had to go after the bandits and rescue Emily.

Most of the people in the wagon train were occupied at the moment with counting the dead and helping the injured, however. More than a dozen of the immigrants had been killed in the raid, including several women and children.

"We drove 'em off, though, by God!" Harding said fiercely a little later as he talked over the situation with Colonel Welles, Conn Powell, and the guide called Mather. Powell and Mather were both wounded, but the injuries were minor. Welles had missed the fight, having been scouting quite a distance ahead of the work crew when the shooting broke out.

"Do you think they were trying to take over the entire train?" Welles asked.

"Aye. They would have murdered all of us and looted the wagons. But we put up too much of a fight." Harding looked at Davis, Grimsby, McIntosh, and some of the other men who were standing nearby and added grudgingly, "And your boys lending a hand like that probably tipped the scales our way even more, Colonel."

"I'm sorry we couldn't have saved your people who died," Welles said solemnly. "If there's anything else we can do to help—"

"We can go after those bastards and bring back Emily," Davis broke in, unable to contain himself any longer.

A look of pain passed over Harding's face, and it wasn't prompted by his wound. "I was going to speak to you about that, Colonel. Our folks are pretty shot up, and nearly every family's got somebody either dead or hurt."

Welles nodded. "Of course. Some of my men can pursue the bandits."

"If we're goin' to, we'd better get started mighty

quick-like," Powell said. A bloody rag was tied around his left arm, but that didn't stop him from gesturing toward the gray sky overhead with that hand. "Could be a storm movin' in. That'd make it harder to track 'em."

Davis stepped over beside Powell. "I'll go with you."

Powell glanced at him, dark, hooded eyes unreadable. "Somehow, that don't surprise me none," he said dryly.

"Count me in," Grimsby said. McIntosh volunteered as well, followed by several other men. Within moments, Powell had a group of a dozen ready to go.

"Take what supplies you need from our wagons," Harding said. "You're liable to be out there in the woods for quite a while."

Powell nodded and said, "Much obliged. We'll take you up on that, Captain."

They couldn't prepare to leave quickly enough to suit Davis. He paced back and forth while Powell gathered up a bag of food and another of powder and shot. After what seemed like an interminable time to Davis, they were ready to go. The damp wind blew in his face as he shouldered his flintlock and walked away from the wagons with the other men.

Powell, who was in the lead, looked back over his shoulder and said, "Watch close, mind you. We could be walkin' into an ambush. I wouldn't put it past that bunch to leave some men behind to cover their back trail, just in case anybody comes after them."

That made sense to Davis. As worried as he was about Emily, though, he didn't think there was much chance of him letting down his guard.

A fine mist began to fall not long after the men were out of sight of the wagon train. Like Powell, Davis was worried about rain making the trail more difficult to follow, but unless there was a downpour, he thought they ought to be able to pick up the tracks left behind by the fleeing bandits. For one thing, riding their horses through the forest had left plenty of brush broken and shoved aside. To a long hunter like Powell, that was a route that had been plainly marked. Even to a relatively inexperienced frontiersman such as Davis, the trail was easy to follow.

But it might not remain that way, he reminded himself. The bandits had been in a hurry to get away from the wagon train with their captive. Later on, they might be more careful about the tracks they left behind.

Besides, the sooner Emily was rescued from them, the better. Davis didn't want the bandits to have time to abuse her.

He wondered why they had kidnapped her. Did they intend to demand a ransom for her from her parents? That was possible, in which case they would have a good reason to keep her alive and relatively healthy. Or perhaps they had grabbed her simply because they hadn't been able to get their thieving hands on anything else. They might take out their anger and frustration at the raid being foiled on her.

That possibility turned Davis's blood to ice in his veins.

The mist stopped, but the wind still blew, soughing loudly in the tops of the tall trees. Lightning flickered in the gloom, and thunder rumbled in the distance. "Tater wagon's rollin' over," Grimsby commented. "That's what my ma used to say whenever it thundered."

Davis just grunted, not interested in such homespun childhood memories at the moment. He just wanted to find Emily, wanted to take her into his arms and pull her against him and feel her warmth and know that she was all right.

But instead of vital and alive, she might already be as cold as the clay, and that thought gnawed at his brain almost constantly no matter how much he tried to banish it.

Davis knew that, with the overcast sky, night was going to fall early. Powell seemed to be just as aware of that, so he pushed the men at a hard pace. They climbed hills, slipping carefully over the crests so that they wouldn't be silhouetted against the sky, dim and dreary though it was. A keen-eyed observer might still spot them if they weren't cautious. They splashed through creeks and made their way along wooded ridges. Always, Powell trotted along in the lead, but Davis was usually right behind him. The logging work had hardened Davis even more than he had been to start with, and he moved tirelessly, driven as well by his concern for Emily. Even if he had been tired and sore, he would have ignored any pain if it meant finding her sooner.

After a great deal of twisting and turning, the trail finally straightened out and led in the direction of a gray-green, rough-shouldered peak to the north.

As mountains went, it wasn't terribly impressive. The taller scarps were far behind them in the Appalachians. But this was the most prominent feature in the surrounding landscape, and Davis wondered if it was honeycombed with caves. He had heard about such things from men who had been in Kentucky before. If that was the case, then the mountain might make a perfect hiding place for the band of highwaymen. Davis's pulse began to pound harder as he looked up at the mist-shrouded peak.

He and Powell were thinking alike again. The long hunter held up his hand, signaling the men to halt. He nodded toward the mountain and said quietly, "Could be they're up there somewhere. It'd be a good place for 'em to hole up. It's close enough to the Wilderness Road to make raidin' travelers pretty easy."

"Let's go," Davis said impatiently. "The trail leads straight to the mountain. Even I can see that."

"Can you see the trap they've probably laid for us?" Powell snapped.

Davis's mouth tightened. "Trap or no trap, we've got to go ahead. The only other thing we can do is turn back, and I'll be damned if I'm going to do that."

"We're going ahead," Powell conceded. "But everybody look sharp, and sing out if you spot anything that don't seem right."

The air was crackling with tension as the men started forward. The trail led into a narrow valley that ran up the side of the mountain. There were quite a few horse tracks in the soft, grassy earth. Davis knew the bandits had come this way, and he was convinced they still had Emily with them. With every mile he and the other men had covered without finding her body, his hopes of freeing her from her captors grew stronger. The rescue party would be outnumbered more than two to one, he judged, but that might not matter if he and the others could strike quickly and unexpectedly. Powell kept them in the trees on the edge of the valley, flitting through the shadows like phantoms.

The precautions weren't good enough. Powell stopped and stiffened suddenly, as if some instinct had warned him, but as he turned and started to wave the rest of the men back, a volley of rifle fire crashed from a nearby thicket. The balls ripped into Powell and threw him backward, dark stains of blood blossoming on his buckskins.

Davis jerked his rifle to his shoulder and fired, aiming into the clump of brush. He heard a whine next to his ear and knew that a rifle ball had barely missed him. Behind him, a man grunted in pain.

More shots ripped through the air. Muzzle flashes lit the gloomy late afternoon. Davis threw himself forward onto the ground to make himself a smaller target and began desperately reloading. He heard men cry out, saw from the corner of his eye as they fell, knocked off their feet by the shots of the ambushers. When his flintlock was charged and loaded again, he aimed at the brush and pulled the trigger. The powder in the pan flashed and made a small noise, but it failed to set off the charge in the barrel. Davis grimaced. This was no weather in which to be fighting a battle with flintlocks, not unless you could stay under cover and make sure all your powder was dry. He rolled over and lunged onto his feet again, heading for a nearby tree so that he could put the trunk between him and the bandits. As he ran, he saw Bill Grimsby sprawled face-up on the ground. An ugly black hole leaked crimson in the center of Grimsby's forehead.

Davis felt a pang of regret as he ducked behind the tree. Grimsby had been the closest thing to a friend he'd had since leaving Virginia, and now the man was dead. So was McIntosh, who was curled up in a ball in the middle of a pool of blood that came from the wounds in his belly. Powell, of course, had been shot to ribbons in the first volley. In fact, Davis saw as he looked around, out of the dozen men who had set off in pursuit of the gang, only three of them were still on their feet. And as he watched, one of the other men was cut down as he dashed unsuccessfully for cover.

A pulse rang like an anvil in Davis's head. His hands trembled as he tried to clear the misfire from his rifle so that he could reload. Finally, he gave up and dropped the weapon. Powell hadn't had a chance to fire any of his guns, so if Davis could reach the long hunter's body, he could get his hands on a rifle and two pistols. He edged an eye around the trunk of the tree and saw where Powell lay. The distance to the man's body was only about fifteen feet.

I can make it, Davis thought. And once he had Powell's weapons, he could duck back into the trees and try to circle around the ambush. It was a slim chance, but the only one left to him.

Then, just as he was about to dash out from behind the tree, he heard a woman scream.

Emily!

It had to be her. She was the only woman out here in this savage wilderness—at least the only one he knew about. Rage exploded inside him. She was alive, but she was scared, or hurt, or both. Without thinking about what he was doing, he emerged from the shelter of the tree and sprinted toward Powell's body, an inarticulate cry of rage welling up his throat. The other survivor of the rescue party was right behind him, also shouting.

The other man's bellow was cut short as a rifle ball struck him and threw him backward. Davis was vaguely aware that he was charging the gang alone now, but he was far beyond caring about that. He paused for a fraction of a second as he passed Powell's body, just long enough to bend down and jerk the foreman's pistols from behind his belt. Then Davis was running toward the hidden gunmen again, screaming and firing both guns. He flung the empty weapons aside, ready to do battle barehanded.

He never got there. Something slammed into the side of his head with an awful impact, harder than anything he had ever felt before. He reeled to the side, tried to keep his balance, but failed. What felt like a finger of fire drew a line of agony across his side as he fell. He tasted grass and dirt in his mouth.

The rains that had been threatening all afternoon finally came then, pouring down from the sky, washing away the blood that welled from the wound in his head.

Davis never felt the cold, hard rain.

13

He did feel something underneath him, however, when he woke up an unknowable time later. Something sharp and prodding and uncomfortable, but not nearly as uncomfortable as the pain that rampaged through his head.

For one dizzying moment, he thought he was back in Constable Peter Abernathy's jail in Elkton. He remembered waking up there, but everything after that was a blur. Gradually, as he lay there unmoving, some instinct warning him not to announce the fact that he had regained consciousness, other memories came back to him.

The trial for Faith's murder. The lies that Andrew had told. The escape from the jail, the days and weeks of hiding and running. And then the Wilderness Road . . .

And Emily.

Despite the fact that he was trying to lie completely still, Davis's jaw clenched tightly, and his fingers twitched. He knew now what had happened. The raid on the wagon train was clear in his mind. He remembered following the bandits along with Powell, Grimsby, McIntosh, and the other men.

They were all dead now. All dead . . . except Davis himself. And he knew damned well that he was alive because no one who had passed beyond this life could possibly hurt so much.

He recalled as well Emily's scream, just before the final charge against the bandits. Did she still live, too? If they had kept him alive, surely they hadn't killed her. A beautiful young woman had to be worth more than a grizzled, soul-weary fugitive from the law.

As he lay there, a few more things penetrated his consciousness. He heard the low-pitched voices of several men. Something tantalized his nose for long moments before he realized it was the smell of frying bear. Then he heard hollow echoes of footsteps somewhere nearby.

Davis opened his eyes, just the barest fraction of an inch.

At first all he could see was a strange, flickering, reddish light. It came from a fire, he figured out after several seconds. He could smell the wood burning. Somebody laughed, and a man said, "Pass me that jug."

He was in the bandit camp, Davis decided, probably in a cave in that mountain he had seen before the ambush, judging by the echoes he heard. For some reason, they had dragged him in here after shooting him. He was lucky to even be alive.

Or, depending on what his captors had in mind for him, maybe not so lucky at all.

He tensed his muscles and tried to move his arms and legs a little, not enough to let the bandits know he was awake. He had to find out whether or not he was free. It took only a moment for him to realize that he was bound hand and foot, and pretty tightly at that. His fingers and toes were going numb.

Footsteps approached him, and he tried to lay as limp as possible. The masquerade didn't help. A booted toe nudged under his shoulder and then roughly rolled him over onto his back. Cold water splashed in his face, its touch as shocking as the blow of a fist. Sputtering, he shook his head from side to side, the reaction instinctive and violent.

"'Bout time you woke up, mister," a man said. His rough voice sounded like it had been filtered through gravel. "Thought for a little while there you weren't goin' to make it. That gal was carryin' on somethin' fierce over you."

Davis felt a spark of hope blaze into life inside him. The woman this man was talking about had to be Emily. She was the only one in these parts who would "carry on" just because she thought he might be dead.

Blinking water out of his eyes, Davis looked up at the man looming over him. From this angle, lying on the floor of the cave, it was impossible to tell how tall the man was, but his spread of shoulders and his long, powerful arms were impressive. He wore buckskin pants, a linsey-woolsey shirt, and a broad-brimmed black hat shoved back on curly dark hair. His beard hung down almost to his chest.

The man had his hands on his hips and a self-satisfied expression on his face. "You know who I am?" he asked.

Davis shook his head, even though the movement made fresh pain throb behind his eyes.

"They call me Shadrach. I'm the leader of these boys."

"Can't say as I'm . . . pleased to meet you," Davis managed to grate.

Shadrach threw back his head and laughed, the booming sound echoing from the high ceiling of the cave. "No, I don't imagine you would be," he said. "But you're here, and there ain't a blessed thing you can do about it. What's your name?"

The question caught Davis by surprise. He answered, "Davis."

"Well, Davis, old son, you been shot a couple of times, in case you were wonderin'. You got pinked in the side and creased on the noggin, but I reckon you'll be all right. Leastways, you would be if we wasn't plannin' on doin' what we're plannin' on doin'."

"And what would . . . that be?" Davis forced himself to ask.

Again the uproarious laugh came from Shadrach. Whatever he was about to say amused him so much that tears leaked from the corners of his deep-set dark eyes. "Why, we're goin' to give you to the Shawnees, old son. Ain't nothin' they like better'n a white man to torture and kill ever' now and then, and you sure enough fit the bill."

The shock of the statement almost made Davis pass out again. He had survived two battles with the bandits, had lived through being shot, only to discover that he was still doomed. And if he died, Emily's hope of being rescued probably died with him. Captain Harding might send out another search party, but he might not. When Davis and the others didn't return, the captain might be so discouraged that he wouldn't risk the life of anyone else. He might even convince himself that Emily was already dead and the only choice remaining was to move on and get the wagon train to its destination. Davis doubted that Colonel Welles would send anyone else, either. The colonel had already lost his foreman and half a dozen of his workers. He would be for pushing on with the job at hand—and Davis couldn't blame him for feeling that way.

"It'll be a while 'fore we turn you over to the savages, though," Shadrach went on. "You might as well get used to our hospitality. That little gal's been pitchin' a fit from wantin' to take care of you, so I reckon we'll let her do that. Just don't get no ideas. You're bound for a Shawnee fire, and you ain't endin' up nowheres else."

Davis let his head slump back against the hard rock floor underneath him. Despite the grisly fate that awaited him, he was going to see Emily again. He could at least reassure himself that she was all right.

Shadrach turned away and said to someone Davis couldn't see, "Untie the girl." The bandit leader walked across the cave, moving out of Davis's vision. A moment later, he was replaced by a much prettier sight, at least in Davis's estimation. Despite the fact that her face was smudged with dirt and a worried frown cut deep creases in her forehead, Emily looked positively lovely as she hurried over and knelt beside him.

"Davis!" she said, catching hold of one of his bound hands. "Are you all right?"

That was a pretty foolish question under the circumstances, but he managed to smile anyway. "Sure. I'm a little bunged up, that's all."

"Shot up, you mean. Those . . . those devils nearly killed you."

They *had* killed eleven other good men, Davis thought. It was only by sheer chance that he had not made it an even dozen.

Or maybe it was more than that, he told himself. Maybe there was a reason he had been chosen to live. He hung on to that thought, because it meant that maybe there would be a chance for him and Emily to get out of here after all.

"You poor man," she murmured. "Let me look at those wounds."

Her probing fingers were as gentle as possible, but her touch still set off explosions of agony through his head as she explored the wound left above his ear by the rifle ball that had grazed him there. He gritted his teeth together to keep from crying out. Then she moved his shirt aside and examined the crease on his side, a procedure that was almost as painful as the first one. When she was done, she looked off to the side and asked, "Can I get a rag and some water?"

"Sure," Shadrach's gravelly voice replied. "Fix him up good, darlin'. Don't want them Shawnees to think we're tryin' to trade 'em any shoddy goods."

That was all he was to these bandits—goods to

be traded to the Shawnee Indians. What Shadrach and the gang of highwaymen would get in return, Davis didn't know, but he would probably find out, and all too soon at that.

Shadrach brought Emily a rag and a pan of hot water. As he set the water down beside her, his left side was turned toward Davis, and Davis saw something he hadn't noticed earlier. Shadrach was wearing a sheathed knife on his left hip, which came as no surprise. Most frontiersmen carried a knife. But this one had a distinctive silver knob on the end of its handle. Davis had seen one just like it somewhere before, but the rest of the memory eluded him.

The next moment, he forgot about it entirely in the wave of pain that swept over him as Emily began cleaning his wounds. She swabbed away the dried blood from his head and side with the wet rag, and he saw the cloth turn red as she used it. He must have bled like a stuck pig, he thought.

The ordeal lasted only a few minutes, and to tell the truth, Davis didn't even mind the pain that much. As long as Emily was kneeling beside him and leaning over him, as long as he could see her face and smell the light brown hair that occasionally brushed feather-soft against his features, he was content even though he was hurting.

While she was close to him, he whispered, "Are you all right? Have they . . . hurt you?"

She gave a tiny shake of her head and whispered in reply, "I'm fine. Just . . . scared. Very scared."

Davis could understand that. He was frightened, too. There had been a time, not that long ago, when he had believed that he had nothing left in life to lose. Now he was beginning to understand just how wrong he had been.

"That's enough," Shadrach said. "Don't go spoilin' him. The Shawnees won't treat him so gentle."

Emily turned on the bandit leader, and the look on her face was fierce. "How can you do that?" she demanded angrily. "How can you just turn another white man over to the Indians to be ... to be ..." She couldn't bring herself to put Davis's fate into words.

Shadrach shrugged. "It ain't a bit hard. The Shawnees like to have themselves some fun ever' now and then, and as long as we help 'em get what they want, they let us do pretty much what we want around here."

"So you turn over your captives to them, and they let you raid wagon trains and settlements and then hide out here in this cave," Davis said.

"That's right," Shadrach said. "It's a mighty fine arrangement, if you ask me."

Davis wasn't going to debate that point with the bandit, especially when Shadrach reached down and took hold of Emily's arm, hauling her to her feet and being none too gentle about it. "Leave her alone!" Davis exclaimed.

"You ain't in no position to be givin' orders, old son," Shadrach pointed out. "Lay there and keep your mouth shut, or we'll gag you. This little lady ain't goin' to be hurt. She's worth too much money the way she is."

That should have been reassuring, Davis

thought, but somehow it wasn't. Emily's face was pale and her expression was shaken as Shadrach dragged her away. Davis closed his eyes and tried not to give in to the surge of nausea that gripped him.

It didn't matter how badly he was hurt or how much he was outnumbered, he told himself. He was alive and he was going to stay that way, and he was going to find some way to get them out of this danger. He had to, for Emily's sake.

The fact that his hands and feet were tied made it awkward, but after determining that the wall of the cave was right behind him, he was able to wriggle himself into a sitting position and lean back against the cold, damp stone. From there he could look around and see the entire cave.

It had a high, vaulting ceiling and had evidently been naturally formed, judging from the water that still dripped from the ceiling here and there. The walls of the cave formed an irregular circle, and Davis estimated the diameter at fifty or sixty feet. On the other side of the cave, a narrow tunnel sloped upward toward the surface. The campfire was built in the center of the underground chamber. Smoke from the blaze rose straight up to curl around the ceiling and gradually dissipate. There had to be some natural chimneys up there through which the smoke filtered out of the cave. They would be too small to offer any hope of escape, however. The tunnel appeared to be the only practical way in or out of the place.

Overturned crates served as seats around the fire, and more than a dozen men were gathered there eating a meal of panbread, bear, and beans. The smell of the food made Davis's stomach growl and reminded him of how long it had been since he had eaten. Other men were sprawled on bedrolls scattered around the cave, dozing. Still others passed around a jug and played cards on a blanket that had been spread out on the floor. Shadrach was in this last group, and he had Emily sitting on a crate next to him, keeping her close since she hadn't been tied up again.

Davis wondered where the gang's horses were. They probably kept the mounts in a hidden pen somewhere outside near the entrance of the cave, he thought. He supposed he should be grateful they didn't keep the animals here in the cave. The air was a little stale to start with, and it would soon get utterly rank if a herd of horses was in here as well.

Shelves had been built along one wall, Davis noted, and they were full of supplies. Supplies that had no doubt been stolen from travelers or nearby settlements, he thought bitterly. The bandits had all the comforts of home here, and yet if the entrance to the cave was cleverly concealed, it would be very difficult to root them out of their hiding place. There was very little law around here to start with, so the gang could operate without having to worry too much about anything except the Indians.

And as long as they paid off the savages with white captives to torture—like him—Shadrach and his men were safe even from that threat.

Emily glanced across the cave at him, and Davis

met her eyes squarely, gave her what he hoped was a reassuring nod. He certainly didn't feel very confident. Everything he had seen in this cavern made his hopes ebb that much more. There was no way out, even if he could manage somehow to get free. All the bandits were roughly dressed and rugged looking, cut from the same ruthless cloth as Shadrach. And they were well armed. They could cut him down before he had taken three steps toward that tunnel.

After a little while, Shadrach looked over toward the prisoner, saw that Davis was sitting up, and turned to speak to Emily. He inclined his head toward Davis and said, "You can take him something to eat if you want."

Davis's stomach clenched again at the words.

Emily was evidently thinking of escape, too, because she said, "His hands will have to be untied for him to eat."

Shadrach grunted. "Not likely. You can feed him. I reckon he'll like that, anyway."

Emily sighed and looked at Davis. He nodded. Regardless of whether his hands were tied or not, he had to eat, had to keep his strength up. When the opportunity he was waiting for finally came about, he didn't want to be too weak from hunger to take advantage of it.

One of the men at the fire put some beans and fried bear on a tin plate and handed it to Emily along with a hunk of panbread. She brought the food over to Davis and knelt beside him. "What are we going to do?" she hissed, too quietly for any of the bandits to overhear.

"You're going to feed me," Davis said, forcing a degree of calm into his voice that he didn't really feel. "Then we're going to wait for a chance to get out of here."

"Do you really think we will?"

"Of course," he said, and he was a little surprised to discover that it wasn't a well-intentioned lie. Despite everything, he really did believe that they were going to escape. He couldn't allow himself to believe anything else.

But he had believed that he and Faith would love each other forever, too, a perverse part of his brain reminded him.

Davis shoved that thought out of his head and concentrated on the beans and chunks of bear that Emily spooned into his mouth, the bites of panbread he chewed off the piece that she held up to his lips. The bread and the bear had both been cooked too long, and the beans hadn't been cooked long enough. But it all tasted good to Davis, because he could feel strength flowing back into his body from the food.

"Do you know what they intend to do with you?" he asked Emily quietly. He didn't want to upset her, but he needed to know what the bandits were planning.

She took the question calmly enough, evidently understanding why Davis had asked it. "The one called Shadrach said there's a man who comes over here from a big river somewhere to the west. He's a Spaniard, and he . . . he's a slave trader. Shadrach says they can get a good price for me."

"When does he expect this Spaniard?"

Emily shook her head. "I don't know. Not right away, though. I got the impression it'll be a while before the man comes through here again."

"That gives us some time."

"Not much," Emily said grimly. "He plans to turn you over to the Shawnees in less than a week."

"We'll be long gone by then."

"I hope so," Emily said. "I sure hope so, Davis. Because if anything happens to you . . . well, I don't intend to let them sell me to that Spaniard. I'll get my hands on Shadrach's knife and put it in my own heart before I'll let that happen."

She still sounded calm enough, but the fervent tone of her whisper convinced Davis she was telling the truth. She might be better off dead than sold into slavery. He couldn't make that decision for her.

But she had said *if anything happens to you . . .*, as if his life was just as important to her as her own.

Davis didn't know what to make of that, didn't dare try to read too much into it. Not now, not when it looked like both he and Emily might be able to number the rest of their lives in mere days.

"It won't come to that," he told her. "I'll get us out of here somehow. You just be ready when the time comes."

She nodded, and he knew from the look in her eyes that he could depend on her. All they needed now was an opportunity . . .

"Finish shovelin' that grub in him and get back over here," Shadrach called to Emily from his seat next to the card game. "My luck's gone to hell since you ain't been beside me, gal."

Davis felt pretty much the same way. He knew

that his luck—his life—had changed when he met Emily Harding.

Reluctantly, Emily fed Davis the rest of the food and then stood up. "I'll get you something to drink," she said. Ignoring the glare Shadrach sent her way, she fetched a jug from one of the shelves and brought it over to Davis. There was water in the jug instead of whiskey, but that was all right with him. He wanted to keep his head clear. The water was stale and brackish, but it tasted good to him as it ran down his throat.

After that, Emily had no choice but to resume her seat next to Shadrach. The bandit leader put his hand on her shoulder for a moment as she sat down, but he didn't try to paw her. Davis was grateful for that.

The card game broke up a short while later, and more of the men headed for their bedrolls. Inside this cavern, it was impossible to tell if it was day or night outside, but from the way the bandits were acting, Davis was convinced it was night. Shadrach and another man came over to Davis, and the second man untied the ropes around his ankles. For a second, Davis thought about trying to jump them and get his hands on a gun, but he discarded the wild idea. His wrists were still tied, and his feet were so numb that he was pretty wobbly when Shadrach took hold of his arm and hauled him upright.

"We'll take you outside and let you take care of your business," Shadrach said, "but don't get no ideas. There'll be a gun at your head the whole time."

Davis nodded. Prodded along by the two bandits, he stumbled toward the mouth of the tunnel. The second man picked up a flaming brand from the fire to use as a torch.

Davis was tall enough so that he had to stoop slightly to keep from scraping the top of his head on the ceiling of the tunnel. He followed it for perhaps fifty yards before it made a sharp turn and rose even more steeply. Davis had to put his hands down to steady himself as he climbed toward the surface. Shadrach and the second bandit were right behind him with their pistols drawn and ready.

When he stepped out into the night, Davis drew a deep breath of air that had been washed clean by the afternoon's storm. It invigorated him, cleared away some of the cobwebs that had gathered in his brain during his underground captivity. He wished he could just cut and run. Shadrach and the other man might miss their shots, and if they did, he could be out of range of the flintlock pistols before they could reload.

But that would mean leaving Emily behind to face whatever fate they had in store for her, not to mention the anger they would feel at his escape. He couldn't condemn her to that, not even to save his own life.

He unbuttoned his trousers and relieved himself, with the other two men flanking him. True to Shadrach's word, the bandit leader held his pistol pressed to Davis's head. Davis remembered something that had puzzled him earlier, so he said to Shadrach, "That's a mighty fine looking knife you're wearing. Where did you get it?"

Shadrach chuckled. "You ain't goin' to have a chance to find one like it, Davis, even if there is another one anywhere in these parts, which I doubt."

Davis fastened his trousers and shrugged. "Indulge my curiosity. What can it hurt?"

"True enough." Shadrach lowered his pistol and took a step back. The clouds had all cleared away now, leaving the moon and stars shining brightly in the night sky overhead. The light glinted on the silver ball at the end of the knife's handle as Shadrach slipped it from its sheath. "Won it in a card game, I did."

Davis's heart started to thud heavily in his chest. He thought he remembered now where he had seen a knife like that before. "From whom?"

"Just a gent in a tavern over at Boonesborough. I don't like to go into the settlements much, but every so often a fella's got to have a roof over his head and sleep in a real bed with a willin' wench."

"The man you won the knife from . . . what did he look like?"

Shadrach frowned. "What the hell business is it of yours? He was just a fella I'd never seen before. Young, dressed pretty fancy for Kentucky. The trollops workin' in the tavern seemed to think he was handsome, the way they were flockin' around him and ignorin' the rest of us. I tell you, I was glad to clean him out in that card game." Shadrach paused, then went on, "What the hell's the matter with you? You ain't about to have a fit, are you?"

Davis's breathing had gotten faster and faster until he was almost panting. The ache in his head, which had subsided a little, came roaring back as his pulse began to hammer unmercifully.

Andrew! The name screamed through Davis's brain. The man Shadrach had described could have been Andrew Paxton. Andrew had disappeared from the Shenandoah Valley just like Davis himself had disappeared. What better place for any man to vanish than out here on the nearly trackless frontier? Andrew was the only man alive other than Davis who knew the truth—the bloody truth—of what had happened in the Hallam cabin on that wintry day. It was possible that knowledge had eaten at him, just as it haunted Davis, and Andrew could have feared that someday, somehow, the truth would come out. If that ever happened, he would want to be far away from the Shenandoah Valley.

Those convoluted thoughts shot through Davis's head in a split second. He realized that Shadrach was talking to him, and he forced his racing mind and his galloping pulse to slow down. Dragging a deep breath into his lungs, he let it out with a sigh and said, "No, I'm not going to have a fit. I'm all right now."

Shadrach grinned. "Thinkin' about those Shawnees and what they're goin' to do to you, eh? Don't reckon I can blame you for that. It'd be weighin' heavy on my mind, too, if I was in your place, Davis. Maybe you'll be lucky. Maybe they'll kill you quick."

Davis doubted that. He knew little about any Indians, let alone the tribe called Shawnee, but he had heard lurid stories about the savages and their love for torture, especially when their victim was white. During the Revolution, Kentucky had also been called the Dark and Bloody Ground because of all the massacres that had taken place here as the British enlisted the Indians in their fight against the rebel colonists. Obviously, even though the British had been defeated, the Indians were still here and still had a thirst for blood.

Shadrach took hold of Davis's shirt collar and jerked him back toward the tunnel entrance. "Come along," the bandit leader ordered. "We've been out here long enough."

The three men retraced their steps back to the cavern, Davis sliding awkwardly down the steepest part of the path. Emily looked up as they entered the cave, relief flooding her face when she saw that Davis was all right. She must have been worried, he thought. Anyone in his or her right mind would be, under the circumstances.

He nodded to her, even managed to smile a little, and then Shadrach prodded him over to the rear wall and made him sit down. Once more, Davis's legs were tied together.

"Better get some rest," Shadrach advised him.

The very idea of sleeping seemed impossible to Davis. He didn't see how he could relax enough to doze off.

But once again, he surprised himself. He closed his eyes, and a few minutes later his head drooped forward onto his chest as he was claimed by slumber.

A scraping sound woke him. At first he wasn't certain of that, but then the noise was repeated. It came from somewhere nearby, but he couldn't locate it.

The fire had burned down to a pile of embers that gave off only faint light. Davis looked around the cave and let his eyes adjust to the darkness.

After a moment, he could make out quite a few motionless figures wrapped up in their bedrolls. He saw Emily lying near a bulky shape that had to be Shadrach. Despite everything he had expected, the bandits hadn't molested her, and he was grateful she had been spared that horror. Obviously, she would fetch a better price from the Spaniard as a virgin, and money meant more to Shadrach than slaking his lusts. He controlled this band of highwaymen with a strong enough grip so that Emily was safe from their advances, too. But that wouldn't last. Once she was in the hands of the slave trader, Emily could look forward only to a life of shame and degradation.

Davis heard the tiny scraping sound again. He stiffened. It was close now, very close.

A hand wrapped around his arm in the darkness.

He started up, but the hand's grip was like iron. Another hand clamped itself over his mouth, silencing any involuntary outcry he might make. If there had been more than one man, he would have expected a knife blade to come slicing into his body at any second, but the man beside him had both hands on him, and Davis could sense that he was alone.

"Don't raise the alarm, you damned fool," a voice hissed, the man's lips so close to Davis's ear that they were practically touching it. "I've come to get you out of here."

Davis's eyes widened in shock as he recognized the voice. It belonged to a man he had never expected to see again, a man who had been torn and bloodied by rifle fire the last time Davis had seen him.

Crouched beside him in the darkness was Conn Powell.

14

The hand pressed against Davis's mouth went away, and he whispered, "Powell! How—"

"Shut up, blast it!" Powell breathed in his ear. "You want to get us all killed?"

Powell was right, Davis knew. At this moment in time, it didn't matter how Powell had survived or how he had gotten into the cave. What was important was that he was here, and he had come to help.

But the problem still seemed hopeless. They were surrounded by bandits, any of whom might wake up at any time. The odds were still overwhelmingly against them. In all likelihood, the only thing Powell had succeeded in doing by sneaking in here would be to get himself killed a second time.

Davis didn't want to think about what a crazy idea that was. Maybe Powell really was dead. Maybe he was a ghost, a "haint," as Davis's grandmother would call it. It was even possible that he was imagining the whole thing, Davis told himself.

But Powell's rough touch hadn't felt like the hands

of a ghost. Nor was there anything imaginary about the tugs Davis felt on his wrists and ankles as Powell used a knife to slice through his bonds. The ropes fell away, and blood rushed back into Davis's extremities with a painful tingle. He flexed his fingers to get as much feeling into them as quickly as he could.

Powell pressed something into his hand. Davis recognized it as the hilt of a knife. "Where's the girl?" Powell asked, his voice still just a slender shaving of sound.

Davis pointed in silence, knowing that Powell's keen eyes could follow the gesture. He thought he saw Powell nod, then a hand on his arm urged him to follow.

Moving slowly and carefully, making as little noise as possible, Davis crawled behind the foreman. Powell led him along the rear wall of the cave. Davis didn't know where they were going, and every instinct cried out for him to go to Emily instead. But Powell knew what he was doing, Davis told himself.

He had damned well better.

Suddenly, a darker patch of shadow loomed up on Davis's right. He put his hand out toward it, expecting to feel the rough, gritty texture of the stone wall, but instead his fingers encountered only cool, empty air. The black patch was the opening of another tunnel, he realized. His heart slugged heavily. This was a way out, it had to be. Powell must have gotten into the cave through this tunnel, since Shadrach had posted guards at the main entrance. Maybe Shadrach didn't even know this tunnel was here.

Davis certainly hadn't seen it earlier when he was looking around the cave. He felt around, touched a large rock only a foot away. The rock might have been covering the tunnel entrance, he thought. That was the only reasonable explanation.

"Stay here," Powell hissed at him. "I'll get the girl."

For a second, Davis almost protested. *He* was supposed to be the one who rescued Emily. But then reason took over, and he knew that Powell was right. The long hunter would have a much better chance of getting her away from Shadrach than he would. All that mattered was saving Emily's life, not who got the credit for rescuing her.

He stayed where he was as Powell crawled away into the shadows. Davis used the time to explore the opening of the second tunnel. It was small, perhaps two feet wide and not much more than that tall. A good-sized man would be able to wedge himself through it, but there wouldn't be much room to spare. Davis wondered where it led.

He looked back over his shoulder to see what Powell was doing. The sleeping bandits were all still motionless except for an occasional twitch of arm or leg. Their snores filled the cave and helped cover up any small sounds Powell might be making. Powell was almost at Emily's side.

But then he started to circle around her, and Davis's eyes widened in fear. Powell was crawling toward Shadrach instead! He must have mistaken which sleeping figure Davis had indicated.

Davis wanted to call out, to warn Powell that he was about to wake the wrong person, but then he saw that *he* was the one who had made the mistake. It wasn't Powell's intention to rouse Shadrach from sleep.

On the contrary, he was going to make sure that Shadrach never woke up again.

Powell loomed over the bandit leader, his right hand rising above his head. Davis saw the very faint reflection of the glow from the embers of the campfire on a knife blade. Then Powell's left hand locked over Shadrach's mouth as the right hand fell in a savage thrust. Davis heard only a muffled thump as the blade drove into Shadrach's chest. Powell's other hand kept the bandit from crying out as he died. Shadrach's feet kicked once, convulsively, in the blankets wrapped around him, then they were still.

Powell pulled the knife free and wiped it on Shadrach's bedroll.

Davis realized he was holding his breath. He let it out softly. Powell's knife must have penetrated Shadrach's heart on the first try, otherwise the bandit would not have died so quickly and quietly. Obviously, Powell knew quite a bit about killing. Davis was glad he had never made an out-and-out enemy of the man.

Shadrach had died so quietly that Emily was still sleeping undisturbed beside him. Powell sheathed his knife and woke her as he had Davis, one hand on her arm, the other clamped over her mouth to prevent any outcry. Davis could tell that much from the movements he glimpsed in the shadows of the cave, but he couldn't hear anything Powell might have whispered in Emily's ear.

A moment later, however, she pushed her blankets aside and came up on hands and knees to crawl toward Davis, and he felt a surge of relief. She had understood who Powell was and what he was trying to do. Now it was just a matter of crawling through the narrow tunnel before any of the bandits woke up and realized what was going on.

Davis reached out to Emily as she came up to him, pulling her unashamedly into his arms and embracing her. "Are you all right?" he whispered to her. He felt her nod, her soft brown hair brushing against his cheek.

Powell moved up beside them and tapped Davis on the shoulder. He gestured toward the tunnel. Davis nodded, understanding that Powell wanted him to go first. That was probably for the best. He would lead the way, then Emily could follow, and Powell would bring up the rear. The fact that Powell trusted him to take the lead told Davis that the tunnel most likely ran straight to the surface without diverging anywhere along the way, otherwise Powell would have had to go first to make sure they took the correct turns.

Stretching his body out on the floor of the cave, Davis slithered into the roughly circular patch of darkness marking the tunnel entrance. With his elbows and toes, he pushed himself through the opening into the stygian blackness. For a moment, panic gibbered wildly inside his head as the dark enveloped him completely. But he was able to force himself to keep crawling, his shoulders and back scraping against the sides of the tunnel, and after a couple of minutes his nerves calmed down slightly. His own breathing was loud in his ears, but he could hear Emily behind him, too, making her way through the tunnel.

The rough floor of the tunnel tore the elbows of his shirt and the knees of his trousers and abraded his skin. He ignored the pain and continued crawling. From time to time he heard Emily gasp and knew the rocks were probably hurting her, but there was nothing that could be done about that. Better a few scrapes and bruises than the fate that had awaited her at the hands of Shadrach and the rest of the bandits.

The tunnel seemed endless to Davis, and the horrible thought flashed through his mind that he would spend eternity here, crawling through darkness and never reaching the end of it. But then he realized that somewhere far ahead of him was a tiny patch of gray instead of black, and he began to move faster. The blob of lighter shadows grew steadily larger, and finally he could make it out for what it was: the other end of the tunnel, illuminated by the moon and stars. He pulled and pushed himself along, desperate to reach it.

His head emerged into open air, the oppressive walls of the tunnel falling away around him. His hands felt dirt and grass and his fingers dug into the earth and pulled hard. He slid out of the tunnel and tumbled down a steep slope, rolling over a couple of times before he caught himself and stared up in joy at the star-dotted sky overhead. A wild laugh bubbled out of his mouth.

He heard a soft cry and turned to see Emily emerging from the tunnel. After that utter blackness, the night seemed almost as bright as day. Emily began to slide down the side of the mountain, just as Davis had done, but he was there to catch her and keep her from going head over heels. She was panting for breath, and as he held her he could feel the wild beating of her heart. The long crawl through the tunnel had been as hard on her as it had been on him.

But they were free now. They had come through the darkness and into the light.

A moment later their deliverer slithered out of the black hole in the side of the mountain. Powell motioned them toward a clump of brush nearby.

Once they were crouched there, Powell whispered, "Didn't want to talk too much there by the openin' of the tunnel. That hole would've funneled any sounds right back down to the cave."

"I thought you were dead!" Davis exclaimed in a low voice. "I thought the bandits killed you in that ambush!"

"They shot me up pretty good," Powell admitted. Now that they were out of the cavern, Davis could hear how weak the man's voice was. In the light of the lowering moon, he could see as well the large dark bloodstains on Powell's buckskins. "It'll take more'n a few rifle balls to put me under, though," the long hunter went on. "I woke up while those bastards were lootin' the bodies and just played possum until they were finished. It was damned lucky none of 'em decided to slit my throat to make sure I was dead."

"How did you find us in there?" Emily asked.

"Shoot, I've known about that cave for years," Powell replied. "When I heard that big fella with the beard talkin' about it, I knew where he meant to take the two of you. Reckon they didn't know about the back door. There was rocks coverin' both ends of that little tunnel, and if you didn't know it was there, you'd never find it. I knew."

"You saved our lives," Davis said. "We can't ever thank you—"

"Don't waste your breath on that now. We got to get out of here. Soon enough, those boys'll find out you're gone, and then they'll be all over this mountain." Powell reached into the brush beside him and brought out a flintlock rifle. The stock was shattered and broken off. He handed the weapon to Davis, along with a powderhorn and shot pouch. "This is all I was able to salvage except for a couple of knives. They took everything else. The lock's all right on that rifle, so it'll fire, but it'll be hard to handle without a stock."

"I can manage," Davis said grimly.

"Figured you could. Hang on to it, 'cause you're liable to need it 'fore we get back to the Wilderness Road."

Powell came to his feet, then abruptly swayed and almost fell. He would have if Davis had not leaped up and grabbed his arm. "You're too weak to travel far," he said.

"Don't have any . . . choice. We got to get movin'—"

At that moment, Davis heard a shout. The sound was faint and hollow, and after a second he realized it had come from the nearby mouth of the tunnel.

"Damn it!" Powell grated. "Somebody must've stumbled over the body of that big fella." He grunted. "Well, now they know you two are gone. Won't take 'em long to notice that second tunnel, and then some of 'em are likely to come boilin' out of it as quick as they can. The others'll go around the long way. Come on."

He started off in a stumbling run down the slope. Davis took hold of Emily's arm with his free hand, and they followed Powell. They were on the far side of the mountain from the spot where the bandits had ambushed the rescue party, Davis realized as he glanced up at the dark bulk of the peak rising above them. It wouldn't have taken long for him to become hopelessly lost if he had been alone. Luckily, Powell evidently knew this country like the back of his hand.

When they reached a ridge that ran along the side of the mountain, Powell led Davis and Emily to the left. The ridge petered out after several hundred yards, ending in a deep, narrow gully. Powell followed the gash in the earth, always heading downslope. Every so often, Davis thought he heard a shout in the distance, but he couldn't be sure about that. It could have been his imagination, he supposed.

After half an hour, they were on relatively flat land again. "I think we got down before they could . . . circle around us," Powell said. He leaned over, put his hands on his knees, and drew in several deep, ragged breaths.

"You need some rest," Davis began.

Powell straightened. "Not as bad as we need to put more distance between us and those bandits," he said. His voice sounded a little stronger, but Davis didn't put much stock in that. He knew that Powell had to be utterly exhausted and weak from loss of blood.

They pushed on, Powell stumbling now. Davis

had to reach out and grasp his arm to steady him several times. Another quarter of an hour passed, and the three of them reached a narrow creek that was flowing fast from the recent rain.

Gasping for breath, Powell signaled a halt. "Figured we'd . . . get here pretty soon," he managed to say. "This crick'll take you back . . . almost all the way to the road. Just stay with it . . . until you get to a hill with . . . two trees on top of it. Wait there 'til . . . morning . . . then head due south. That'll put you back on the road . . . pretty quick."

"Wait a minute," Davis said with a frown. "Why are you telling us all this? Can't you just lead the way?"

Powell looked at him. The moon had set a little while earlier, and Davis couldn't make out the man's face in the faint starlight. Not that it would have helped much if he had been able to see Powell, Davis thought. He had never been able to tell what the long hunter was thinking.

"I ain't goin'," Powell said. "I'm just too . . . wore out. Goin' to sit down here by this crick an' . . . have me a little rest."

Davis's frown deepened. "What about the bandits?"

"Ain't likely they'll . . . find any of us. They're probably . . . still back up on the mountain . . . tryin' to figure out how you two got out of that cave." Powell leaned against the trunk of a small tree and slid down it with a groan until he was sitting at its base. "If they do come along, I'll . . . slow 'em down for you."

"With what? One knife?"

Powell chuckled. "I'm better with a knife . . . than any of those boys are with flintlocks. I'll be . . . all right, Davis."

"Damn it, Conn—"

"I didn't . . . give you leave . . . to call me by that name," Powell said. His voice seemed to be weakening even more. "Now go on . . . ge' out of here . . . "

Davis swallowed hard and looked over at Emily. Both of them knew what Powell meant. He was dying, and he didn't want to hold them back. His reprieve from death had only been a temporary one, and he had spent the time he had been given rescuing them from the bandit gang. If they disobeyed him, if they threw away their lives now, his sacrifice would have been for nothing.

Davis nodded to Emily. She knelt beside Powell and put her hand on his shoulder. "Thank you, Mr. Powell," she said softly.

"You're . . . mighty welcome . . . ma'am." Powell lifted his own hand and awkwardly patted Emily's. "You know that . . . Davis here . . . he's in love with you . . . don't you?"

Emily looked up at Davis. "I . . . I . . . "

"Ne' mind," Powell said. "Ain't none o' . . . my business. Jus' . . . stay alive . . . both of you."

"We will," Davis promised. "Thank you."

"G'wan . . . git."

There was nothing else to say. Davis reached down, took hold of Emily's hand, and helped her to her feet. His fingers squeezed tightly on hers for a moment as they both looked down at the half-conscious man sitting beside the tree. Davis knew they would never see him again, but at least he had given them a chance for life.

They couldn't waste it now.

"Come on," he said to Emily, and they walked quickly, hand in hand, along the edge of the creek. When Davis looked back a moment later, he had already lost sight of the tree where Conn Powell was resting for the final time.

Even in the darkness, the creek was easy to follow because of the rushing sound of the water. Davis held Emily's hand in one hand and carried the flintlock with the broken stock in the other. They moved as quickly as possible, making their way through the brush and trees along the bank of the stream, until Davis judged they had put at least another mile behind them. Then he stopped and made sure the flintlock was loaded and charged. If they managed to elude the bandits, it was unlikely they would run into any other trouble that would require the use of the weapon, but Davis wanted to be ready just in case. There were Shawnee in these parts, he knew that for a fact.

Davis listened intently for any sounds of pursuit, but other than the normal noises—which ceased when he and Emily got close enough to the birds and small animals that made them—the night was quiet.

Until suddenly, the distant boom of a shot came to their ears, followed by several more. Emily gasped and stopped short, her fingers tightening on Davis's. Davis turned his head and stared back in the direction from which they had come, but it was impossible to see anything.

"Do you think they found Mr. Powell?" Emily asked in a half-whisper.

"I'd say it's likely," Davis replied. Regret stole through him. They should have stayed with Powell, he thought for a second. Then, the foolishness of that wild impulse became clear to him. If he and Emily had stayed, all three of them would have died. It would have all been for nothing.

He tugged on Emily's hand and said, "Let's go. Powell just bought us some more time. We have to use it."

If the bandits had just found Powell, that meant they were still several miles behind Davis and Emily. Davis felt hope growing inside him. It couldn't be too much farther back to the Wilderness Road. They ought to be reaching that hill Powell had told them about any time now. And there was a narrow band of gray in the sky to the east, signifying that dawn was approaching. Powell had said for them to wait on the hill until the sun came up, then head due south. Davis wasn't sure they would have to linger that long. He could locate south once sunrise was a little closer.

Emily began to stumble a little now and then, and Davis couldn't blame her. They had been traveling at a hard pace ever since escaping from the cave. She had to be exhausted. Davis certainly was. But he kept putting one foot in front of the other, unwilling to slow down.

Finally, Emily stopped, pulling her hand free from Davis's grip. "I can't keep going," she said breathlessly. "I have to rest a little while."

Davis glanced at the sky, saw that the arch of gray in the east was now tinged with red. He saw something else, too. Up ahead of them, perhaps a hundred yards away, was a small hill topped by a pair of trees.

"There's the place Powell told us about," he said, pointing to the hilltop. "If you can make it that far, we can rest."

Emily was swaying back and forth slightly. She stiffened her shoulders and managed to nod. "I can make it."

Davis took her hand again. "I thought you could."

They set off, moving more slowly now, and trudged up the slope to the trees. Davis sat down, put his back against one of the tree trunks, and let Emily sit down and lean against him. The back of her head rested on his left shoulder, leaving his right arm free. He kept the flintlock clutched in that hand, just in case.

Emily sighed heavily as she closed her eyes and settled back against him. Davis longed to stroke her hair, but he didn't want to let go of the gun. He settled for moving his head so that her hair seemed to caress his cheek.

"Davis," she said in a soft, sleepy voice, "was Mr. Powell right?"

"About us getting away?" he asked.

"No. About you being in love with me."

Davis's breath caught in his throat. He hadn't known Emily for very long, didn't really know her well. And despite everything Faith had done to help bring her fate down on her head, Davis still mourned for her. He had been completely convinced that any capacity for love he possessed had died that cold day along with his wife.

But he knew now that wasn't true, had never been true, even in the darkest days. He had never stopped loving his children, even though they were lost to him forever. And the feelings that had grown up inside him for Emily had taught him that not everything in his soul had died along with Faith.

"Powell was right," he whispered. "I love you, Emily."

She sighed, and even after the horrible ordeal they had endured, he knew it was a sound of contentment. "I love you, too," she said. His left arm went around her, tightened.

They fell asleep that way, as dawn rushed toward the wilderness from the east.

He hadn't meant to doze off, and when the sharp crack of a foot stepping on a branch woke him, he knew right away what a terrible mistake he had made.

"Ain't that a pretty sight?" a man's voice said.

Davis's eyes flew open as he instinctively pulled Emily closer. She had shifted around while they were both asleep so that she was halfway facing toward him now, the side of her face pillowed against his chest. She stirred, and Davis said, "Don't move, Emily."

That made her gasp in fear. She would have been even more frightened if she had been able to see the man standing about ten feet in front of them. He was a rawboned, lantern-jawed man with ginger chin whiskers and a nose that had been broken and twisted sometime in the past. Davis recognized him as one of the bandits. He seemed to be alone at the moment, but that situation wasn't likely to last.

"Thought you could get away, didn't you?" the man said with a sneer. "Don't know how you found that other tunnel, or how somebody like you managed to kill Shadrach, but it ain't goin' to do you any good. You're comin' back to the cave with me, both of you."

The man had a rifle in his hands, but he held it casually, the barrel pointing at the ground about halfway between him and his newfound prisoners. Davis was stunned at his lack of vigilance until he realized that a fold of Emily's long skirt had fallen over the flintlock with the broken stock when she moved around in her sleep.

The bandit didn't know Davis had a gun.

Davis's hand was still on the rifle, although his grip had relaxed. Now he tightened it unobtrusively, all too aware that he would get only one chance to use the weapon. The bandit took a step forward, his amused expression vanishing to be replaced by a scowl as he started to lift his rifle and said, "Get on up, now. I'm tired of chasin' after—"

Davis didn't wait for him to finish. He tilted up the barrel of the flintlock and pulled back the hammer as he raised the rifle. Emily gave a short, involuntary scream as he pressed the trigger and the flintlock roared, firing through her dress.

The ball caught the outlaw in the chest and threw him back, his face contorting in shock and pain. He dropped his own rifle as he sprawled on the ground. Davis shoved Emily aside, dropped the now-empty flintlock, and sprang after the bandit. He yanked out the knife Powell had given him and drove it again and again into the bandit's body, gripped in a frenzy unlike anything he had ever experienced before. Crimson splattered his hand and forearm as the knife rose and fell.

Then he became aware that Emily was holding his shoulders and saying urgently, "That's enough, Davis, that's enough! He's dead! We've got to get out of here!"

She was right, of course, and the realization finally penetrated Davis's hate-fogged brain. He shuddered, then nodded his head in understanding. Pulling the knife free from the bandit's mutilated body, he wiped off the blood on the grass of the hillside, then picked up the man's fallen rifle. It was loaded and unfired, and it would serve him better than the rifle with the broken stock.

Davis intended to take the broken gun with them anyway. He picked it up and handed it to Emily as he stood up. "Come on," he said. "The others must've heard that shot, and they're probably not far off."

He glanced at the sun to confirm the direction, then started off toward the south. It was still early in the morning, and he judged the sun hadn't been up for more than an hour. The two of them moved at a trot, anxious to reach the Wilderness Road and find the wagon train.

A shout sounded somewhere behind them. Davis glanced back and saw several men running through the trees. Emily saw them, too, and cried out in alarm.

"Come on!" Davis urged her as he broke into a run. He kept her hand locked firmly in his. He wasn't going to leave her behind. If the bandits caught up to them, he would sell his life dearly defending her.

Then, suddenly, he heard the sound of hooves over his own thundering heartbeat. Several riders swept out of the trees in front of them, and pistols cracked. Davis threw Emily to the ground and stood over her, shielding her with his body. The horsemen were practically on top of them.

The riders raced past, but not before Davis saw Colonel Tobias Welles and Captain Harding and Asa and several other men he recognized from the work crew and the wagon train. They must have heard the shot, too, and came to investigate, thinking that it might be the rescue party returning.

Well, that was true, Davis thought as he lifted Emily back to her feet and put his arms around her. The two of them were all that was left.

"Davis, that . . . that was my father!" Emily said.

"I know."

"Then . . . we're safe? It's over?"

Davis looked over his shoulder as more shots sounded. The bandits were fleeing, disappearing back into the savage wilderness from which they had come.

"Yes," Davis said quietly, putting his hand under her chin and lifting her face to his. "This part is over . . . and everything else is just beginning."

15

This time, Davis received a warmer welcome at the wagon train than he or any of the other men from the work crew had gotten so far. He had brought Emily back safely, something that no one had really expected.

"We ought to go find our men who died and give them a decent burial," Colonel Welles said with a frown when Davis had told him everything that had happened.

Davis was sitting with the colonel beside one of the cooking fires in the wagon train camp, sipping gratefully from a cup of hot tea. He said, "Aye, but if you did that, you might be walking right into another ambush. Those bandits will be mighty angry about everything that happened."

"Davis is right," Captain Harding said. "Much as I hate to abandon the bodies of our friends, I think we should push on and not tempt fate."

Welles nodded slowly. "I had some of the same concerns." He put his hands on his knees and pushed himself to his feet. "All right, I'll get the men back to work, and we'll proceed as quickly as possible. It may be difficult, though, since we've lost several men."

"Let me replace them," Harding offered. "I'm sure I can find some young men here in the wagon train who'd be glad to help. They can swing an ax or anything else you need."

"And some men to stand guard," Davis suggested. "Just in case we run into more bandits, or the Shawnee."

"An excellent idea," Welles said. He smiled faintly. "This has been a tragedy, of course, but you have to admit, Captain—we're working together now."

"That we are," Harding agreed. "I reckon we've all learned that's the only way to survive out here."

Davis was glad to see the improved relations between the immigrants and the work crew, although, like the colonel, he wished the circumstances which had brought the two groups together had been less bloody and tragic. At least Emily had come through the ordeal relatively unharmed. That mattered more to him than anything else.

Emily had disappeared inside the Harding wagon with her mother when they reached the camp, and Davis didn't know when he would see her again. In the meantime, there was work to do. He drained the last of the tea from his cup and stood up. "Let me get my ax, Colonel," he said to Welles, "and I'll be ready to get back to work."

The officer looked at him in disbelief. "Davis, it hasn't even been twelve hours since you were a prisoner of those bandits!" Welles exclaimed. "Don't you think you should get some rest?"

"I'll be all right," Davis insisted. "Besides, you said we're short-handed—"

"Don't you even think about it, lad," Harding said sternly. "You're going to take it easy for a day or two. Nothing's too good for the man who saved my daughter from certain death."

Davis was about to object that Conn Powell deserved more of the credit for saving Emily than he did, but at that moment, Emily herself climbed out of the back of the Harding wagon and came toward Davis. She had changed her dress, replacing the torn, gunpowder-scorched garment with a fresh one. Her hair had been brushed, and she had washed the grime off her face. Davis thought she looked beautiful. He could have stood there and watched her for hours.

She came up to him and put a hand on his arm. "I heard some of that discussion," she said. "You should rest. You deserve it."

"Well . . . I don't suppose a man with any sense should be arguing with a gal as pretty as you."

Emily smiled in surprise and pleasure. "Are you flirting with me, sir?"

To his astonishment, Davis realized that he was. A grin spread slowly across his face. "I reckon I am."

"Good," Emily said. "Now, go back to your camp, get some rest, and come back here this evening for supper." She looked at Captain Harding. "Is that all right with you, Father?"

"It sure is," Harding said. He stood up and slapped Davis's shoulder. "You're welcome here any time, son."

Davis thought about the way Hammond Larrimore had treated him. Captain Harding hadn't been too friendly starting out, either, but his attitude had changed. Larrimore's never had.

Change was sometimes a good thing, Davis decided as he said his goodbyes and started back toward the other camp with Colonel Welles. His old life had been destroyed, and he was still filled with sharp regrets for what had been lost. But now he had a chance to build a new life.

No matter what it took, he was going to make this one work.

Two weeks later, the government work crew, aided by an ample supply of volunteers from the wagon train, reached Logan's Fort, the terminus of the Wilderness Road. If anything, progress had been faster following the raid by the bandit gang and Emily's rescue—the new spirit of cooperation between the immigrants and the workers made that possible. Everyone was thrilled to reach the end of the journey.

Except Davis Hallam.

The past couple of weeks had been better for him than he could have dreamed possible a few months earlier. The work was still hard, of course, and his muscles sometimes ached at the end of a long day swinging an ax. But he could look forward to the evenings with Emily and her family. The meals prepared by Emily and her mother, the singing around the campfire, the new-found camaraderie between the two groups . . . all of those things made Davis feel as if he truly belonged where he was. And then there was the courting . . .

He was too old for such things, he told himself,

but the stern mental admonition did no good. Walking with Emily under the trees, holding her hand, stealing a quick kiss in the shadows, all the little rituals that went with a man and a woman coming to know each other had Davis in a constant state of emotional turmoil. But it was incredibly delicious turmoil, and he welcomed every moment of it.

Now it was coming to an end. As the wagons rolled into the good-sized settlement that had grown up around the original fort, he felt his heart sinking. It was over, and he had no idea what to expect next.

Davis was leaning on his ax after felling what would likely be the last tree that would have to be chopped down. The Harding wagon and several of the others in the train had already gone past him. Colonel Welles rode up and reined in. "Be sure to come by the trading post and collect the rest of your pay, Davis," he said with a grin. "You've earned it. All the men have."

Davis nodded. "I'll be there in a bit, Colonel."

Welles leaned forward in his saddle and looked around at the settlement and the rolling, wooded hillsides that surrounded it. "This is fine country. Now that there's a good, wide road leading to it, there'll be plenty of settlers coming in here. Why, I wouldn't be surprised if there were enough people in another year or two for Kentucky to petition for statehood."

Davis frowned a little. "You really think so, Colonel?"

"Why not? Have you ever seen a better place to settle?"

"No, can't say as I have," Davis replied honestly.

"Once people make a place their home, they're

going to want churches, and schools, and everything else that makes it civilized."

Like law and order, Davis thought. If what Welles said was correct, Kentucky might not stay a frontier for much longer. That murder conviction might come back to haunt him, and he might have to move on to escape it.

Davis didn't want to think about that. He was still a long way from the Shenandoah Valley. If he made a life for himself in Kentucky, it would be as Hal Davis. He would still be safe.

The reassurance sounded hollow, even to him.

But there was nothing he could do about the situation right now. He had more pressing matters with which to concern himself—such as Emily Harding and the relationship that had grown up between them. He had to deal with that first. And he had been thinking more and more about Andrew, as well. Shadrach had said he won that knife in Boonesborough, from a man who could have been Andrew. That settlement was only a few days' journey from Logan's Fort. It was possible Andrew was still around somewhere up there.

As much as he might try to deny it, the need for vengeance still burned within Davis. He could go take a look around Boonesborough, maybe ask a few questions. It wouldn't hurt anything.

But first . . . Emily.

Davis put his ax over his shoulder and walked up to the supply wagon. He turned over the ax and picked up his weapons: the flintlock he had brought with him to the Block House, the one he had taken from the outlaw he'd killed on the hill, and the rifle with the broken stock that Conn Powell had pressed into his hands that night outside the little tunnel. Davis had never thought of himself as a sentimental man, but he was going to hang on to that broken flintlock, he had decided, to remind him of what he and Emily had gone through together, and to remind him of the long hunter as well.

From the supply wagon, Davis walked on to the settlement. The people who already lived here had turned out in large numbers to greet the newcomers, creating a large, bustling crowd. Life on the frontier was often difficult and lonely, and these pioneers usually seized any excuse for a get-together. There would be plenty of drinking and laughing and fiddle-playing and dancing tonight, Davis thought. He was sure Emily would enjoy the celebration.

But would this be the last time the two of them danced together?

"My goodness, you're loaded for bear, aren't you?" Emily asked with a laugh as Davis came up to the Harding wagon carrying the three flintlocks.

He managed a smile. "Man never knows what he's going to run into out here."

"I suppose that's true." Emily stepped down from the tailgate of the wagon. "Why don't you leave two of those rifles here, and we'll take a look around the settlement?"

That sounded like a good idea to Davis. He had wanted to talk to her privately, without her parents and brothers and sister around, and this might be the best opportunity he would get. He set the broken flintlock and one of the others inside the wagon for safekeeping, then linked his arm with hers as they strolled toward the high stockade walls of the fort. Although most of the buildings in the settlement were outside the walls, the citizens could retreat inside the fort in case of Indian trouble. So could the farmers who worked the blue-green fields in the distance.

"What do you think of the place?" Emily asked. "After passing through all that wilderness, did you think we'd ever see a settlement again?"

"I figured we would."

"Well, of course, I know that. We knew all along that Logan's Fort would be here, and so would Boonesborough, and Harrodsburg, and Bryan's Station and all the others."

"Colonel Welles says that in a year or two, he thinks there'll be enough people hereabouts for Kentucky to become a state."

"Really? That would be wonderful!" Emily exclaimed.

Davis wasn't so sure about that, but he didn't want to say anything to ruin her good mood, not yet, anyway. He asked, "Where are you and your family thinking of living?"

"I don't know. There's still plenty of land just waiting to be claimed. I think Mother would like to be somewhere close to the settlement, though. She's had enough of the wilderness." She shivered, and Davis felt the tiny movement. "To tell you the truth, so have I. I'd just as soon stay here if . . . if everything works out all right."

Now, what did she mean by that? Davis wondered. He started to ask, then checked himself, not sure he wanted to hear the answer just yet.

They walked around the fort, Emily exclaiming

in surprise at all the places doing business in the settlement. "I thought there might be a trading post, but that would be all," she said. "Why, there's a milliner's, and a lawyer's office, and even a doctor!"

"And a blacksmith shop and a mill and a stable," Davis pointed out. "Pretty much everything anybody would need."

"They say that nothing can stop the march of civilization."

Davis was afraid she was right about that.

"I've heard there's going to be a dance tonight," Emily went on after a moment.

"Figured there would be," Davis answered shortly. Whenever he was worried about something, he generally retreated back into his old reticence.

"Are you going?" she asked bluntly.

"Well . . . sure." He took a deep breath. "And you're going with me."

Her smile was as bright to him as the sun. He would have a talk with her later, after the dance, he decided. He didn't want to spoil this day for her. Better to postpone the hard choices.

Because hard they would be. He had reached another decision, the most difficult one of all.

If there was ever going to be anything lasting between the two of them, Emily deserved to know the truth about him.

No matter how much it hurt.

Music filled the night, wafting into the air from a dozen or more fiddles, a handsaw, and a tub with a broom handle stuck through the bottom of it so that

a string could be attached. Several hundred pairs of
hands clapped along with the robust melodies.
Skirts swirled, feet flew, and the biggest celebration
that ever hit Logan's Fort in its relatively brief
existence continued long into the night.

Davis danced until it felt as if his feet were going
to fall off. Emily was light, almost buoyant, in his
arms, but he *had* spent most of the day chopping
down trees and clearing brush over the final half-
mile or so of the Wilderness Road. Besides, he had
more on his mind than dancing.

Still, as they whirled and spun to the music,
Davis couldn't help but be carried away by the
joyousness of the occasion. He smiled more that
evening, he figured, than he had in a year.

Trying not to puff and pant after a particularly
fast-paced song, he led Emily out of the big clearing
where the dancing was taking place. Tables had
been set up around the edges of the clearing, and
they were practically groaning from the platters of
food and jugs of cider with which they were laden.
Davis picked up one of the jugs, uncorked it, and
poured cider into cups for himself and Emily.

"Thank you," she said as he handed her the cup.
"All this dancing has made me thirsty."

"You want to sit out a while?" he asked.

Emily considered, then nodded. "That would be
fine."

Davis felt a mixture of relief and dread. He had
been waiting for an opportunity to have his talk with
her. This might be the best chance he would get.

"Why don't we take a walk?" he suggested.

"Unchaperoned?" Emily asked with a smile.

"I won't tell your ma and pa if you don't," Davis said. "Besides, my intentions are strictly honorable."

"Well . . . not *too* honorable, I hope," she said boldly over her shoulder as she turned to stroll toward the trees where the wagons were parked.

As a matter of fact, Davis thought as he hurried after her, his intentions were so damned honorable that he wondered if he was making a terrible mistake. Either way, he knew he had to go through with it. He cared too much about Emily to live a lie with her.

Shadows claimed them as they walked side by side underneath the trees. There were a few people around the wagons, of course, but no one close enough to be within earshot. Davis made sure of that before he had Emily sit down on one of the wagontongues. All the oxen and mules had been unhitched and were penned up in a corral near the walls of the fort.

Emily took a sip of her cider, then said solemnly, "I have a feeling you brought me out here for a reason, Davis."

He nodded, wishing he could see her face a little better in the shadows. "Yep. I did." He fell silent.

"Well? Are you going to tell me what it is or not?"

For an instant, Davis felt like bolting. But he knew he couldn't do that, so he drank down the rest of the cider, hoping it would give him a little courage. To his dismay, it didn't seem to help one blasted bit.

He took a deep breath, then said, "All right. I just figured that since I love you and you love me—"

She reached up and touched his cheek with her fingertips. "I never tire of hearing you say those words," she murmured.

He frowned, distracted by her gentle touch. Forcing himself to go on, he said, "I figured that you ought to know the truth about me. I already told you my name's Davis Hallam, not Hal Davis like I told the colonel and everybody else."

"I don't care about that."

"Well, there's a reason for it, and you may care about it." He wiped the back of his hand across his mouth. "I had . . . some trouble with the law back in Virginia."

"All right," Emily said steadily. "I think I know you well enough by now to know that you're a good man, no matter what you might have done in the past."

"I didn't do what they said I did," he went on hurriedly. "You've got to believe that."

"Of course I do."

Her trust in him strengthened his resolve to go through with this. "I was married," he said. "I had a wife . . . and children."

Emily's chin lifted a little as she regarded him intently. "What happened to them?"

"The children are all right . . . I hope. I haven't seen them since last winter. I don't reckon I'll ever see them again. My wife . . . " He had to swallow hard before he could continue. "My wife is dead," he said flatly. "I was accused of killing her, and the magistrate found me guilty and sentenced me to hang. I got away and . . . wound up here."

It was Emily's turn to take a deep breath as she tried to cope with what he had told her. After a long moment, she said, "I see. Did you kill your wife, Davis?"

"No! Dear Lord, no! I never touched her." His

hands shot out and gripped Emily's shoulders, pulling her up so that her face was close to his. "I swear by everything that's holy, I didn't do it, Emily. But . . . I know who did."

He felt her trembling and knew that he was probably frightening her. But she said, calmly enough, in a voice that was little more than a whisper, "Tell me about it."

He did. For the next few minutes, the story poured out of him—the problems between Faith and him, the growing suspicion of Andrew's involvement, the terrible discovery he had made on that wintry day . . . Faith's death at Andrew's hand. He told her all of it, and tears welled from his eyes, and her arms went around him and held him tightly as great shudders wracked him. With anyone else, he would have been ashamed and humiliated to be seen this way.

Somehow, though, with Emily it was all right. Before he was finished, she was crying with him.

Finally, he made himself ask, "Do you still believe me?"

"Of course I believe you! You're a good man, Davis Hallam. I know you'd never hurt someone you love."

"I'd never hurt you," he whispered. She lifted her face to his, and their lips met.

Reluctantly, Davis ended the kiss only a moment later. "There's more," he said. "I think Andrew may be here in Kentucky."

Emily pulled back from him a little. "What makes you think that?"

"Remember that knife Shadrach had, the one with the silver ball at the end of the handle?"

"If you say so," Emily replied doubtfully. "I never paid that much attention to it. I was too scared of him."

"Well, I got a good look at it. Andrew had a knife just like that."

"There must be more than one knife made that way."

"Maybe, but Shadrach said he won it in a card game from a man in Boonesborough. The man he described sounded an awful lot like Andrew."

"So . . . what are you going to do, Davis?"

"I don't know. I thought about going up to Boonesborough and taking a look around to see if maybe I could find him."

This time Emily stepped back completely out of his embrace. "And what if you do? Will you kill him?"

Davis blinked in surprise at her reaction. "I don't really know. I never thought that far ahead." His fingers clenched and unclenched. "He deserves killing."

"I won't argue that, but you don't know for certain he's anywhere around here, Davis. If you don't find him in Boonesborough, what then? Will you go to Harrodsburg, or Bryan's Station?"

"I don't know," he said.

"How long will you look for him?"

"I . . . don't know."

"Davis . . . " She caught his right hand in both of hers. "Listen to me. You want revenge on your brother."

"I want justice," he said stubbornly.

"No, justice is something meted out by the law . . . or God. You just want vengeance. And if you go seeking it, you may be consumed by it. It can destroy you, just as sure as anything."

"I won't let that happen."

"How can you be sure? None of us know what the future may bring, none of us!" She stepped closer to him, and his arms instinctively went around her. "Davis, I thought you brought me out here tonight to tell me that you're going to be staying here. I thought . . . I thought you were going to ask me to marry you."

"That's what I want," he said in a voice choked with emotion. "That's what I want more than anything else in the world."

"Then I'll be yours," she whispered, "but only if you give up searching for Andrew. Let the law handle it."

"The law said I was guilty," Davis said bitterly. "The law wanted to string me up from a gallows."

"I can understand why you left the Shenandoah Valley. No man should be punished for something he didn't do. I'm not asking you to go back. I'm just asking you to let your brother find whatever justice Fate has in store for him."

Davis felt himself weakening. When he had headed west, finding Andrew and wreaking vengeance on him had been the furthest thing from Davis's mind. He had been concerned then only with survival. It was only since the encounter with Shadrach that thoughts of settling things with Andrew had steadily grown stronger in Davis's mind.

Had it become an obsession with him? Was Emily right? Davis had never felt himself consumed with the need for revenge.

But if the search was unsuccessful in

Boonesborough, what then? Maybe he *would* move on, seeking Andrew in some of the other settlements. Maybe he would forget about what he had walked off and left here at Logan's Fort. Maybe he would abandon the future he might have had, in exchange for a bloody past that wouldn't let him go.

He couldn't risk it. He had come too far, endured too much, to throw away a second chance at happiness that he had never figured to have. He took a deep breath, the rightness of the decision filling him.

"Emily Harding," he said, "will you be my wife?"

"What about Andrew?" she asked tautly.

"I don't care. Whatever happens to him is in God's hands, not mine."

"Davis . . . "

She kissed him again, her answer to his question in the soft warmth of her lips. Davis felt his passion growing as her body pressed insistently against his. He could feel, too, the rapid beat of her heart. Likely there was a preacher here in the settlement who could marry them, he thought. *There had damned well better be!*

And the best part of all was the resolve spreading through him, telling him that he was doing the right thing. The decision he had made was the only one he could have reached. Just as he had told her, Andrew's fate was in other hands now, and that was the way it should be. Davis Hallam wasn't going to look back any longer.

From now on, he would look only to the future . . . the future he was going to share with Emily.

16

Davis climbed down the ladder, stepped back, and looked up in appreciation at the sign he had just nailed to the log building above the door. He had spent a long time burning the letters into the thick plank with a heated iron. Emily had helped him a little with the spelling.

The largest letters on the sign read *THE BROKEN FLINTLOCK*. Below it in smaller letters were the words *Tavern and Inn*. Emily had suggested that he put his name on the sign, too, but Davis had declined. If anyone ever did come looking for him, he didn't want to make their job any easier than it had to be.

Emily emerged from the open front door of the building, wiping her hands on the apron tied around her waist. She smiled at Davis, then turned to look up at the sign with him. He slipped his left arm around her shoulders and drew her close against him.

"It looks mighty fine, Davis," she said. During the past year, people around Logan's Fort had

become accustomed to hearing her call him by
what everyone else thought was his last name. "You
did a good job on it. Now when folks hear about the
inn, they can find it easier."

He nodded. "I'm glad you talked me into it."

"I just want the place to be as successful as
possible."

"I'd say it's had a good start," Davis commented.

Indeed, in the time since the tavern and inn had
opened its doors, the establishment had done a
brisk trade. Logan's Fort was growing steadily as
the flow of settlers into the area grew as well. This
settlement was more than the terminus of the
Wilderness Road. It was actually the beginning of
several other trails leading to the other settlements
scattered around Kentucky. Practically all the
immigrant traffic into the area passed through here.
Davis and Emily hadn't lacked for customers. Men
from the wagon trains stepped in for a drink before
going on their way, and travelers on horseback
often stopped to spend the night in one of the
rooms on the second floor of the big building.

"Come along inside," Emily said. "I have supper
just about ready."

Davis nodded and walked with her into the
tavern. As they entered the building, they passed
underneath the weapon that had given the place its
name. The broken flintlock was hanging inside on
pegs just above the door. The story of how Davis
used it to kill one of the bandits who had kidnapped
Emily was common knowledge around here. Davis
was more than a little uncomfortable with the
notoriety, and he supposed displaying the weapon

like that only made things worse. He had not been able to bring himself to part with the gun, however, and he liked being able to look up and see it hanging there when he was behind the bar pouring drinks for the customers.

At first the men had tried to get him to tell the story of the broken rifle every evening, but his reluctance to do so soon became as well known as the tale itself. The drinkers had to be content with spinning the yarn themselves, and it soon grew to truly epic proportions. Some of the tellers had Davis killing a dozen bandits and two dozen Indians with the broken gun. Davis just smiled wearily, shook his head, and said, "Not the way it happened."

The first floor of the building consisted of one main room with a couple of small storerooms behind it. The bar, made of puncheons laid across empty whisky barrels, ran across the back of the main room. Rough-hewn tables and benches filled the floor. To the right was the staircase leading up to the second floor. There was nothing fancy about the place, but to Davis it had become home.

Any place where Emily was would be home to him, he knew.

The year of marriage to her had been better and happier than he'd had any right to expect. She was a sweet, loving wife, but she had opinions of her own and never hesitated to express them. When the nightmares still occasionally came to him, making him sit bolt upright in their bed with cold sweat bathing his face and great shudders wracking his body, she was always there to hold him and soothe him and remind him that he had come through the bad times in the past.

She had taken to lovemaking with joyous abandon, too, and he felt a stirring of desire now as he watched her walk across the room. She always aroused those emotions in him, and he hoped fervently that she always would.

Several men were standing at the bar drinking, although it was early yet. The crowd would be much larger later, and Davis would probably have to work the bar himself, instead of trusting it to his helper, a young man named Willy Malone who was tapping the kegs for the customers at the moment. In the meantime, Davis and Emily could have their supper in the small living quarters that were built onto the back of the tavern building.

He followed her through the storeroom that connected with their quarters. Several dozen kegs of whiskey were stacked in the room. Trains of freight wagons arrived regularly now over the Wilderness Road, and as Davis watching the settlement expanding and trade booming, he took pride in the fact he had played a minor part in the growth, as one of the group that had widened the trail. Only a little pride, though, because he had never managed to forget completely that with the onrush of civilization came an increasing chance that someday his past would catch up with him.

He would deal with that when and if it ever happened. Until then, he was going to enjoy the life he was building here with Emily.

When they were settled down at the dinner

table, Emily looked at her plate and blushed slightly as she said, "I want you to know, Davis . . . I'm not in the family way after all."

"Oh," he said. He frowned and cast about for more words to say. "Well. That's all right. Perhaps one day . . . "

She reached across the table and caught hold of his hand. "I'm sorry, Davis," she said. "I know how much you were hoping that this time—"

"I said it's all right, and I meant it." His fingers tightened on hers. "I love you, Emily, and that love doesn't depend on whether or not we have children."

"You must miss your little ones terribly, though."

Davis took a deep breath. It was true that not a day went by when he failed to think about Laurel, Mary, and Theodore. He did miss them and still felt their loss as a sharp pain deep inside him.

When he didn't say anything, Emily went on, "We might be able to send for them—"

He shook his head sharply. "No! It's too late for that." She had made the same suggestion before, more than once, and each time he had refused. "By now they're lost to me. They're Jonas Kirby's children, and I hope he's raising them well. But they're sure to have been told how I went insane and murdered their mother, then escaped from jail and fled into the wilderness. They'll never want to have anything to do with me again, and I can't blame them for feeling that way."

"You can't *know* that's what they believe," Emily insisted.

Again Davis shook his head. "I'm sure enough of it. No, Emily, we'll just keep trying to have children of our own, and if we don't . . . well, at least we have each other."

"Yes," she said softly, putting her other hand on his. "We'll always have each other."

Davis just wished that cold fear would not ripple through him every time she said something like that.

Their second summer together turned into autumn. The leaves on the trees blazed brightly, swaying red and orange and gold on the branches before relinquishing their grip and falling to the earth as the wind grew colder. There was enough of a chill in the air each night so that the fires Davis lit in the tavern's big fireplace felt welcome indeed. Winter was coming, and unlike the previous year, when the snow had brought too many memories with it, Davis believed that this year would be different. His life was not perfect, but he was happy with it.

Then, on a day full of bright sunshine and crisp, cool air, a ghost walked into the tavern.

That was what Davis thought at first. He was alone behind the bar in the middle of the afternoon. There were no customers, and Emily was back in their quarters doing some mending. Davis was drowsy, and he thought about sitting down in the rocking chair next to the unlit fireplace for a short nap before men began drifting in during the late afternoon for a drink. Then he heard a step in the open doorway and looked up from where he was leaning his elbows on the bar.

The man who stood there was difficult to

distinguish at first because of the brilliant sunshine behind him. But after a moment, Davis could make out the lean figure and the long hair underneath a floppy-brimmed hat, the long-barrelled rifle the man carried and the swaying fringe on the buckskins he wore. A shock of familiarity shivered through Davis as the man limped toward the bar.

"Don't just stand there gawkin'," Conn Powell said. "Pour a man a drink, why don't you?"

"You're alive," Davis said. It was all he could think of.

"Any man with eyes in his head could see that. I'm told you serve the best whiskey in Kentucky. Care to prove it?"

Automatically, Davis reached for a tin cup on the shelf behind the bar. He tapped one of the kegs and let the liquor splash out into the cup, then placed it on the bar. Powell picked it up, took a sip, nodded appreciatively, then tossed back the rest of the drink.

"Looks like that part of the story was the truth, anyway," he said. "Not like the other things I've heard about you."

"What have you heard?" Davis asked, suddenly wary. As startled as he was to discover that Powell wasn't dead after all, he was still in the habit of being careful about revealing too much.

"Oh, that you killed a hundred bandits to rescue that pretty Harding gal you up and married later. Or was it two hundred?" Powell said dryly. "I tend to disremember."

"I never claimed that. I told the truth of what happened. It was other folks who made it into some sort of legend."

Powell nodded. "I figured as much. You're a lot of things, I reckon, but I never had you pegged as a liar and a braggart." He reached across the bar and for a brief moment clasped Davis's arm with fingers that felt like iron. "You may not believe this, but it's good to see you again, Davis."

Davis knew he ought to call out to Emily and let her know that Powell was here, but he was still too dumbfounded at this unexpected visit by the long hunter. "We thought you . . . we thought—"

"You thought I was dead," Powell finished for him. "I reckon I damn near was. But after I sat there by that tree for a while, I got to feelin' a mite better. Decided I wouldn't wait for those bastards to find me and kill me." He laughed coldly. "So *I* went lookin' for *them*."

Davis could believe that.

"I jumped one of 'em," Powell went on, "and killed him with my knife. Once I had a rifle and plenty of powder and shot, the odds got even better. Thought about lyin' down and dyin' a time or two while we were all out there in the woods, but damned if I was goin' to give 'em the satisfaction. After I'd put two or three of 'em under, they was so spooked they started shootin' at each other. I figured then the time had come for me to get out of there, so I did."

"I'm sorry," Davis said sincerely. "We should have stayed and helped you—"

"Hell, no! You did what I asked of you. You got that gal back safely to her folks. Where is she?"

"Out back, where we live. I'll get her." Davis started out from behind the bar.

Powell stopped him by holding out a lean, deeply tanned hand. "Hold on a minute. The first time I saw you, Davis, I didn't trust you. Figured you were hidin' something."

Davis hesitated, then said, "I was."

"Whatever it is, it ain't none of my business. But does *she* know?"

"I told her all about it before we were married."

Powell nodded. "Good. Maybe you ain't such a bad sort after all. If you were, that gal wouldn't have married you."

That approval from the man, grudging though it might have been, meant a lot to Davis. He couldn't stop himself from grinning as he went to the door of the storeroom and called through it, "Emily, can you come out here? We have a visitor."

She walked into the tavern a moment later, saying, "Who is it, Davis?" Then she stopped short, and the shirt she had been mending slipped from her fingers and fell unnoticed to the floor. Still grinning, Davis picked up the shirt as Emily stared at Powell.

"It can't be," she finally murmured. "It just can't."

Powell smiled, one of the few times Davis had seen such an expression on the normally grim face of the long hunter. "I reckon it's me, all right," Powell said. "You look like marriage is agreein' with you, ma'am. You're as pretty as you were back there on that wagon train."

"Thank you," Emily said distractedly. "How . . . how can you be here, Mr. Powell? We thought—"

"We've been over that already, Emily," Davis told her. "It seems our friend here decided he wasn't ready to die just yet . . . so he didn't."

Powell nodded. "Stubbornness'll carry a fella a long way sometimes. And I've always been mighty stubborn, 'specially about things like dyin'."

Davis stepped over to one of the tables and pulled back a bench. "Sit down," he said. "You've got to tell us what you've been doing. It's been over a year since that day."

"Sure," Powell said easily, "but bring a jug."

Davis complied with that request, filling a jug from the keg and carrying it to the table along with Powell's cup and a cup for himself. Emily never drank anything harder than cider.

Powell downed another cup of whiskey, then wiped the back of his hand across his mouth and said, "First thing I did after spookin' that bunch of highwaymen was to find me a place to hole up. There are caves all around that mountain that nobody knows anything about 'cept me and some Shawnees. I found one of 'em and crawled into it after I'd packed my wounds with moss again. Probably would've died in there if I hadn't been so blasted stubborn, like I said. There's a little spring inside the cave, so I had water. I just laid up there for three or four days—I ain't sure which—and fought off the fever that come over me. When it finally broke, I was mighty hungry, so I crawled back out and made a snare. Didn't want to do any shootin', since I figured it wouldn't be a good idea to call attention to myself, weak as I was. Caught a rabbit that night, and it tasted mighty good, even raw."

Emily repressed a shudder, and Davis felt a little queasy himself. He had eaten rabbit plenty of times but always roasted. He supposed that if he had been in the same situation as Powell, however, he might have torn into the animal just the same way.

"That gave me a little strength," Powell went on. "Figured since I wasn't dead by then, it just wasn't my time. I headed for the Wilderness Road . . . leastways that was what I intended." He lifted a hand and pointed at Davis as he continued sternly, "If you ever let on to anybody about what I'm fixin' to tell you, I'll not only deny it, but I'll come back here and settle up with you."

"Whatever it is, Mr. Powell, I won't say anything about it," Davis promised solemnly.

"Call me Conn. Anyway . . . " Powell took a deep breath and looked uncomfortable. "I reckon I took a wrong turn. I got lost. And maybe I was still a little out of my head, too. Anyway, I wound up back in Virginia 'fore it was all over. By then I'd pretty much recovered from those rifle balls that ventilated me, so I went back to long huntin'. I've had enough of bein' a guide, and I don't *ever* want to work for the gov'ment again."

"So you've just been . . . wandering?" Emily asked.

"That's how a man like me is the most satisfied, never stayin' in one place for too long."

Davis said, "Why haven't you come to see us before now?"

"Didn't know you were here," Powell said. "Oh, I admit I was a mite curious whether or not you got back safe to that wagon train, but I figured you did. Then, later on, I heard the stories about you, heard how the two of you got married and built this tavern. Figured I'd come through these parts sooner or later." He shrugged. "And here I am, so I reckon I was right."

"It's good to see you, Conn, it really is." Davis shook his head in wonderment. "I still can't get over it. We really thought you were dead."

"You know," Powell said dryly, "a fella could get tired of hearin' that."

"You'll stay with us, of course," Emily said, "for as long as you like."

"Never sleep as well with a roof over my head as I do with sky . . . but I'll bide here a day or two. Say, you ever hear any more about those bandits?"

Davis shook his head. "I suppose after all the trouble they had when they raided the wagon train, they gave up and moved on. They haven't been seen around here in the past year."

"Well, maybe so," Powell said. "But if that's what happened, they ran out of easy pickin's elsewhere and decided to try their luck in these parts again. They hit a train of freight wagons day before yesterday."

Davis's eyes widened in surprise, and Emily said, "Oh, no."

Powell nodded. "Yep. Saw it with my own eyes."

"We haven't heard anything about it," Davis said.

"That's because the freighters—what's left of 'em—ain't limped into the settlement yet. They ought to be here tomorrow. I can move faster by myself, so I come on ahead."

"You say you saw the attack?"

"That's right. I was on a hill about a quarter of a

mile away. Wasn't much I could do to help. Time I
got there, it was almost over."

"How do you know it was the same group of
bandits?" Emily asked.

"I got a look at some of 'em ridin' off just as I
came hustlin' up. I recognized 'em . . . 'cept for one
young fella I guess joined up with 'em since that
time a year and a half ago. Heard one of the others
call him Paxton."

Davis couldn't stop his hands from clenching
into fists. "What?" he said, his voice taut with
surprise.

"Paxton," Powell repeated. He looked shrewdly
at Davis. "Why? That name mean somethin' to you,
Davis?"

Davis glanced at Emily, saw how her face had
gone pale. Powell was too keen an observer to have
missed the reaction of either one of them. The long
hunter had to know he had stumbled onto
something.

But Davis shook his head anyway and said, "No.
The name means nothing to me."

"Whatever you say. I took a shot at him and
damn near knocked him out of the saddle. Would've
if he hadn't ducked. That's when one of the other
fellas yelled at him to come on."

"Well, I certainly don't know who he was," Davis
said, knowing that he was professing his ignorance
too vigorously but unable to stop himself.

For a moment, a strained silence hung over the
table, then Powell said, "I reckon that gang's liable
to stay around here for a while. Lots of traffic on the
Wilderness Road these days. You ought to know

that, though, since you see most of it comin'
through here."

"Yes." Davis nodded, still stunned by what
Powell had said. "Lots of traffic."

He was aware of Emily's gaze on him, but he
couldn't bring himself to meet her eyes. The news
that Andrew was not only in the area but running
with the same bandits who had raided the wagon
train was just as unexpected as Powell's return from
the dead. Davis had to take it all in, decide what it
meant to him.

Powell pushed himself to his feet. "I've walked a
far piece today. You got a bunk where a fella can lie
down?"

"Of course," Emily said hurriedly as she stood.
"There are rooms upstairs. I'll show you."

"Do you have a horse?" Davis asked. "I'll take
care of—no, that's right, you said you're afoot. I'm
in the habit of asking."

Powell hefted his flintlock. "This old girl and
some powder and shot and a good knife are all I
really need."

Davis knew that to be true. And when it came
right down to it, Powell could survive with even
less. His presence here today was proof of that.

Emily took the long hunter upstairs, and Davis
settled back down on the bench. As happy as he
was to know that Powell was alive after all, he
almost wished the man had never walked in. Now
he knew that Andrew was likely somewhere close
by, probably within a day's ride of Logan's Fort.
Davis leaned forward, ran his fingers through his
hair, and sighed.

The past might go away for a while, but it always—*always!*—came back.

That evening, Conn Powell regaled the tavern's customers with tales of the adventures he'd had since coming over the Cumberland Gap into Kentucky with Daniel Boone seventeen years earlier. Willy Malone dashed from one end of the bar to the other to keep up with the shouted demands for more whiskey and beer and cider. Davis, however, walked out back of the building and looked up at the stars shining so bright in the cold night sky and wondered what he should do.

He had listened to Powell's yarns for a while, including what the long hunter insisted was the one and only true version of how he and Davis had rescued Emily from the bandits. The story had been heavily colored, however, and had given Davis far more credit than he deserved. This tale-spinning was a side of Powell that Davis had never seen before. When they had been working together on the Wilderness Road, Powell had always seemed taciturn and even rather dour. Here in the tavern, his caustic wit and colorful speech had his listeners hanging on every word and bursting out in frequent laughter.

Finally, Davis had given in to the worries that occupied his mind and slipped out the rear door, avoiding the living quarters he shared with Emily as he did so. But she must have heard him anyway, or perhaps just sensed his presence, because he had been outside in the chilly air only a few minutes before she appeared beside him, pulling a shawl tighter around her shoulders.

"It's a lovely crisp evening," Emily commented without looking at him. Like Davis, her gaze was directed up at the stars overhead.

"Aye," he agreed. "Lovely."

Emily was quiet for a moment, then she said, "You're thinking about him, aren't you? About Andrew Paxton?"

"He's here, Emily," Davis said, his voice breaking a little. "I can feel him."

"There's more than one man named Paxton in the country, you know. And that description Mr. Powell gave you could fit hundreds, even thousands of men."

Davis nodded slowly. "You're right. But I still know it's him. It's what he would do, joining a band of thieves. Andrew never did an honest day's work in his life."

Emily turned toward him, caught his arm in both of her hands. "What if it is him?" she demanded. "You don't have to go after him. It's not up to you to bring him to justice, Davis."

"No one else is going to do it," he said stubbornly. "Andrew has the devil's own luck. If he keeps riding with those bandits, he'll get away no matter what happens to the rest of them. Andrew always gets away."

"Someday his luck will run out," Emily whispered.

Suddenly, anger flooded through Davis. He looked down at her and said, "Damn it, woman, that man did me the greatest hurt of my life! He killed my wife, he caused my children to be lost to me forever, he made me run for my life to escape being hanged for a crime I didn't commit! And you want me to just . . . let him go?" He shook loose from her grip. "It seems to me that if you loved me, you'd want vengeance on Andrew just as much as I do!"

Emily's face was bleak in the moonlight as she returned his angry stare. "It's because I love you that I don't want you to go after him. If anything happened to you, Davis, I . . . I don't think I could bear it."

Her words penetrated his fury and touched his heart, but they couldn't make the feelings raging inside him fade away. Still, he wanted to try to make her understand. "This has been hanging over me for more than a year now. I've given up on clearing my name with the law. I . . . I just want to be at peace again with myself. And I know now that I never can as long as Andrew is riding free."

"So you're going after him?"

Davis took a deep breath. "I think I have to."

"If you do, I may not be waiting here for you when you get back . . . if you get back." Emily's voice was flat, tightly controlled, not giving away the turmoil she had to be experiencing. Davis thought he knew what an effort this conversation must be costing her.

He certainly knew what it was costing him.

But he said anyway, "I'll be riding out first thing in the morning to see if I can pick up the trail."

Emily made a sound that was half-sob, half-gasp. "Will you . . . will you at least take Mr. Powell with you?"

Davis shook his head. "I have to do this myself."

Now her voice was bitter as she said, "Then may God go with you, if you won't allow anyone else." She turned and stalked back to the building.

Davis didn't watch her, but he heard the door slam and knew that he was alone again—maybe for good. Maybe he had always been alone. Perhaps those moments when people believed they were touching someone were only illusions, fantasies that the heart and mind created to deal with the awful, inescapable fact of human solitude.

Davis stood there for a long time, breathing in the cold night air.

17

Davis was up early the next morning, when the sky in the east was only a faint gray and the air was cold enough to make his breath fog in front of him as he walked toward the barn behind the tavern. The little building was more of a shed, really, but it was enough to shelter the two horses he and Emily owned.

Several times in the past, they had taken the horses and gone riding, not straying far from the settlement. It was far enough, though, so that when the weather was warmer, they had felt comfortable enough about being unobserved to make love in the lush blue-green grass of the Kentucky hillsides. Davis recalled those times now, recalled the warmth of the sun on his back, the heat of Emily as she had wrapped herself around him.

This morning the air was cold against his face, and the bed he shared with his wife had been cold as well. There might as well have been a mountain between them for all the closeness Davis felt to her.

He didn't think she had even noticed when he got up, dressed, and left their living quarters.

Roughly, he shoved those thoughts out of his mind. He hoped that when he got back, he could work things out with Emily, but if not . . . he still had no choice about what he was setting out to do this morning. He could never be a whole man again until he had dealt with the specters of the past that were haunting him.

Even though the light was bad, he had no trouble saddling the horse, working mostly by feel in the pre-dawn gloom. He almost had the animal ready to go when he heard the step behind him.

Thinking it was Emily, come to plead with him again not to go after Andrew, Davis stiffened, unwilling to have this argument again. But it was Conn Powell's voice that came to him.

"Fixin' to ride out, Davis?"

"There's something I have to do," Davis said.

"Aye, most men feel that way. They have a task facin' 'em, and they know it won't go away."

"Exactly."

"But you know what happens when a fella goes out and takes care of whatever it is that's doggin' his trail?"

Davis turned his head and looked at the shadowy figure behind him, but he didn't say anything.

"Then there's just somethin' else waitin' for him," Powell said after a moment. "Right up until a man dies, there's always somethin' waitin' for him."

"What are you saying?" Davis demanded. "Since all the problems can never be solved, it's best just to ignore them and not even try?"

Powell shrugged. "Or walk away from 'em."

Davis wondered if that was what the long hunter had been doing all his life. Spending months at a time tramping through the wilderness boiled everything down to a matter of survival. A man who spent his days in that manner wouldn't have much time to worry about sins of the past, or lost loves, or things left undone, words that had never been said. He wondered briefly just what had driven Powell to the wilderness.

But it was none of his business, and besides, he had his own concerns this morning. He had no time for some homespun lecture. He had already eaten a sparse breakfast, and he had a bag of supplies that he had slung over the back of the horse. He was ready to ride.

Turning to face Powell squarely, he said, "I have to be going now."

Powell nodded. "Sure. Reckon I understand." He scraped a thumbnail along the line of his jaw. "Could be those bandits are usin' that cave as a hideout again. That part of the country's 'bout as wild as it ever was."

Davis hesitated, then said, "Thanks."

"You want company? I got no place I have to be."

Davis shook his head and said, "No, that's all right. I can handle this."

"I hope you're right."

So do I, Davis thought as he swung up into the saddle. *So do I* . . .

*   *   *

Emily sat up straight in the bed, shivering. She was cold despite the thick nightgown she wore and the quilts wrapped around her. She wasn't sure what had woken her. Her head felt thick and fuzzy, and her eyes were still raw and sore from crying. She looked over at the other side of the bed, not really able to see a thing in the darkness of the room.

But she didn't have to see to know that he was gone.

She reached over, let her hand rest on the thin pillow where his head should have been. The pillow was cold, not retaining even the slightest bit of his warmth. She wondered how long he had been gone.

Her head jerked back the other way as she heard the sound of hoofbeats outside, the noise only faintly audible because of the thick shutters over the window. But she was sure she wasn't imagining them.

Without thinking about what she was doing, she threw the covers back and swung her legs out of the bed. The floor was icy when she put her bare feet on it, but she ignored the discomfort as she ran to the window and fumbled with the catch on the shutters. After long seconds that seemed like hours, she got the catch loose and was able to swing the shutters outward. The sun was not yet up, but there was enough light for her to make out the flicker of motion as he rode away from the shed where the horses were kept.

A desperate cry welled up in her throat, but she caught it before it could escape. If she called after him, begged him not to leave, made her pleas pathetic enough, she might be able to shame him into staying, she knew.

But she couldn't bring herself to do that. She had already told him how she felt, had made it clear that she didn't want him to go after his half-brother. He had made his own choice. If tracking down Andrew Paxton was more important to him than the life he had made here with her, then so be it.

That determination not to cry out for him didn't stop her from sinking to her knees beside the window and sobbing, though.

There was only so long that Emily would allow herself to give in to her emotions. Then she forced herself back onto her feet, dried the tears from her eyes with the sleeve of her nightgown, and began to get dressed. She had to stir the embers of the cooking fire and bring it back to life so that she could start breakfast for the travelers who were staying in the rooms upstairs. Just because Davis could saddle up and ride away from his responsibilities didn't mean that she could turn her back on them as well.

Conn Powell came in from outside while she was in the kitchen cooking. She looked up at him in surprise, not expecting to see him there.

"Mornin', Miz Davis," the long hunter greeted her.

"What are you doing up and about, Mr. Powell?" she asked. "It's barely light outside."

"I'm an early riser," Powell explained, "and these eyes of mine don't need much light. My eyesight ain't goin' yet."

"I didn't mean to imply that," Emily said quickly. She turned back to the pot she had simmering on the fire. "I'm afraid breakfast won't be ready for a while."

"That's all right." Powell moved over to the table and took a seat. "I'm in no hurry. I was just takin' a walk."

"Did you . . . " Emily paused, then forced herself to ask the question. "Did you see my husband?"

"Yep. He saddled one of the horses in that shed out back and rode off. But you already knew that, didn't you, ma'am?"

She should have known that she couldn't fool this shrewd frontiersman. Without looking at Powell, she said, "I heard Davis leaving. Did the two of you talk before he rode out?"

"We exchanged a few words. Mind if I light my pipe?"

"No. Go right ahead."

Powell packed the long-stemmed briar and lit it with a sliver of wood from the cooking fire. As he settled back on the bench beside the table, he puffed a couple of times on the pipe and blew out a cloud of fragrant smoke. The smell reminded Emily painfully of Davis, who often smoked an early morning pipe as *he* sat at the table while she was cooking breakfast.

As Emily blinked away the tears that had sprung into her eyes, Powell went on, "You know, ma'am, the first time I met that husband of yours, I didn't like him at all. Didn't trust him. I could tell just by lookin' at him that he was hidin' somethin'. I don't reckon he's hid much from you, though. I don't reckon I ever saw a fella as much in love with a woman as he is with you."

Emily drew a deep breath. "I hope you won't take offense at this, Mr. Powell, but despite your knowledge of the woods, you don't strike me as a man who knows a great deal about the human heart."

"Could be you're right," Powell said with a grim chuckle. "But I ain't totally lost, either, and I've figured out that I was wrong about Davis. He has his secrets, right enough, but he's a good man."

"I knew that the first moment I saw him," Emily said softly.

"Some trails are easier to follow than others. A fella's got to travel wherever the path leads him. Don't do any good to go wanderin' off."

"That's very philosophical, but it doesn't bring my husband back to me."

"He'll be back," Powell said confidently. "Soon as he does what he's got to do."

"If he's still alive, you mean."

The long hunter shrugged. "Every time you draw a breath, ma'am, you don't know if you're goin' to draw another one. Same's true for everybody else. But if we spent all our time thinkin' about such as that, we'd all go crazy. Life's a gamble."

Emily shook her head. "Perhaps you're right, but I just can't see it that way. I want to know that the man I love will wake up beside me today and tomorrow and all the mornings after that."

"Then you're bound to be disappointed, ma'am, and I hope *you* don't take any offense at that." Powell pushed himself to his feet, tapped out the ashes from his pipe into the small fireplace where Emily was cooking. "I'll be movin' on soon as I've eaten."

Emily turned toward him. "Can't you stay until—" She couldn't finish.

"Until Davis comes back? No, I've got to b movin' on."

"You saw him leave. Which direction did he go?"

For a moment, Powell didn't reply. Then he saic "East. He headed east."

"Which direction are you going?"

"West. Davis didn't want any help with hi chore. He wouldn't take it kindly was I to horn in."

"But if you—" Again, Emily stopped abruptly She sighed. "You're right, Mr. Powell. He wouldn' want any help."

"Not from me, anyway." With that, Powel turned and limped out of the room before Emil could ask him what he meant.

But she thought about the comment for a lon time.

Powell left after breakfast, as he had said he wa going to, walking off toward the west with a casua wave of his hand. Emily didn't know if she woul ever see the man again. She felt gratitude towar him, because he had helped save her life when th bandits kidnapped her, but she didn't particularl like him. There was too wide a gulf between them i the way they looked at things.

That day was a long one. She had never had t take care of the tavern by herself before. Of course she wasn't completely alone. She had Will Malone's help, and she was grateful to the youn man for the way he pitched in uncomplainingly. Sh had no answer for him, however, when he aske how long Davis was going to be gone.

She couldn't bring herself to tell Willy that Davis might never come back . . .

The next morning was even worse because she spent a near-sleepless night tossing and turning in the empty bed. She had never realized how much his mere presence meant to her until he was gone. She wasn't sure she would ever be able to adjust to his absence if he never returned.

Still, there was work to do, no matter how bad she felt, so she tried to shove her weariness and self-pity aside and concentrate on the chores that went with running a tavern and inn.

Around midmorning, she was sitting outside the front door of the tavern churning butter. Although autumn was advancing steadily and the leaves on the trees were a riot of gaudy color, there were still days when the sun was bright and warm. This was one of those days, and Emily thought she would have been enjoying it, if only Davis had been here to share it with her.

The tavern was on the edge of the settlement, near the woods that came almost to the buildings. It was close enough, though, so that Emily could hear all the normal noises of the other settlers going about their business. A shouted question, a laugh, the creak of wagon wheels, the ringing of the blacksmith's hammer on the anvil . . . the sounds, often heard but seldom really noticed, blended together like a piece of music.

Another noise, the sharp *clip-clop* of approaching hooves, caught Emily's attention, and she looked up from her churning to see a man riding toward the tavern. She had never seen him before, but there was certainly nothing unusual about a stranger riding up to the place.

But as she watched this man riding toward her, her fingers tightened on the handle of the churn until they turned white and numb.

He didn't appear particularly threatening. He was just a middle-aged man, stern-faced man with gray hair underneath a black tricorn hat. His coat and trousers showed signs of long wear, but they were well cared for. The same could be said for the big chestnut horse the man rode. As he came up to the front of the tavern, he reined in and lifted his hand to the brim of the hat.

"Good day to you, missus," he said with a nod. "Is your husband about?"

For a moment, Emily couldn't find her voice. Then she realized how tightly she was gripping the handle of the churn and pried her fingers loose. She managed to say, "No, sir, he is not. Can I help you?"

"You *are* the wife of the man who owns this establishment?"

Emily nodded. "I am."

"Then you'd be Mrs. Davis Hallam."

She made an effort to remain calm. It wouldn't do to let this man see how his visit was really affecting her, no matter who he might turn out to be. "You're mistaken, sir," she said. "My husband's name is Davis, but it is his last name. I'm Mrs. Hal Davis."

The stranger smiled, but the expression didn't reach his eyes, which Emily now noticed glittered like ice. "I think not. If anyone has made the mistake, madam, it is you. May I step down from my horse?"

Emily's chin lifted defiantly. "*I* think not, not i

you insist on being both mysterious and offensive. Who are you, sir, and what do you want here?"

The man had taken his right foot out of the stirrup and shifted his weight, preparing to swing down from the saddle. At Emily's crisp words, he stopped the motion and settled down on the horse's back once again. "Very well," he said. "Since you already seem to know who I am, I see no harm in admitting it. My name is Peter Abernathy. I daresay your husband has mentioned me."

"I've never heard of you before," Emily lied, her voice as cold as Peter Abernathy's eyes.

"What about the village of Elkton, in the Shenandoah Valley of Virginia?"

Emily shook her head.

"And Faith Hallam?" Peter Abernathy asked softly. "Does *that* name mean anything to you?"

"Nothing." Emily had control of her rampaging emotions now, and she was determined not to let the reins slip.

"I see." Abernathy pursed his lips. "Then you have either deluded yourself, madam, or you have been lied to by a master. Meaning your husband, Davis Hallam, of course."

Emily came to her feet. "Mr. Abernathy," she said, "if you would like to buy a drink, or if you have need of a room for the night—even though it is very early and you could travel on a good distance before sundown—then, please, come in. We here at the Broken Flintlock will be happy to serve you. But if you intend to sit there and make insulting, lying remarks about my husband, then I'll thank you to ride on and trouble me no longer."

The false smile disappeared from Abernathy's face, and a frown that was much darker but also much more genuine took its place. "I represent the law, madam."

"You represent nothing but an annoyance to me, sir. The people of Logan's Fort have elected a constable, and you are not he."

"I'm from the Commonwealth of Virginia—"

"And this is Kentucky, soon to be a sovereign state." Emily stepped away from the churn and closer to the door of the tavern. "Now, I have a helper inside who would be more than happy to come to my aid if I call for him, not to mention that there are quite a few men here in the settlement within earshot. If I should scream—"

Abernathy held up a hand, palm out, to stop her. "Very well," he grated. "I'll leave. But be warned, Mrs. Hallam, or Mrs. Davis, or whatever you call yourself. I've spoken to enough people around here to know that your husband is the man I'm seeking. He matches the description perfectly, and the name is too similar to be coincidence. Wherever he is, I *will* find him. He cannot escape justice for what he did in Virginia." Abernathy's right hand went to his left arm and rubbed it, and Emily noticed for the first time how Abernathy seemed to favor that arm, as though it had been injured in the past.

"And one more thing," the man continued. "A word of warning, madam, in case you really *don't* know what this man did. He murdered his wife in a frenzy of rage and tried to kill his own brother. I wouldn't sleep too well at night if such a man were in bed beside me."

Emily fought back a shudder. "You are too bold, sir," she gasped. "Please leave."

"I'll be back," Abernathy promised grimly. "I've searched for Davis Hallam for more than a year. I'll find him."

The man's bleak confidence sent another shudder through Emily. He wheeled his horse and trotted it back toward the fort. She stepped inside the tavern, her head spinning wildly as she did so.

For the first time, Emily was glad that Davis wasn't here. If he had been, Abernathy would have tried to take him into custody, and Davis would have fought him, and quite likely one of them would have died. Davis had made it plain to her that he would never return to Virginia to face a hangman's rope for something he hadn't done.

And she still believed that he was innocent of his wife's murder. Now, after seeing Peter Abernathy, she was more convinced of it than ever. The man had no mercy in him, no ability to listen to reason. Once Abernathy had made up his mind about something, nothing would ever sway him from that belief.

Emily could understand now why Davis had been willing to take any chance to escape from Abernathy's jail.

But what was the constable from Virginia doing in Kentucky? Despite what Abernathy had said, Emily knew he had no legal right to arrest anyone here. Davis would be well within his rights to refuse to go anywhere with Abernathy, and if Abernathy tried to force him, then Davis would be the injured party. The law would be on *Davis's* side this time if he tried to fight back.

That meant Abernathy's pose as a lawman was a sham, probably just a sop to Abernathy's own conscience. Obviously, he had tracked down Davis as a matter of revenge. He probably intended to kill his quarry as soon as he found him.

Emily's hand went to her mouth to stifle a gasp as that realization hit her. A second later, she jumped and cried out as Willy Malone asked her from behind the bar, "Ma'am, are you all right? Miz Davis?"

Emily shook her head, not in answer to Willy's question but to try to clear it. She said, "I'm fine, Willy, just fine."

"Well, I hope you'll excuse me for sayin' so, ma'am, but you don't really look it. You look about as shook up as my Uncle Seth did the time he nearly sat down on a rattlesnake."

A rattlesnake, Emily thought. That was a pretty good description of Peter Abernathy. Something evil had been coiled inside the man, just waiting to strike.

Davis had been right. The past couldn't be avoided forever. Sooner or later, no matter how well someone hid from it, it caught up. And most of the time, the past brought with it only trouble. Nothing lived longer than trouble.

Those thoughts were whirling through Emily's mind as she walked slowly over to the bar. She placed her hands on the rough wood and leaned on it for support. "Willy," she said, not really thinking about the words coming from her mouth, "can you go out back and saddle the other horse for me?"

Willy stared at her. "Saddle the horse?" he repeated. "But, ma'am—"

"Please," she interrupted. "Don't ask questions, just go do as I asked."

She knew she was being curt with him, and she regretted it as soon as she saw the hurt in his eyes. But he nodded and said, "Yes, ma'am, sure. I'll do that."

Emily stayed where she was, leaning on the bar, as Willy hurried out of the tavern. She heard the back door open and close as he left the building and headed for the shed.

She had no real idea what she was going to do. But Conn Powell's words from the day before echoed in her mind. *Not from me, anyway.* That was what the long hunter had said in reply to Emily's statement about Davis not wanting any help.

Would he accept help from her? Emily had no idea, and she certainly couldn't be of any assistance in helping him find Andrew Paxton.

But Davis had to be warned that he wasn't the only manhunter in this part of the country. He had to be told that Abernathy had been here looking for him. Emily knew she had handled the conversation with Abernathy badly, but she had been too upset with Davis leaving and too surprised by Abernathy's arrival in the settlement to think straight. Then too, Abernathy had been almost brutal in his questioning of her, and she could see now that he had most likely done that on purpose to keep her off-balance.

No one would have believed her when she denied knowing anything about Davis Hallam, she thought bitterly. Abernathy had to know that his long search had finally brought him to the right place and the right man.

She could make it up to Davis by warning him. Somehow, she had to find him.

Willy came back into the tavern. "That horse is saddled and ready to ride, just like you wanted, ma'am," he said. "Is there anything else I can do for you?"

"Can you stay here and watch the tavern for the rest of the day?" Emily asked.

"Well, I reckon I can. I know it's none of my business, but what in the world—"

"Please, Willy," she interrupted with a smile. "Don't ask any more questions. Just take care of the place while I'm gone. I'll be counting on you."

"I won't let you down, ma'am." The young man was still frowning in confusion, but he didn't press Emily for any more answers.

She was glad of that. She had enough on her mind as it was. Leaving him there in the big public room of the tavern, she went to the living quarters, pulled a small trunk from underneath the bed, and opened it.

In a hardwood box inside the trunk was a pistol, along with a powderhorn and shot pouch. Emily took all three items from the box and placed them on the bed. With fingers that trembled slightly, she began to load the weapon.

By the time she finished, her fingers weren't shaking at all.

18

Davis crouched behind a large boulder that crowned a wooded hill. He had worked his way up here because the spot gave such a good view of the surrounding countryside. Several miles behind him was the mountain where the bandit lair had been when Shadrach was leading the gang.

The day before, Davis had spent hours riding around the mountain in a fruitless search. He had been unable to find anything indicating that the highwaymen had returned to their former hideout. That had come as something of a surprise. Davis had been convinced that Conn Powell's cryptic comments were meant to tell him something. Now it appeared that Powell had merely been speculating.

Not even Conn Powell knew everything, Davis had told himself as he continued looking, and even a good guess could be wrong.

Yet he had to have a starting place in his search for Andrew, and the mountain was as good as any. Davis had made a cold camp the night before—and cold it had been without a fire, indeed!—then started riding again this morning, circling out wider, putting more distance between himself and the peak.

At least the weather was a bit nicer. In fact, it was a glorious autumn day, filled with bright sunshine. The air still had a bite to it, but that was all right. It kept the sun from being too warm.

By mid-afternoon, Davis had reached the hill where he now leaned against the boulder. From here he could see several miles in each direction. To the north and south were rolling hills, to the west the land that gradually grew flatter, to the east the foothills of the Cumberland Mountains and in the faint distance, the Gap itself. He could see a winding line in the trees that marked the route of the Wilderness Road. In a few places, he could see the road itself, the dirt bare and hard-packed from the countless wagon wheels, hooves of horses and mules and oxen, and human feet that had followed it.

The path of civilization itself, Davis thought.

He sighed and slid down the boulder so that he was sitting on the ground with his back resting against the stone surface. Although he had left the tavern prepared to spend as long as it took to find Andrew, he could already feel disappointment and restlessness growing inside him. He had hoped to locate the bandits quickly and find out if the young man called Paxton who was now riding with them was indeed his half-brother. Davis had been confident the man Powell saw was Andrew, but it was always possible he was mistaken. It wasn't as if he had never been wrong before, he told himself with a grim smile.

If the bandit *wasn't* Andrew, then he would look almighty foolish when he returned to the tavern and Emily, Davis thought. She wouldn't try to make him feel worse about it, though, he felt certain of that. They had disagreed on whether or not he ought to go looking for Andrew, but she was a woman with a good heart, and she loved him.

Of course, he was assuming that she would even be there when he got back, he reminded himself. She had warned him that she might not be. But he couldn't bring himself to believe that she would really leave him. She wouldn't end their marriage. They loved each other too much for that.

Ah, if only love was enough . . . but Davis knew from bitter experience that sometimes it wasn't. "Faith," he muttered, his voice low and torn by the pain of memory.

His mind began to turn back to those terrible times, but suddenly something else caught his attention, snapping him back to the present and making him sit forward to peer intently toward the Wilderness Road. He saw something moving along the trail. Squinting, he followed the movement along the road to a spot where the trees thinned and he could get a better look at the travelers.

Wagons—quite a few of them, and all pulled by teams of oxen. Judging by the number of brutes in each team, the wagons were heavily loaded, which meant they were likely carrying freight. This wasn't an immigrant train, like the one headed up by Emily's father. The men driving these wagons were not settlers. They were businessmen, coming to Kentucky to make money.

Davis started to lean back against the boulder again when more movement caught his eye. This came from the thick woods along a ridge behind which the Wilderness Road ran. Sunlight struck a glint off metal there, and although the reflection would not be visible to the freighters approaching on the trail, Davis could see it plainly from where he was.

And as his breath caught in his throat, he remembered Powell telling him about the way the bandits had attacked a train of freight wagons.

Davis sprang to his feet while the thought was still only half-formed in his brain. The bandits had successfully struck a train of freighters only a few days earlier. It was entirely possible that they were about to try again. Davis knew he was looking at an ambush in the making.

Holding his flintlock tightly in his hand, he started down the far side of the hill toward the spot where he had left his horse. Half-sliding, half-bounding down the slope, he ignored the way the underbrush tugged at his clothes and scratched his hands and face. The bandits, including perhaps the man he was looking for, were less than a mile away. Once he reached his horse, he could be there in a matter of minutes. From what he had seen of the speed with which the wagons were traveling, Davis thought he had a chance to get to the ridge before they passed beneath it, their drivers tempting targets for the guns of the gang. To be honest, Davis thought wildly as he made his way down the hill at a breakneck pace, he was less concerned with warning the freighters than he was with finding

Andrew, but if he could ruin the ambush the gang had set up, so much the better.

When he reached his horse, the animal was dancing around nervously, spooked by Davis's crashing progress through the brush. Davis yanked the reins free and then lunged for the saddlehorn with both hands. He grabbed it and swung up onto the horse, the long-barreled rifle held crossways in front of him. His booted heels drove into the animal's flanks and prodded it into motion.

A fast trot was the best Davis could manage as he rounded the shoulder of the hill. There was too much brush to allow the horse to gallop. But a few minutes later he hit a narrow game trail that meandered toward the Wilderness Road. He pushed his mount to a faster pace.

His pulse drummed wildly in his head, seeming as loud to him as the sound of his horse's hooves. Soon he might be face to face once more with Andrew Paxton. The fact that Andrew was his half-brother, blood of his blood, had long since ceased to have any meaning for Davis.

No, if he had the chance, he would shoot Andrew down like the mad dog he was and feel the same way he would have if he had chopped the head off a venomous snake. But, at the same time, a small part of his mind was glad their mother had never lived to see this day, when her two sons would face each other and only one would live to walk away.

That would come about only if he reached the bandits in time, however, so he put aside those thoughts and concentrated on guiding the horse

around the twists and turns of the game trail. Withi
minutes, he saw rising in front of him the ridg
where the bandits lurked. The Wilderness Roa
came into view again, ahead and to his left. The lea
wagon in the freight caravan was approaching.

Davis hauled back on the reins, slowing th
horse to a stop. Neither the highwaymen nor th
freighters seemed to have noticed him yet. He coul
slip up behind the bandits and use the opportunit
to get a good look at them, increasing his chance
of finding Andrew. While he was doing that
however, the freighters would come within range c
the ambush. Or he could fire his flintlock now an
ride straight toward the wagons, yelling a warning
If he did that, the bandits might decide to abando
their plan and flee instead, taking Andrew wit
them.

It was a grim choice, and Davis had only
moment to make it.

In the end, he did the only thing he could. H
lifted the barrel of the rifle toward the sky, eare
back the hammer, and pressed the trigger. Th
booming roar of the shot rolled over the Kentuck
hills.

While the sound was still echoing, Davis drov
his heels into the flanks of the horse once more an
galloped toward the wagons stretched out along th
Wilderness Road. "Bandits!" he bellowed at the to
of his lungs. "Bandits on the ridge!"

For an instant, he worried that the freighter
would think *he* was attacking them and star
shooting at him, but then the ambushers conceale
on top of the ridge opened fire, revealing thei

position. From the corner of his eye, Davis saw that some of the bandits were on horseback, and they were riding hurriedly down the slope toward the road, firing as they came. They were going to try to salvage this raid, even though they had lost the element of surprise.

The wagons had come to a stop, and the drivers were leaping down from their seats and taking cover behind the heavy vehicles. Davis headed for the wagons as well. He heard something whine past his head and knew the sound had come from a rifle ball that had almost hit him. The bandits must have been furious at having their ambush spoiled, and they would especially want to see him dead.

The freighters were firing at the charging riders. Davis was coming in from a different angle, but he waved his rifle over his head anyway to let the men know he wasn't a threat. He aimed for a gap between two of the wagons and sent his horse squirting through it. As soon as he was clear, he reined in hard, bringing his mount to a sliding halt.

Davis was out of the saddle almost before the horse stopped moving. He tied the reins to the brake lever of a nearby vehicle, then turned and ran toward the lead wagon, powderhorn and shot pouch slapping against his hip as he loped along beside the caravan. A burly, bearded man crouched beside the first wagon. He was probably in charge of the group, Davis thought. The man turned to face him as Davis ran up.

"You'd be the fella who fired that warning shot?" the bearded man demanded.

Davis nodded. "That's right. I happened to see

those bandits hiding up there on the ridge, and
didn't take long to figure out what they were up to."

A grin split the man's face beneath the dark
bushy beard. "Then you have our gratitude, friend."
He thrust out a hand. "I'm Benjamin Cobb."

Davis shook hands with him and said, "Call m
Davis."

"All right, Davis. I reckon we'd best get back t
fighting these scoundrels. They don't seem to wan
to give up."

That was true enough. Guns were booming a
along the wagon train, but the rifle fire had failed t
blunt the charge by the highwaymen. The rider
swept around the train, firing pistols as they cam
close to the vehicles and forcing the caravan'
defenders to dive underneath the wagons for cove
Davis joined Cobb under the lead wagon.

He reloaded his flintlock, then extended th
barrel past one of the wagon wheels, searching for
target. He was searching, as well, for a familiar fac
among the mounted raiders. So far, he hadn'
spotted Andrew. He rapidly drew a bead on one o
the other bandits, however, and squeezed the rifle'
trigger. The weapon boomed and bucked agains
Davis's shoulder, and the bandit toppled out of th
saddle with a high-pitched scream. Davis didn'
waste any time congratulating himself on the shot
He just started reloading.

The roar of battle was deafening, and the cloud
of acrid powdersmoke that hung over th
Wilderness Road stung Davis's eyes and nose. H
had never wanted anything except to live
peaceful, happy life, yet violence and death ha

seemed to dog his trail for such a long time that he could barely remember anything else. There had been intervals of peace, of course, but they were just lulls in a continuing storm of tragedy.

There would be time later to mull that over—if he was lucky, Davis thought. For now, he turned his attention to reloading, aiming, firing, and starting the whole process over again. At the same time, he tried to get a look at the face of every would-be robber who galloped past the wagons.

That was difficult, considering the smoke and the way Davis's eyes were watering. So far, though, he hadn't seen Andrew. It was possible that even if Andrew was part of the gang, he was still up there on the ridge and not one of the riders who had attacked the train. If that was the case, he would undoubtedly get away—again.

Then, as Davis lifted the flintlock to his shoulder once more and settled the sight on the back of one of the raiders about forty yards away, the man suddenly wheeled his horse around, bringing him face to face with Davis.

For the first time in over a year, brother stared into the eyes of brother. And Andrew Paxton's eyes widened in shock at the sight of Davis aiming a rifle at him.

Davis pulled the trigger.

He knew as soon as he fired that he had rushed the shot too much. Andrew jerked aside as the ball whined past him, high and wide. He flung up the pistol in his hand and fired. Davis flinched as Andrew's shot chewed splinters from the spoke of the wagon wheel behind which he crouched.

Through narrowed eyes, Davis saw Andrew jerk his horse around and kick it into a gallop, heading north. Davis scrambled out from under the wagon on the other side and looked around wildly for his own mount. He spotted the horse nearby, the reins tied to a wagon's brake lever where he had left them. Davis yanked them loose and hit the saddle, slamming his heels into the horse's side.

Vaguely, he heard Cobb shouting questions after him as he flashed past the first wagon, but he ignored the bearded man. He had done what he could for the freighters. Now they would have to fight off the attack on their own, without his help. He had to go after Andrew, who had obviously abandoned the rest of the gang and was fleeing for his own life.

As Davis rounded the front of the wagon, he caught a glimpse of Andrew's horse disappearing into the trees below the ridge. Andrew glanced back as he vanished, and he had to see Davis coming after him.

Like a ghost, pursuing Andrew out of a nightmare-haunted sleep, Davis thought. The idea gave him a second of savage satisfaction. Right about now, Andrew had to be wondering if he had lost his mind and had only imagined his vengeful half-brother coming after him.

Andrew would find out soon enough just how real he was, Davis vowed.

He galloped after Andrew, but before he could reach the trees, one of the bandits on horseback suddenly loomed up in front of him, face contorted with rage, pistol in hand. The gun snapped up toward Davis, who realized suddenly that his flintlock was still unloaded. He did the only thing he could and ducked low over the neck of the horse as the highwayman fired.

The ball slammed harmlessly past Davis's head, but the bandit still blocked his path and the man had another pistol tucked behind his belt. The bandit was reaching for the second gun when Davis reversed his grip on the rifle and swung it by the barrel. The stock slammed into the man's head with crushing force and drove him out of the saddle, but the impact also splintered the stock.

Another broken flintlock, Davis thought as he dropped the weapon. The first one had served him well, but a glance at the workings of this one told him the lock itself had been damaged. It was useless.

Davis dismounted rapidly and bent over to jerk the loaded pistol free from the belt of the man he had just killed. Holding the gun in his right hand, he swung back up into the saddle and urged his horse into a run again.

He rode into the trees, still hurrying but at the same time alert for any signs of an ambush. He certainly wouldn't put it past Andrew to double back and try to shoot him from hiding. Once he had gone several yards into the woods and the noise of the fighting around the wagon train had diminished a little, Davis reined in and listened intently.

He thought he heard the sound of hoofbeats somewhere ahead of him. Andrew was still running, Davis thought grimly. He wished he knew what was going through his half-brother's mind at that point,

then decided that he wouldn't want to know after
all. Considering everything that Andrew had done
back in the Shenandoah Valley, his brain had to be
little more than a writhing mass of evil.

Davis rode as fast as he could through the
forest. The shooting behind him diminished in
volume and then began to die away entirely. Davis
didn't know how the battle had ended, and while he
hoped the freighters had emerged victorious, it was
beyond his power to do anything about it now.

He had his own battle to fight, a battle that had
been waiting for him for a long time . . .

After skirting the ridge, he reached the edge of
the trees and saw a narrow grassy strip in front of
him, bordering a bluff that fell away sharply. As he
reined in, he could hear the bubbling chuckle of the
stream that flowed swiftly through its channel at
the base of the bluff, some thirty feet below. The far
side of the little river was lined with cottonwoods.
Beyond the stream, the forest stretched away into
the distance, presenting a pretty picture, especially
at this season of the year. Davis didn't have time to
appreciate it.

Because with a sudden rustle of dead leaves
that was his only warning, something came out of
the trees behind him and slammed into his back,
knocking him off the horse. The world spun dizzily
around him for an instant as he fell, then the ground
came up and crashed into him.

A weight pressed down on him, making it
difficult to breathe. Davis gasped for air as he tried
to arch his back and throw off the burden. A fist
struck the side of his head and made everything

turn black and red around him for a second. He heard Andrew screaming obscenities at him.

Part of Davis's brain was still working logically, despite everything that was happening to him. Andrew had come back to wait for him, as Davis had suspected he would. But for some reason, Andrew hadn't lain in ambush with a gun. He had decided instead to finish this hand to hand. Andrew's sense of honor was non-existent, Davis knew, so it was pretty clear that something had happened to his rifle. It had misfired or fouled or in some other way become unusable.

That was all right. Davis had a pistol, the one he had taken from the bandit whose skull he had crushed, but he didn't intend to use it. He was going to choke the life out of Andrew with his own two hands.

With an incoherent shout that packed into it all the rage and hurt and despair of the past year and a half, Davis heaved himself up off the ground and cast Andrew aside. He turned to see Andrew rolling on the grass near the edge of the bluff and lunged after his half-brother, catching hold of Andrew's collar before Andrew could plunge over the brink.

Davis hauled Andrew to his feet. Roaring like some sort of animal, Davis swung a backhanded blow that sent Andrew staggering away. Davis went after him, tackled him, brought him down. He hooked punches with both hands into Andrew's belly.

In desperation, Andrew gouged at Davis's eyes. With a shout of his own, he shoved Davis away from him, rolled over again, and came up on hands and knees. Davis was scrambling back to his feet nearby.

Davis stepped forward, swinging his foot at Andrew's head. The kick would have probably killed Andrew if it had landed, but the younger man flung himself back and reached up to grab Davis's foot. He twisted viciously, forcing Davis either to fall to the side or have his ankle broken.

The impact of falling jarred Davis loose from Andrew's grip. He slid backward and met Andrew's next charge with the heel of his boot in Andrew's belly. Davis lifted his leg, and Andrew sailed over his head, once again sprawling at the edge of the bluff.

Both men were out of breath and showing the effects of the brutal battle. They climbed back to their feet, getting upright at about the same time. They came together toe to toe, swinging their fists in punches made awkward by weariness. Davis didn't know how long this fight could go on, but at this rate, he and Andrew were going to beat each other to death.

If that was what it took, then so be it, he thought as he looped an overhand punch at Andrew's head.

Unfortunately, the blow missed, throwing Davis off-balance. He stumbled into Andrew, and suddenly he felt Andrew's hands fumbling at his belt. The fingers of one hand closed around the butt of the pistol and jerked it away from Davis's body, while the other plucked Davis's hunting knife from its sheath. Davis froze, fists still upraised to strike, as Andrew stumbled back a couple of steps and trained the pistol on his chest. A crazed laugh rippled out of Andrew's mouth.

"I don't know how you found me, Davis," he said breathlessly, "but, by God, you're going to die this time!"

Emily rode frantically through the trees, ignoring the branches that whipped at her and her mount. All she could think about was the fact that Davis was somewhere up ahead of her, perhaps fighting for his life. At least, that was what the big bearded man called Cobb had told her. She had ridden up to the wagon train in the aftermath of an awful battle, and it had taken her only a moment to discover that the freighters had been attacked by a group of bandits. Davis had warned them in time to prevent a massacre, Cobb had said, and the thieves had been routed. Davis, however, had ridden off like a bat out of Hades in pursuit of one of the fleeing bandits.

Since leaving Logan's Fort that morning, Emily had stayed on the road, asking everyone she met if they had seen Davis. This was the first time she had found someone who could point her in the right direction. Of course, Davis and Andrew Paxton—for Emily was certain it had been Andrew that Davis was pursuing—could have gone almost anywhere in these thick woods, but she was counting on luck to be with her and lead her to Davis. It just had to.

The trees thinned abruptly, and as Emily slowed, she heard grunts of effort and puffs of breath, as well as the thud of fists striking flesh and bone. The sounds of battle made her urge her horse ahead recklessly, but just before she emerged from

the trees, common sense asserted itself and made
her rein in. She didn't know what she was riding
into, and she might put Davis in even more danger
by bursting in on whatever was happening. She slid
down from the saddle and hurried forward on foot,
bending over so that she was screened by some of
the brush at the edge of the trees. She saw
movement up ahead, movement that resolved itself
into the struggling forms of two men trading blows.

Davis! And the man fighting with him had to be
Andrew. The younger man's face was smeared with
blood, as was Davis's, but Emily thought she could
see a faint resemblance.

She slipped her hand into the bag slung over
her shoulder and closed her fingers around the
pistol she had brought from the tavern. If Davis
needed her help, she would be there for him.

Just as she should have been there all along,
she knew now. She understood why he had been
compelled to go after Andrew, understood how the
burden of the past finally had to be confronted if it
was ever to be lifted. The anger and hatred she had
felt for Peter Abernathy had taught her to
understand.

She could have killed Abernathy for the threat
he posed to Davis. Davis's need to settle things with
the man who had actually stolen away his wife, his
children, and his freedom had to be even stronger.

Every harsh word she had said to Davis came
back to haunt her now as she watched the two men
slugging each other. They were so close together
that there was no way she could get a clear shot at
Andrew. And if she stepped out of hiding and called

out for Davis to step back, she might distract him and give Andrew an edge in their battle. Besides, both of them were standing too close to the edge of the bluff to take a chance on startling them.

But then everything changed suddenly as Andrew darted back away from Davis, a pistol in his hand. Emily didn't know exactly where he had gotten the weapon, but that didn't matter. The only important thing was that he was threatening Davis with the gun.

And Emily finally had a chance to step out and shoot.

Before she could do so, an arm encircled her and a strong hand clamped over her mouth, stifling any outcry she might have made. She was jerked back roughly, and another hand reached around her to pluck the pistol from her fingers.

"Let's just be quiet, shall we, Mrs. Hallam," Peter Abernathy hissed in her ear, "and see what happens next."

19

Davis knew he was staring at his own death. He couldn't possibly leap toward Andrew and knock the pistol aside in time to prevent him from firing. But if he was going to die, he wanted at least to clear the air between them before Andrew pulled the trigger. After all this time, he deserved that much.

"You're going to kill me, are you," Davis said harshly, "the same way you killed Faith?"

Andrew's left hand, the one holding the knife, was trembling slightly as he lifted it and wiped the back of it across his bleeding mouth. His right hand, the one with the pistol in it, was rock-steady. He said, "Faith's death was an accident. I didn't mean to shoot her. You were the one I wanted dead, Davis."

Davis's voice shook as he said, "Accident or not, you killed her, Andrew. You took away my wife and children, and I was thrown in jail for what *you* did. They were going to hang me for it!"

"Better you than me," Andrew said. "But I didn't

really take Faith away from you, Davis. You gave her to me. You drove her into my arms with your cold, sullen ways." He laughed again. "You just didn't know what a hot-blooded woman you had!"

The mocking words were more than Davis could stand. Even though he was only hastening his death, he threw himself toward Andrew with a choked cry.

The pistol boomed, smoke and flame geysering from its muzzle, and what felt like a giant fist punched Davis in the chest. He was thrown backward, and suddenly there was nothing underneath his feet.

He was falling, the world spinning madly around him.

Emily had known as soon as she heard Abernathy's whispering voice that she had done the wrong thing again. He had goaded her into looking for Davis and then followed her, and now here he was, ready to step out of the brush and either try to arrest Davis or more likely just shoot him down in a mockery of the justice the man claimed to represent.

But as the angry words flowed back and forth between Davis and Andrew, the accusations and the admissions, she had felt Abernathy's body stiffen against hers. What he was hearing now utterly destroyed every belief that had led him to search for Davis for more than a year. Davis had been telling the truth all along. *Andrew* was the guilty one, the one who had killed Faith Hallam. Faith's death might have been a tragic accident, but

Andrew laying the blame on Davis for it had been a
act of coldly calculated evil.

Then suddenly, Davis was leaping toward
Andrew and the pistol in Andrew's hand fired, and
Davis was thrown backward toward the edge of the
bluff—

As Davis disappeared over the brink, Emily's
teeth sunk into the ball of the hand clamped over
her mouth.

Cursing in pain, Abernathy flung her aside.
Emily sprawled on the ground at the edge of the
bushes. With a look of anger, the constable from
Virginia stepped over her and emerged onto the
grassy strip along the bluff. He leveled the pistol in
his uninjured hand at Andrew, who stared at him in
stunned disbelief.

"Andrew Paxton," Abernathy boomed in his
stern voice, "you are under arrest!"

Emily watched, her eyes almost as wide with
shock as Andrew's, as her husband's half-brother
twisted and lifted his left arm. In his hand was the
long-bladed hunting knife. A flick of Andrew's wrist
sent the knife spinning through the air toward
Abernathy.

Abernathy tried to dart out of the way, but the
blade struck him high on the left side, biting deep
into his shoulder. At the same instant, Abernathy
fired. Emily's stunned gaze saw droplets of blood fly
out from Andrew's side as the ball struck him.

Then Andrew, too, was gone, plunging
completely out of sight over the edge of the bluff.

* * *

The shock of hitting the icy water jerked Davis back from the fog of pain that had wrapped itself around him. He plunged underneath the surface of the river, and water rushed in through his open mouth. The stream was perhaps a dozen feet deep along the base of the bluff. Davis cut through the water, jarred against the rocky bottom, and kicked hard for the surface. When his head broke into the air once more, he gasped for breath, gagging and choking on the water he had swallowed. The fact that he had come up instead of staying down was as much luck as anything else, he knew.

The horrible pain that had bloomed in his chest when Andrew's shot struck him was dulled by the chilly water. In fact, he seemed to be numb all over. But instinct made him struggle toward the far bank anyway.

He had gone only a few feet when another shot sounded somewhere above him. He heard the report of the gun vaguely, but then there was a tremendous splash near him. Water swept up over him, engulfing him, but this time he managed to grab a lungful of air before he went under.

The usually crystal clear stream had been roiled and muddied somewhat, but when Davis opened his eyes underwater, he was able to see the figure flailing and struggling nearby. His brain was still dazed by everything that had happened, but not so much so that he didn't recognize Andrew.

Fate had delivered his half-brother to him once more. Davis wasn't going to let this final opportunity escape him.

He kicked hard, launching himself toward Andrew.

His grasping hands closed on Andrew's shirt
hauling the younger man around. Davis saw tendrils
of blood coming from Andrew's side and knew
Andrew was wounded. How that had come about
Davis had no idea, but neither did he care. At this
moment, there was no one else in the world except
the two of them, and his entire existence had boiled
down to this battle. With his left hand bunched in
the front of his half-brother's shirt, Davis drove his
right fist into Andrew's face.

Andrew struggled to pull loose from Davis's grip
and when he couldn't, he began to fight back. Their
heads broke the water, giving each man a chance to
gulp down a fresh breath before going under again.
They grappled fiercely. Time meant nothing to Davis
and he had no idea of up or down, either. Sometimes
water enclosed them, and sometimes there was air
sweet air. As they fought, Davis became aware that
the current of the stream had caught them and was
sweeping them along with it.

He didn't know this river, had never traveled
along it, but one of the times when he and Andrew
were wrestling on the surface, he heard a roaring
sound and glanced up to see white foam on the
water ahead of them. They were nearing some
rapids. Davis had no idea how rugged the rapids
were or how long that stretch of the river might be
nor did he really care. He had long since given up
on surviving this confrontation.

The only thing that mattered to him was seeing
Andrew die first.

He slammed his fist into Andrew's face again and
then tried to hold him under the surface. Andrew's

struggles were growing weaker, it seemed to Davis, but he didn't trust his impressions, knowing that he, too, had been shot and was probably in pretty bad shape. What happened in the next moment seemed to confirm that, as Andrew twisted around with a fresh burst of strength and caught Davis with a vicious punch. Davis sagged in his half-brother's grip.

The current was even stronger now, and despite its chill, the water seemed to be boiling around them as they entered the rapids. The roar filled Davis's ears . . . or maybe that was his own blood he heard. He felt Andrew's fingers close around his throat as he went down the river backward.

Davis knew that the air was filled with noise, but a vast silence seemed to enfold him as Andrew's grip on his neck grew stronger and stronger. He was dying. That much seemed certain. And he had failed, because Andrew's eyes, wide and staring and perhaps more than a little insane, were still filled with life.

The way Faith's had been, before Andrew killed her.

With the last of his strength, Davis twisted in the water, bringing Andrew around so that he was going backward, rather than Davis. Davis caught just a glimpse of the gray, jagged rock protruding from the surface of the river, and then in the next instant, Andrew slammed into it. Both men hung there, locked together by the grip of Andrew's fingers around Davis's throat, pressed up against the rock by the current. From a distance of mere inches, they stared into each others' eyes.

And then the light faded from Andrew's gaze as

blood welled from his mouth. His fingers fell awa
from Davis's throat.

Davis tore himself free and grabbed the rock a
the current tugged Andrew loose and carried hir
on downstream. Andrew's body rolled in the wate
revealing to Davis's stunned eyes the huge dent i
the back of his skull. Hitting that rock head on ha
killed Andrew.

And Davis was still alive.

The question was, for how long?

He had lost a lot of blood, he knew that. Th
pistol ball was probably still buried somewhere i
his chest. The icy water had drained most of hi
strength. The simplest thing to do would be to jus
let go of the rock and allow the river to sweep hir
under the surface, out of this life.

Then, over the roar of the rapids, he hear
something he had never expected to hear again.

He heard Emily calling his name.

He lifted his eyes toward the heavens, thinkin
that surely he was mistaken. What he heard wa
Faith calling out to him, welcoming to whatever la
beyond death. Davis had never been a particularl
religious man, but he firmly believed in th
Kingdom of God and the idea that someday h
would once again see all those who had gone o
before.

But not yet, he realized numbly, becaus
through the wet hair that had fallen over his eyes
he saw Emily running along the edge of the bluf
overhead. Behind her was someone else Davis ha
never expected to see again in this life—at least h
had hoped not to.

Peter Abernathy.

For an instant, the hope that Davis had felt at the sight of Emily faded. Abernathy had tracked him down after all, had come all the way to Kentucky to arrest him and take him back to the gallows. Now, with Andrew dead, so too had died Davis's final chance of making Abernathy believe the truth.

Of course, Davis told himself with a grim laugh, it was entirely possible that he wouldn't live to hang, that he wouldn't even live long enough to feel the touch of Emily's hand once more.

But he wasn't going to give up, not now, not after everything that had happened. He let go of the rock.

And swam toward shore with every bit of strength left in his body.

Far above him, Emily cried out his name, tears streaming down her face, and Davis pulled himself toward her through the current, her voice a beacon in an endless sea.

"The ball passed right on through," Abernathy grunted as he wound strips of cloth tightly around Davis's shoulder. Emily had already patched up the knife wound in the constable's shoulder. He and Davis were going to have matching bandages, a thought that brought a grim smile to Davis's face.

"I think maybe you can sit on a horse long enough to get back to your place," Abernathy said, "but then you're going to be laid up for a good long time while that wound heals."

Davis had a blanket from Abernathy's pack

wrapped around the lower part of his body. He was sitting on a log near the roaring fire Emily had built up, letting the heat from the blaze seep back into him and drive out the chill of being in the river. His clothes were drying on sticks nearby. Emily sat on the log beside him, his right hand held tightly in both of hers.

"You're a lucky man," Abernathy went on. "The shot missed the collarbone. Ought to heal nicely, although you'd do well to keep the wound clean and the bandages changed regularly."

"He won't have to worry about that, Constable," Emily said. "I'll see that he's cared for properly."

A ghost of a smile played over Abernathy's lean face. "Yes, I imagine you will, madam," he said.

When he was finished bandaging the wound, he drew the blanket up around Davis's shoulders. Earlier, Davis had been shaking too badly from the cold to talk. Now, after taking a healthy swallow of whiskey from the flask Abernathy fetched from his saddlebags, Davis was able to say, "What are you going to do now?"

"About what?" Abernathy said.

Davis glowered at him. "You know what I mean. Do you intend to take me back to Virginia?"

Abernathy exchanged a glance with Emily, then looked squarely at Davis and said, "I see no reason to do that. You've been a law-abiding citizen since you came here to Kentucky, haven't you?"

Davis nodded.

"And your wife and I both heard Andrew Paxton admit to killing the first Mrs. Hallam," Abernathy went on. "That's what I intend to tell everyone back in the Shenandoah Valley when I return. As far as the law is concerned, you can come home, Hallam."

Davis looked at Emily, and for the first time in what seemed like an eternity, he laughed softly. "I *am* home," he said.

Abernathy shrugged. "Whatever you wish." He hesitated, then added, "I was wrong about you, Hallam, but I make no apologies. I was doing my job as I saw fit. Now, my job is to set things right. If you don't want to come back to Virginia, I'll see what I can do about arranging for your children to come out here to Kentucky."

Davis's smile widened into a grin, and Emily clutched his arm in excitement. "Thank you, Constable."

Abernathy took a swig from the flask himself and sat down on the other end of the log. "Hammond Larrimore is going to be a very disappointed man . . . and I don't really give a damn if he is."

"Larrimore," Davis repeated. "He's the one who sent you after me."

Abernathy nodded. "He paid me to resign from the constable's position in Elkton and track you down. I'm convinced he expected me to kill you outright when I found you, but I never intended to do that. I'm a lawman, not an executioner."

He was still a stiff-necked bastard, Davis thought, but at least Abernathy had finally believed the truth when he heard it from Andrew's own lips. And his offer to help arrange for the children to come out here showed that he did indeed want to make things right.

Davis closed his eyes, and Emily said, "Lean on

me, Davis. You need to rest before we start back home."

"Home," Davis murmured, liking the sound of it. He knew now that he had been wrong. A man might spend most of his life in solitude, but there were moments of truth, moments of togetherness, moments when he wasn't alone after all.

"You can go back to using your real name now," Abernathy said. "You can be Davis Hallam again."

Davis nodded, not bothering to open his eyes. He felt the touch of Emily's hand on his forehead, her fingers cool and soft. He rested his head on her shoulder. The fire crackled merrily.

After all the months, all the miles, all the tears, he knew that soon he would be exactly where he was supposed to be.

Once more, the Wilderness Road was going to bring him home.

A professional writer for the past nineteen years, **JAMES REASONER** has authored dozens of novels and nearly a hundred short stories in a variety of genres. Many of his novels have concerned the American frontier, including the best-selling *Westward!* (written under the pseudonym Dana Fuller Ross). A graduate of North Texas State University with degrees in English and Film, Reasoner considers himself primarily a storyteller whose first goal in his work is always high-quality entertainment.

James Reasoner is married to award-winning mystery novelist L. J. Washburn, creator of private detective Lucas Hallam. She was kind enough to allow Reasoner to tell the story of one of Lucas's relatives in *The Wilderness Road*. Washburn's heritage includes the Blackfoot Indians of early-day Montana Territory. One of Reasoner's ancestors was the mountain man Jacob Reznor, who was a member of the first American fur-trapping expedition to journey up the Missouri River to the Rockies in 1809. Jacob Reznor was later killed and scalped by hostiles in 1814, leading to speculation that perhaps one of Washburn's ancestors was responsible for his death. Unlikely to be sure, but stranger things have been known to happen. . . .

For Fans of the Traditional Western:

Critical Acclaim for Douglas C. Jones:

"Slowly, but with infinite grace, Douglas C. Jones is creating a masterful fictional history of America"
—*The Washington Post*

"Jones . . . achieves the nearly impossible: he recreates the American West in a manner so fresh and compelling as to banish every Hollywood cliché."—*Kirkus Reviews*

Elkhorn Tavern
The Civil War swept through the border states of Missouri and Arkansas, and the hill people of the Ozarks quickly chose sides. But it would take guts, decency, and more to weather the furious winter of '62 and ride out the storm into the sudden spring that followed.

Gone the Dreams and Dancing
Jones's thrilling narrative of a proud and powerful peoples' surrender to the white man's world captures the pain and triumph of a difficult but inevitable journey, while weaving an engaging tale of majesty, surrender, and acceptance.

Season of Yellow Leaf
A ten-year-old girl is captured on a South Plains raid in the 1830s. Reared by the Comanche tribe, she survives the pain of losing her world and becomes a unique witness to a vanishing way of life.

AN ORDINARY MAN
by J. R. McFarland

A drifting lawman with a knack for killing, MacLane was a lonely man—until an odd twist changed his fate. Only then did he have the chance to change the course of his life and become an ordinary man with an extraordinary message to deliver.

GRAY WARRIOR
by Hank Edwards

Jack Dalton was a rebel who would never surrender—even if it killed him. But the love of a beautiful woman brings changes all the killing in the world could not. In a savage wilderness of bullets and blood, Dalton finds something bigger and better than himself, something worth living for.